FIRE
EYES

FIRE
EYES

D.F. BAILEY

Douglas & McIntyre
Vancouver/Toronto

Douglas & McIntyre Ltd.
1615 Venables Street
Vancouver, British Columbia V5L 2H1

Canadian Cataloguing in Publication Data

Bailey, D. F. (Donald Frederick), 1950 –
   Fire eyes

   ISBN 0-88894-537-X

   I. Title
PS8553.A54F5 1987   C813'.54   C86-091593-X
PR9199.3.B35F5 1987

All the characters, events and places in *Fire Eyes* are entirely fictional. Any resemblance they may bear to real persons, experiences and locations is illusory.

Cover illustration by Dave Webber
Cover and book design by Barbara Hodgson
Typeset by The Typeworks
Printed and bound in Canada by D. W. Friesen & Sons

For Audrey

CHAPTER 1

The bomb went off a little after one in the morning. It was a beautiful thing. There was blues and greens and thick yellows that blended in with the smoke to make it all look like mustard gas in some World War I movie. And the sound of it was much louder than I thought. I guess it could have been the noise alone that brought the cops. But the look of it—the colours—they were much more than I hoped for. Damn it, they were *beautiful*.

But what happened to Renee, that's something else. It was the last thing I expected. She tried to make everything so casual, carrying the bomb the way she did under her arm. First she spins around and smiles like there's no care to the world and moves up the sidewalk in her dream of ballet. She points her toe to the ground once, twice—then, as she turns on one foot, the bomb explodes and breaks the night into a thousand smoking greens and yellows and reds, with a huge blast like a rocket burst echoing off the walls of the mountains. And then it's all over before you can really see it and in the end she's worse than dead because the bomb blew everything apart. There's a crater gutted into the sidewalk and suddenly all the lights in the First City Electric building black out. A minute later there's a flicker of light in the windows and then the power surges back to life. Only the front door has any sign of damage, two windows shattered from their steel frames. And along the sidewalk, halfway up from the road, her handkerchief rests where it fell. Except for that, there's nothing left at all. Not even the baby.

Yes, *she's* the one that didn't come back. I remember her saying it would be like a war, and in a war there's always some that don't come home. I always thought she was talking about me. Specially when I put the bomb together in the lab.

"No, no," I tell her, "I'll be careful. I always tamp real careful when I'm making these things."

Making the bomb is when the Power comes into my mind. That's when the danger is worst. So I tamp the guts of it down into the shell with cotton balls. Cotton's best because it keeps the moisture of my fingers away from everything so none of the electrics can short out. And it's soft enough so I can build the most dangerous parts in a gentle way.

"Just be sure," she says and backs to the corner of the room near the mattress. She thinks she can dive under it if anything triggers accidental. She doesn't know that if something triggers she'd be dead before she could even *see* it.

"I am," I tell her, "just don't even breathe." I can hear her footsteps backing to the mattress. It's the kind of noise that gives me the Power. Everyone else backing off and there I am doing the impossible. Nobody else can touch it but me.

"Steady out your fingers," she says.

"Just quit your talking." Any interruption's like poison. Finally I tamp the last of the explosives into the cannister and seal the shell off with a waterproof cap. That way I can leave it outside in a pinch and if rain comes there's no problem. Just wait her out till I'm ready. And I can either set it automatic or by remote. Hell, the remote's a dream these days. Some even do it with one of those garage closers. I heard of one guy who's triggering them with remote-control T.V. channel changers. That's a tough one to believe. But can't you see it? Parking a block down the road and just waiting till the cops come, then click it to channel 13 and WHAM!—they're goners.

But there wasn't a remote on Renee's. I should've put one in but it was her fault, because she wanted it timed for thirty-three-and-a-third minutes. Just like a record, she says. That's rule one. Never allow no one else in the lab. But she was a forceful one. She'd come in anytime she pleased and stick around and seldom do as I told her. You've got to admire that in a way, because most of these modern women's bitches are just hot air and no bras. Not Renee, though, she'd stick it out to the end whether there was shit in the hole or not.

That's why she took the shell instead of me. That and the fact she could pass the security check. It's the one thing they gave her for working there three years: a little plastic badge with her picture on one corner that pins to her shirt so they don't stick a knife in her guts just for walking in the front door after hours.

We drove there together and had the banger rolled in flannel blankets in the back seat. We even borrowed one of those baby harnesses that lock into the seatbelts. If the cops stopped us then it'd look like some baby sleeping on the way home. Even cops wouldn't disturb no baby.

"Roll it up nice and easy," I tell her when we're setting out.

"It's so cute," she says, "what'll we call him?"

"Nothing. And you shouldn't fix yourself on the idea of having a kid." But to keep her happy I add on a new touch. "Or we could call it Billy Junior, if you really want to."

She starts laughing like this is the joke-of-the-week. "When you name it after yourself it shows you're egotistical."

"Nothing wrong with a little pride," I tell her as she pulls the blanket right over the baby's head so he can sleep like a newborn kitten.

We drive to the electricity offices in the Camaro. It takes about an hour and a half altogether, when you add in the time for the stop at the 7-Eleven and then the half-hour stop we made when she started crying. At least that's how it began. After that I think she went a little crazy on me. She was looking up at the stars and her whole face was wet from the tears and then she tried to explain everything between us. It's the kind of thing you don't want to dwell on. People will stop trusting you if you talk about the truth. Especially when you lay everything out person to person.

Anyway, we just about forget the bomb, it looks so much like a baby and the music blasting out of the radio is such a lure away from what we're really doing. When we get to the building she grabs it up very softly, just like a kid, under the ass and around the belly. I sit back and watch her go up the sidewalk. She starts to dance a little, like she's got one of those Fifties songs in her head, and pretends to be dancing at the prom. Christ, how ridiculous. Then a handkerchief slips from her pocket and drifts to the ground. She turns around without noticing it and pulls the baby to her chest and shows me how she's breast-feeding the newborn like a good mother should do. For a second I even think about being that little baby and sucking on the mother-nipple and how good it's got to taste.

She strides up the walk and does a little ballet turn. But it's no place to play ballerina, so I get out of the car and whisper up to her as loud as I dare.

"Stop that assin' around, Renee. Just drop the baby off and stop that jerk-off stuff."

She smiles that devilish smile she uses when she knows she's gone one step farther than I ever would. It's like a contest between us. Sometimes we'll try to out-chicken the other. When someone finally backs off, it shows where all the nerves really are. The winner gets to leer it into the loser and it's a big deal until the next time comes. Then it's really up to the loser. He's gotta *shine*.

But with this baby there shouldn't be no goof-assing. I've seen guys lose anything from their fingers to their life in one sudden flash. It'd be so quick you'd blink to shut it away, then open your eyes and the whole world has changed. A guy dead here. One guy with a hand off there. Maybe another guy with his stomach ripped open and his kidney flopped onto the ground. And it happens from no cause at all. Maybe God says, "Okay, now you blow up those combat engineers in F-squad. Them soldiers don't matter no more." Then the bomb just flashes and it's over.

"Gentle that baby," I whisper, "until you get inside."

Then she smiles more heavenly than I've ever seen. The Devil part turns into something sweet and she does another ballerina turn along the sidewalk.

And that's where it blows. The gas colours pour out like mustard steam and for some reason my eyes don't blink at all. They just suck it in like a mind volcano so I get to see everything flying apart.

First her smile washes out. Those angel lips fall off like the great hotels dropped by the real demolition experts. They're there one second and the next they're just *gone*. The whole wall of her face, smooth and clear as it is, turns into rubble and falls onto itself until there's nothing left but a pile of broken bricks and bones. There's no look of sadness, no idea that the end has come.

I run up the sidewalk after the first shock passes and look into the smouldering crater. I'm balanced there on the sidewalk, on my toes with one knee bent forward, like a wild deer in the forests ready to disappear into the night bush. But something pulls me in closer, down to where her body should be. The Devil is flying out of her and I squat over and take a good sniff of the blasting powders steaming up from the pit, then I look around and see everything *perfectly*. The brown brick building with two shattered front windows, the parked car, the grass and sidewalk, those prickle bushes next to the link fence. I know *exactly* how to run and break away like that deer in the woods, straight down the sidewalk jumping the lawns and shrubs. I hop the last bush and duck into the car and close the door tight and just listen. If there's squad cars coming you sit tight and tell 'em sweet dick when they ask. But if there's no cops then turn the key soft and pull out as sweet as you please.

And it works just like that. There's no sign of a soul, so I pull out unnoticeable. I dump the baby harness off at the welfare office and no one knows the difference. It's somebody's free donation. Far as they're concerned, some big-heart left it without a trace. They might even give up a prayer in the morning. Who knows how they think it through?

Then I drive round like a bug that just found some dead squirrel. Don't know where to go. Just take all the green lights and whenever there's a red one turn right and keep going. After a while I sort of come to, come right out of this automatic driving and realize how useless it is. Following the lights is crazy cause no one ever took the time to organize it so the lights'll take you somewhere. They don't lead nowhere. Just around.

Then I figure, okay, let's drive back to the building and see what's going on. It's an hour later and I'll just be a guy driving by on his own time. A guy who couldn't sleep specially well and is out for a simple drive. Even at two in the morning that's not so suspicious.

But it's like pulling the plug in a washtub that's full to the top with dirty water. At first, nobody knows the drain's free. Then a minute later the water starts sucking down and the surface rolls back and forth until the whirlpool starts. That's when you know it'll never stop and you can see the tiniest speck caught on the edge, right on the lip of the whirlpool at the one point just after any possible escape. There you are. On the lip. Right on the lip. Then one, two quick swirls and down into the guts of some black animal with no eyes. That's how it is driving back there—a dizzy hell.

When I'm a block away I can see the place has gone crazy with cops. There's at least six squad cars with their lights flashing all blue-red, like the Devil's still with Renee.

I slip the car into neutral and pull up at a coast. They've got a roadblock set up, and two cars ahead of me a cop has his nose poked through the window, yapping at the driver. I take a good clean breath.

After a minute the cop motions for me to unroll my window.

"Evenin'," he says.

"What's the trouble, officer?" I crane my neck and make sure I look surprised to see a roadblock set up so late at night.

"Routine." Then he turns more serious. "What brings you by here tonight?"

"Just out for a drive. Changed my shift today and I couldn't sleep so good."

"Let's see your licence and registration," he says.

I lean over to the glovebox to get the papers and he sticks his head in all the way and starts sniffing the air. You hear him do it twice. Sniff-sniff, just like Porky Pig.

He holds the papers and licence in one hand and checks my face against the picture, asks my name and address and checks my answers against the card. Then he goes to a squad car and makes some notes and radios into headquarters and lingers around his car a while.

If they had the brains for it they might've read my thoughts while I was waiting in the car lineup. But that's not too likely. Usually cops aren't good enough to read your thoughts. Not like the shrinks and special doctors. With a little training some of them could maybe handle it, but on the whole the cops are useless buggers. They're much better at reading how you sweat or how your eyes twitch if there's any little pressure inside you. And that's what I'm doing my best to control. My face is smooth as ice. It's just now that the sweat's starting to come into my palms.

"Okay, on your way."

"Thanks."

He passes the papers to me. I roll the window back up and take a deep breath. With the window up it's like sealing him off and turning him into something stupid and ignorant. Like a cartoon.

Then I drive off slow, obeying all the traffic rules as though I just took my driver's test. When I get close to it I look up the sidewalk to see Renee. But the funny thing is that there's hardly any sign of the bomb. They put a few barriers around the crater, but apart from that there's nothing. Even the building lights are lit up like nothing ever happened. You almost wonder why the cops bothered to show up.

But it's probably another trick of theirs to lure me out of what's really happened. It's the kind of trick that might work on anybody else. It might work on me, too, except that my memory's near perfect and I remember *every* little detail. Up to a point, anyhow.

□   □   □

By the time I get back to the apartment, things have hit in pretty bad. I open a beer and wander around eyeing her furniture and books, sipping the beer and trying to piece it all together.

Then I stop wandering so much and have a look in the mirror. All of a sudden I have to have a good look at myself because something's wrong. It's like waking up after a big drunk with the boys and you realize that somebody shaved off your moustache without telling you. You just look and look and try to figure out what's missing and where it went to. The trouble is that now I'm not sure what's happened. It's like a piece of my face has changed or been moved around. Except it's nothing plain. It's not my nose or my hair or the way my eyes keep darting around. It's more like something *inside* my face has gone missing. Some special prop that kept everything else in place and looking pretty smooth and normal. I try puffing my cheeks out but it doesn't fill in the missing section. Maybe it's Renee. Maybe there was something so special about her that it got built right into my head and turned into part of my face. And now that she's gone, so has that part of my head.

I keep thinking about her and sit down on the bed and take a few pulls on the beer. After a while my mind slips into nothing and I realize that I'm wasting time again. Sometimes it's like that.

Sitting there for hours with my brain on vacation. This time it happens so long that the beer goes flat and makes my tongue curl.

I flush the rest of it into the toilet and lie down so my hands are tucked under my head like a pillow. Then I close my eyes and everything goes dark as a movie house. That's how I do my best thinking. The thinking movie gets so big and loud that everything happens like I'm there right now. And I can sit back and watch and figure out which way to do things, or let the voices in my head do the talking and explain what ought to be done. It's always been like that. If there wasn't somebody pushing me to do something one way, there'd be a voice telling me to do it somehow else. The way you do, you know? Just the way you've always done it.

CHAPTER 2

Right at the beginning it was pretty bad. They'd found me in a brown paper grocery bag next to the highway. Nobody ever believed me when I told them about it, but it's still true. The police came and took me off to welfare. Then they gave me to Carol. That's where everything really starts.

The first thing I remember is when they've got me out with the Dobermans. Carol lifts me by the back of the shirt and drags me down the hallway to the backyard. My feet fall limp and my shoes drag along the floor as I go.

"Don't scuff that floor!" she yells, but it doesn't make no difference on what I do or don't do. For some reason she thinks the more she yells, the louder I'll hear her. But the truth is, it just puts me deeper into ignoring her. When you're seven or eight years old that's the only plan you've got: just keep ignoring them till they run out of steam and their stomachs bleed.

When she has me out the back door she drags me to the kennels and by now I start walking smart, because that concrete sidewalk's damn tough on floppy feet. That makes her think she's won. So she opens the wire cage and puts me in with this winning smile and says, "Now you feed them Dobermans, Billy, or you'll be spending another night in them dog houses."

"You tell me when Nick comes," I warn her.

"You just feed them Dobermans," she spits back.

I sit there after she's gone into the house, and eventually the Dobermans come over to me and start farting around. They're just pups and they don't know when to do nothing. They climb so close I have to bat them away. Then if they snap they've had it. One clip on the nose and they yelp off after finally learning something.

After a long time Nick comes through the back door with a big smile on his face. Then the smile fades and he comes to the kennel and lets me out.

"Hi, Nick." I grab at his waist real hard like it's a tree stump. He's big like a tree and his face is rough like some logger chewed it through with a chain saw and the doctors had to sew it back together.

"Hey, hey, not so tough, Billy," he says and pulls my hand off his pants. "How ya doing, Billy-boy, Billy-boy?"

"Okay. Well . . . not so good."

"How's your counting going?" he asks, and he leads me back into the house by the hand.

"I'm up to a million," I tell him. It's the truth, too. I'd counted up to a million by the time I was six and a half years old. I had a system where I'd keep track of the thousands with my fingers and the hundred thousands with my toes. If I'm counting two hundred and thirty thousands then I'd lock my second finger around my third toe. It's a good system to keep a running count.

"Million, huh? A million's pretty big, you know."

"I know," I tell him. "I took two and a half days."

"A lot of people try and make it to a million," he says. "Hardly nobody ever does."

"I did, an' I'm only eight."

"I thought you were seven."

"Eight," I say, and he sets me on the livingroom chair and just looks me over.

"But how *fast* are you?" And his eyebrows shoot up to the ridge of his head.

"Pretty fast."

"Okay. Let's check you out. I'm gonna go get Carol and you

start counting. By the time we're ready to go we'll see how far you counted."

"All right." I sit back, and starting with one I race up to a hundred before he's even left the room. The reason I count so fast is because my eyes close tight and turn into something like T.V. screens, with the numbers blazing by just fast enough so I can read them clear. There's no number skipping and no cheating. Every number is counted true and I keep track with the finger and toe method I was telling you about.

Nick's looking for Carol for a long time and I can hear them grunting around, wrestling upstairs. That's what gives her those muscles. They're not big but they're tough like golf balls and when she starts dragging me around it shows where the strength is. Sometimes I wish Nick'd lay off her so she wasn't so tough. But I never say anything to him.

"How far'd you get, Billy-boy?" He's got a big smile again and I stop counting.

"One hundred and two thousand, six hundred and four."

"Christ he's a smart one, Carol." He smiles and looks at her.

"Yeah? Well let's see if he was smart enough to feed the pups." She goes out the back door, leaving the two of us pretty happy with one another. Nick is snapping his fingers and cracking his cheeks and tapping his toes on the floor. He does this one after the other as though he's a drummer and he's turned his body into a drum set. The whole thing sounds great, with little drum rolls on his knuckles and a bass drum in his mouth.

Then Carol comes back. "B-i-l-l-y." She says it all stretched out in a low voice. "B-i-l-l-y come here." Nick stops drumming and I freeze. Everything blanks out until I realize she's dragging me down the hall and my feet tops are hurting from scraping on the floor again.

"You shouldn't put the boy in the kennel that way," Nick calls out behind us.

"And the boy shouldn't *not* do his chores," she says.

"Maybe that's not the way for doin' chores."

"Well, listen," and she locks the kennel door on me, "you want honey, you go to the queen bee. Right?" And she smiles at him as though she won the wrestling match.

He just looks down on her, then looks at her feet. "Right," he says. "So what?"

"So this boy's honey to them dogs and he's got to learn to give a little. When he feeds them and cleans them and washes those kennels down, then I'll give the same dues to him—his food and shelter and grooming. And that's the deal. It's the same with you and me and a thousand other folks."

They head off somewhere and she makes a big point of slamming the back door hard as she can. I wish her face was pinched in that door but it's not—so the hell with it.

Then one of the Doberman pups comes up and climbs into my lap. He's just a poor sucker and starts licking at my hands. Then another one comes. And then the other three. One of them gets real stupid, playing around with his mouth wide open and his head swinging back and forth in front of me. Only he's swaying in front of my nose with his tiny needle teeth all strong and tough as steel pins.

That's one thing I can always count on. A dog's always gonna try and outsmart me. They think they've got some trick I can't figure out. So he's swinging bad-mannered with his mouth wide open and I give him a tap under under the chin. It's just what Carol'd do, only she'd try to catch me with my tongue between my teeth so there'd be that sharp lesson to learn. But I don't catch the tongue and the pup comes back for more. Figures he's quicker than me. This time he's got the tongue dolling out of his lips. I give him a firm one on the jaw and the teeth clap shut. He looks a little surprised but thinks he knows enough to really show me what he's made of. He gives a couple of tough yap-yaps and dances around my heels. Then he closes in on my waist. I'm laying down, leaning on the kennel post just waiting. He comes forward with one paw then backs off with another. Back and forth. I start counting it up and he goes through thirty-seven little foot jumps in no time. Just like a boxer. Figures he's going to be a pretty fast fella. Then he comes in closer and romps onto my stomach. "Yap-yap," he says. The tongue's gogged out and I poke him one and miss. Then he jumps up and puts one of those teeth into my nose. It feels all sharp and hot and blood starts oozing out onto my hand.

"No dumb puppy is ever gonna outsmart me!" I grab him by the scruff of the neck and wipe a little of the blood onto his nose. Then I just shake him and start counting. It's one-two-three. I shake and shake, flicking the puppy in my hand every time I hit another number. Pretty soon I'm in the hundreds and thousands and the numbers fly past until I've lost hold of everything but that dog and I'm fixed up in space where no one can find me.

Some time later Carol and Nick show up right out of the blue. Carol's yelling "Stop it! Stop it, Billy!" and shakes me by the shoulders. My eyes blink a little and I come to, but she's not done shaking me. Then she backhands me across the face. "Lookit what you done!" and she swats back on the other cheek. "Lookit what you done!" But the next time when her hand swipes past me I sink my teeth into it hard as I can.

"Let go, you bastard!" She screams louder than I ever heard before but I just let her blast and bite even harder. It's scary as hell, but God, it feels good.

"Let go, you *bastard!*" But I don't. I chomp into her tighter than ever. I've got my teeth into her and I can feel her knuckles rolling around. I can't let go even if I wanted it. Everything's out of control.

Then Nick comes up to try and gentle me. "Take it easy now, Billy," he says. "That's enough boy, that's enough."

I want to stop it cause Nick's so good about it, but I just don't know how to stop.

"Just loosen your jaw, boy, and breathe easy. Just take a deep breath and loosen your jaw." I don't know how he does it but his voice sounds so low and smooth. With Carol screaming and me gurgling and chomping, it's like having three radio stations on at once. So I stop listening to myself and Carol and just tune in on that low voice of Nick's. A voice just like sugar tea.

"Come on, Billy. Come on, slack those muscles down." Suddenly everyone's listening to Nick and I manage to let go of Carol's hand. She looks at it careful and her face whitens.

"Look at that, you bastard." She moves back to the far side of the kennel and wraps the bit fingers in her good ones.

Nick leans down to me and takes the pup out of my hand. I don't even realize that I'm still holding the thing. It's not much more than a ball of dead fluff at this point. All dead and gone. "Come on," he says, "we should all go inside now."

I go ahead of him so there's a barrier between me and Carol. She tags along with a white sheen in her face. Her eyes are dark and afraid like she's just seen a bad movie.

"Now you get into bed," Nick says when he's got me in my

room. "I'm gonna take Carol to the hospital. Then I'll be back after that."

"Then what?" I ask.

"What do you mean?"

"What happens to me?"

"I don't know, Billy." He comes over and pats me on the shoulder. I look at his hand and my jaw doesn't have the least idea of biting into it. It feels good to know I'm not going to bite him, too. "I just don't know," he says.

Later that night they come back. Nick's wearing a worried look on his face and Carol has her arm wrapped in white bandages. Three cops pull in behind them and help me dress. They take me off in the squad car and I never see Nick or Carol again.

They're almost like a dream, except it's the first thing I remember so clear. And the first thing you remember is the most important truth you could ever learn.

CHAPTER 3

It worked out that I landed in the John Balding Children's Institute and had to stay there three years. When I first went in I didn't know a thing. But when I came out I knew enough to read the *John Balding Children's Institute* sign and think it was a pretty good laugh.

"I was never a balding child," I tell Frank, the guard at the gate.

"I don't know." Frank says "I don't know" to everything.

"I wasn't."

"Well," he straightens the knot of his tie, "first time you came in here, Billy, I remember you crying and screaming and holding onto your head like every one of those black hairs were about to fly off like kites!"

"Nah."

"Yes you were."

"No way." But I know he's right. I was there at least half a year before anything good happened. And even when the good came I thought I was going to die from the piss coming out of my eyes.

There was one nurse, Rose was her name, who was pretty special at making things happen. She had a big square face with eyes that never let go of you. And she had big breasts pulled to each side so there was a lot of room between them. Whenever her eyes locked onto me I'd drop mine down to her chest. At least those two breasts didn't look back.

The first time anything good happened it took me by surprise. She kept at me twenty or thirty times with the same old line: "Come on, Billy, tell me about it." Rose could stick right to it, specially when she got me in the one-way room. That's the room with mirrors all along one wall. Except there's only mirrors on one side. On the other side is another room they fill up with shrink doctors and T.V. cameras. The doctors look through the mirrors like windows. And they've got mikes in the ceiling so they can hear everything like radios. All of them shrinks'd live up there and watch and listen and figure your brain out. *Even if you say nothing it means something.*

So I used to tap away on the floor with this special oak stick I'd whittled down from a tree branch. They never let you keep anything that had a pointy tip to it, so my stick was rounded and blunt on the ends. But it was a good tapping stick. I hit on the floor as the nurse talked away and just let my eyes flicker and start counting the number of taps I'd get in.

"Tell me what it was like," Rose says. Her voice is soft and full of sugar water. You almost feel like you could climb onto that voice and go to sleep. Like it's a big stuffed chair.

"Billy, tell me what it was like at Carol's house," she says. This sounds pretty easy to answer but it scares hell out of me. I keep tapping away, counting the taps. Three thousand five, three thousand six. . . .

"Then tell me what it was like before Carol's. Before you ever even lived at Carol's."

That's a good question. I stop tapping the oak stick and just think about it. What *did* happen?

Then a little yellow light switches on near the door and Rose gets up. "Just stay here, okay? They want me outside."

She's gone for new orders. I've seen it when they've got other kids in the one-way room. After a while when things aren't going too hot, the nurse comes out and walks into the viewing room. That's where the shrinks are who tell her what to do. That's their main job: giving orders. They take something that someone's saying or doing and squeeze it and shrink it down into one tiny thing.

Rose comes back with a funny look on her face. I stop thinking and start in with the stick again.

"I'm going to tell you a little story, Billy." Her voice sounds like it's trying to pretend. But it's soft like an armchair. "Only this story isn't make-believe. It's a true story. It's about a little boy who gets lost a few days after he's born. It's all about what happens to him."

I'm still tapping away but not counting any more, sometimes listening to her pretty close but without telling her yes or no.

"Once there was this long highway in the countryside with hardly any cars on it. And one morning this old truck pulls off onto one side of the road. The door opens wide and an Indian girl gets out of the truck. Her name is Sally Deerborn. She's not very old, just five or six years older than you are right now. Let's say fifteen. But she's tired of travelling and sits near the road and puts the packages down beside her. That old truck turns onto a dirt road and leaves her sitting there on her own. All she's got with her, the only thing in the world, are these three packages. One is her clothes and the other is some food. You know what's in that third bag, Billy?"

I tap a little louder so she thinks I don't care about no paper bags.

"It's her little baby: Billy Deerborn, her newborn son that she's taking on his first trip. Now, something happens to her, something that makes her disappear. Maybe it's the wind spirits. Or maybe Jesus calls her into heaven. But something very important, something much bigger than Sally Deerborn, takes her away and leaves her three packages behind. Now the funny thing is, those bags sit there all afternoon. They sit there till the next morning, when the same truck comes by from the opposite direction and sees them next to the road. The truck driver gets out of his truck and looks in the bag and sees the little baby crying away. He's crying so hard he can't stop. He's wrapped in a wool blanket but his head's sticking out and it's cold and he's crying so loudly the truck driver doesn't know what to do. At first he can't believe that someone would just leave a baby like that. But then he believes it when he listens to the baby and looks across the miles of open prairie and sees that Sally Deerborn has disappeared. So he lifts the bag into his truck and drives it into town to the police station."

I stop tapping and feel my arms shaking and my breathing going to quivers. I know what Rose is trying to tell me and feel the piss inside my eyes pushing out like hell itself.

She doesn't say nothing for a while but just looks at me. Then she uses her best voice and says it real simple: "And that's who you are. You're that baby grown up now and your real name's Billy Deerborn."

"No it isn't," I tell her.

She looks like she might start crying, her face turns so gentle on me. "Billy Deerborn's a fine name," she says.

"It is not. It's an Indian name!" I start banging the oak stick onto the floor so she knows I mean business.

"Yes, it's an Indian name. And so is Billy Deerborn. You're part Indian, Billy."

"He is *not!*"

"Yes," she says with the sofa voice, "you are."

"I am not." I bang the stick harder. "My name is Billy . . . Billy *Stick!*" And I smash that stick over and over until it gets a crack and it's finished as a good stick.

Finally she's not saying a word any more. She looks at me and curls up next to me on the floor.

"My name is Billy Stick," I tell her, but she's not believing it. "It's Billy Stick."

I can feel myself tire out like that Sally Deerborn was so tired. Then all of a sudden I start crying. And all the time I thought it was Rose that was gonna cry. But I start crying and fall into her arms crying like that baby, and she wraps me up with those arms and it's like a big soft bed that God invented.

"Okay, Billy, okay," she says and rocks me back and forth. She's gentle everywhere and my head's right between her breasts and she just pushes my head against them like it's all right. "Okay, Billy, okay, okay." She rocks away until I'm dreaming that the clouds have filled up my brain and took me like the wind.

After that I tell her all about Carol and the Dobermans and Nick. Then I tell her more and more and start remembering *before* I lived with Carol. But I don't really remember it perfect and maybe make some of it up. That's fine with Rose. She lets me rock in her arms every time we're in the one-way room and says how lousy it must've been. "I guess you missed a big piece of life. A big piece of loving," she says. "That's your *missing* piece, Billy Deerborn. Loving."

□   □   □

The doctor at the John Balding Children's Institute was pretty good at getting me to open up, too. He'd see me in his office. There wasn't a one-way glass there but he used tape recorders all the time. He wouldn't even try to hide it. He'd ask me to wait a minute while he set the whole thing up. Then he'd put the mike right in front of me and ask if I'd mind being recorded. I never said I minded cause I liked the machine so much.

His office has a black door and a silver doorknob that makes me think about death. But once he opens the door things are okay. He's a big guy with white curly hair and glasses that are so thick I can't see his eyes until he takes the glasses off and sticks one end into his mouth. That's when I see his teeth and how long they are. They're clean white teeth but long, so it's a little scary and it makes me listen to what he's saying.

I step into his office and he does his best to make me feel easy. "Hi, Billy," he says, "how're you today?"

I nod and that's all. It's always hard to say much right off.

I go over to my regular chair, a black one, and sit down. He sits in his chair and there's the little table in between us. I look around to take up the time, but there's not much to see. The blinds are always pulled and there's no pictures on the walls. Just a couple of framed letters with fancy writing. He told me once that those were his *degrees*. He got five of them.

"Look, I got a problem," he says after a while, "and I wonder if you could help me out." He rolls up his forehead so it wrinkles into about ten lines.

"Probably," I tell him. But don't laugh—like any other kid, I fall for it.

"Well, good. I'm glad you're feeling so confident today."

Maybe not feeling too confident, but with those forehead wrinkles I always think he's worried and needs to feel better about things.

"Now look at this." He brings over a lunch tray that's got a white scarf covering it. He sets the thing down on the table near me and just points at it with his finger. He's got one big gold ring on his hand, but he points with one of his clean fingers. "You can take the cloth off that and see my problem," he says.

Well, fine. I take the cover off and see this big mess underneath. It's tubes and wires and knobs. All electric parts sucked from the guts of a radio.

"Wow, where'd you get them parts?"

"My old radio at home. See, I told you I've got a problem. Now, if I can't get those parts together, then that radio's no good."

I'm hardly listening to him because I'm sorting through all the speaker wires and transistors and dials. It's the best thing I've ever seen—having all those electrics right in front of me. I start plugging things together just like a jigsaw puzzle. Pretty soon I've got the outside edges all snapped in, then I try each piece in the middle.

"Why, you're pretty good at that, Billy."

"Uh-huh." I can't bother looking up at him cause I'm so busy with the radio.

"Yes, sir, you've got a real electronic talent."

I keep fitting the pieces together, forcing a few things here and there until finally I've got maybe a third of it figured. Pieces of it fit together right away, some have colours that match up and with others I make a good guess. After ten minutes a third of it's fixed and it looks like the doctor's problem is gonna get solved. But then he asks some tricky stuff and tries to make a few things happen.

"I also hear you're a pretty good talent with numbers, Billy."

"I'm an okay counter."

"That's right. One of the nurses told me you count up to a million."

"Yeah."

"Think you could show me how you do that?" He takes the radio tray and pulls it off the table and sets it on the floor. "You mind if I put this away for a while? I'll put it back when you've showed me your counting, okay?"

It usually bugs me when a guy does something and later asks if what he did is okay with me. But with this doctor I know his word is good most of the time and he doesn't do things just to show he can squeeze me. In fact, if I said no, that would be okay and he'd leave the counting part till later.

"Sure," I tell him and sit back in the chair like it's my own office, not his. "When do you want me to start?"

"How about right now. And let me know when you get to a thousand."

So I count up, and do it slower than normal just so I don't shock him. Then when I'm in the three hundreds he butts in.

"Billy, how do your eyes feel right now?"

"Tight. I always shut 'em tight so the light don't come in. It's because I turn my eyes into T.V. screens. It's like a computer does the counting."

"What would happen if you tried it with your eyes open?"

"Nothin' . . . I wouldn't count up at all."

"Okay. Keep going."

Then when five hundred rolls along he butts in again: "Billy, what does it feel like to be counting like you are?"

"All right. Just counting. It feels like numbers. Fast numbers."

"Okay. You keep going to a thousand and let me know when you're done."

I finish up like it's a race and he's pretty impressed at how fast it ends.

"Where'd you first learn to count like that, Billy?"

That's a good one. It's like asking where you first learned to talk. "I don't know."

"Well, was it at Carol's?"

"No."

"Was it in a house, or in the country . . . or in a car, or on a train?"

"In a car." It *was* in a car.

"Now tell me, Billy, what was happening in that car that made you start counting?"

"I don't know." Maybe counting the telephone poles. Maybe the clouds.

"Well, let's try and figure this," he says and smiles a little. "Tell you what. You sit back in that chair and close your eyes and we'll try some counting. Only this time I want you to start counting backwards from a hundred. But you count out loud so I can hear you and do it as slowly as you can."

I never tried backwards counting before so this is pretty tricky, even with my eyes closed. After a while he tells me to relax and go slower and relax some more. Pretty soon I'm stuck between two numbers and can't remember what comes next, so I'm saying "seventy-seven, seventy-seven," over and over and can't stop. He says to relax and stay where I am and just look around like I'm still in the car counting.

"What do you see in the car, Billy?"

"Nothing much. I'm in the back seat on my own." But it's funny how real it is, how I feel that I'm right back there in this big old seat of a '56 Chevy.

"Who's in the front seat, Billy?"

"I don't know."

"Pretend you can take a look. Just stick your head into the front seat and look."

I do it just as simple as he says. And there they are: a man and a woman. They're hunched together next to the wheel, passing a can of beer between them, and the guy's driving like sixty just beating down the highway. I slip onto the floor and lie low. There's something scary about going so fast.

"Who do you see, Billy?"

"A man and a woman. I don't know who it is, but they're driving pretty fast."

"Take another look up front. Just have a peek into the front seat and tell me what you see."

I get off the back floor and glance over the seat back. Then I look square into their faces. It's Nick and Carol. The two of them giggling and laughing like crazy. Then it gets even more scary because Nick starts passing lots of cars and trucks and honking the horn as he goes. Then out front comes a big truck. I duck down fast. It's going to smack into us for sure.

"There's gonna be a crash!" I'm all pulled into myself and my muscles are shaking. Then I hear my teeth rattling from shivering so bad.

"Just relax, Billy. Take a few deep breaths and count further backwards. Let's start at 77 and go back: 76 . . . 75 . . . 74. . . ."

Then I drift off again. This time he doesn't have to tell me to look nowhere. I've tumbled out the back door and all of a sudden I'm sitting on the side of the road. It's out in the country somewhere and that truck has crunched into the Chevy. I'm just sitting there looking at it and seeing all the other cars driving past real slow. Somebody comes and wraps a blanket around me. All the cars pass by with the windows rolled down, looking at the crash. That's when I start counting them. There's hundreds. Just more and more all the time and I have to speed them up just to get rid of them. Just count and count until I don't know nothing more."

"What's going on, Billy?"

"I'm counting the cars. There's been a bad crack-up and I've been thrown out the back door. I'm just sitting there counting the cars."

"Tell me how that feels," he says.

"Don't feel like nothin'. It's too scary."

"What else is there, Billy? Tell me anything else you see. What about Nick and Carol?"

"Just the Chevy and the truck wrecked up together. Somebody's helping the two of them walk towards me. And there's this blanket around my shoulders. A big red striped wool blanket."

"Who gave you the blanket?"

"I don't know."

"Look into his face," he says. "Who is it?"

I look up to the face. But it's nobody. There's not even a face on the head. It's just a blank spot with no eyes or mouth. No nose or ears either. "It's nobody."

"Who would you like it to be? Let's say you could turn it into somebody. Who would you turn it into, Billy?"

I think a minute and look back into the blank face. Then I see that the face has turned into the doctor's. It's got the wrinkled lines across his forehead and his white hair and that smile with the long teeth. "It's you. The blank face is you!" Then my eyes pop open and he's there next to me but with no smile.

"Just close your eyes again, Billy. Then we'll open them in a minute. First tell me what we do next. Remember that you've got a blanket around you and we're next to the road."

"I don't know." It's just too mixed around and I'm starting to make things up.

He takes a minute to think things over. Then he breathes in so loud you can hear the air rolling up his nostrils. "Listen, Billy. You know why I think you started counting that day? Why you're such a good counter now?"

"No."

"Well, it's because of what happened. Because you were so scared you didn't know what else to do. It's as though counting all those cars driving by was the one thing you could think of to keep all your feelings under control. And with those feelings controlled, you felt safe. Do you feel safe when you're counting, Billy?"

"Yeah. A little."

"I can understand why," he says. "Those were some pretty powerful feelings you had at that accident. I bet they were terrifying." Then he waits some more. "Would you like to tell me more about it?" His voice sounds like he's finished digging into me.

"No," I tell him. "I'd like to fix your radio!" My eyes open again and this time he smiles and nods to show me that it's all right to keep them open.

"That radio's pretty important to you, isn't it?" He puts the lunch tray loaded with all the electronics in front of me.

"Yes, sir."

"Then why don't you take the radio to your room and bring it back in one piece next time? Okay?"

"Sure!" It's a miracle he'd give the whole thing to me. So before he goes back on the promise I cart the lunch tray with all the parts down to my room.

It takes another hour before I figure out there's one bloody piece missing and the whole damned thing's no good. Then another of the mental kids, Barney Williams, comes in and starts bugging me to the point where I have to swat him just to keep him in line. Eventually he goes one step too far and I throw the radio at his head and it explodes into a hundred pieces when it hits the wall. It bangs next to the light switch and all the vacuum tubes explode at once. But the amazing thing is the sound of it. *Whhhhop!* I never thought it could sound so good.

The nurses come charging down the hall when they hear the radio exploding and Barney crying because he's bleeding at the nose where some glass from the radio cut into him. Then I'm given the big needle. That's what happens whenever you break hospital property or hit the nurses or draw blood on one of the kids. The needle is huge and it goes in so hard it feels like they'll suck out all my blood. In three years I had the needle about ten times. But now the sound and the feel of the radio cracking apart make it all worth it. As they shove that needle into my arm I can picture the radio exploding in the air and I don't feel a stitch of pain. And the fact is, it's the last time anyone ever gives me a needle again.

CHAPTER 4

By the time I left the hospital I was twelve years old. It was just about the time you were getting to know me. Funny, when I think back on it. The way you came like a friend when I had no friends at all.

The doctors set up a foster home for me and the foster man and woman started off asking me to call them Dad and Mom. It took about ten months before they'd had it with me and telephoned the social workers and told them to haul me in. Before the social workers got me, though, I packed a bag and stole some of my foster parents' boot money—they always kept spare cash in an old boot in the cupboard—and made a clean getaway. It was the first time I ever hitchhiked anywhere. I escaped over eight hundred miles before the boot money ran out and they caught me stealing fresh bagels from a bakery.

After that, two or three more foster homes turned me away and I graduated to a group home. The group home held anywhere from three to six kids at a time. After a year there I was the old-timer and got the best room. It wasn't bad, really. They allowed me the weekends off and it was then that I roamed around the country and discovered the world. There was one weekend trip that beat all the others to hell. The one with the Lincoln car. It happened just as I put the finishing touches on my hitchhiking routine.

When it comes to hitchhiking, I've got a lot of tricks that guarantee me a ride. First, I butt out my cigarette and make sure my shirt's tucked in. Then I stand on a hilltop or under a street light if it's night—anywhere so they can see me plain. You don't want to surprise anybody and it's best to let a decent picture of me sink into their brains. I also make a strong point of standing clear of any other hiker on the road. That way the drivers don't think they're picking up more than one person. Then I start whistling that special tune: "Ninety-nine Bottles." It's like fishing, only I whistle down the cars instead of fish. Eventually one of them hears me and is lured over and then I've hooked him. Once they've got the window rolled down, it's just feeding them the right line that's important. And the right line works like any other storytelling. I start with something simple but true and build it up until it's a full-blown sailor's yarn. That's how I build this one story about hitching a ride when a wild young broad picked me up for the joy ride of a lifetime. I guess I was just sixteen. Still young. And I'd never had a lay. Funny, you know, when I was a kid, and I had never had it, the thought of making it with a *real* woman just drove me wild. Drove me into the worst places. Places I'd never think to go to once I was grown up a little.

On this one summer day it's hot like six ovens. Some Devil angel scraped all the clouds from the sky and the sun hits down like a whip. I keep my thumb out nice and high and keep whistling and watch the little beads of sweat running off my arm into my shirt sleeve. Taking the shirt off may seem like an idea but it scares most drivers to have a bare-skinned hiker in a car. So I keep it on and sweat it out, hoping to get an air-conditioned Cadillac that's going straight to the Ritz.

After an hour this new Lincoln pulls over. It's going so fast I have to run a hundred yards to where it stopped. I'm running like a pig, sweating every inch, thinking about what a cool cream colour the car is. Just as cool as ice cream.

"Hi. Where're you going?" asks the young chick inside. She's maybe eighteen or nineteen, just old enough so I have to look up to the fact she's not sixteen like me.

"East."

She's got the window cracked just enough so we can talk. I'm bent over leaning on the door.

"East?" She says it like she doesn't have the faintest idea where in the world east is.

"Yeah," and I point down the road. "Straight ahead."

Then she starts sizing me up. She's got on big dark glasses that cover her cheekbones and eyebrows. She's nothing special looking and pretty flat-chested with tumbled up brown hair and skinny legs coming out of her shorts. She keeps looking at me and opening and closing her mouth real slow and clicking her tongue over her teeth.

"Okay," she says. "East it is."

I get in beside her and roll the window down and flick open the vent so the air rushes all over me.

After a while she starts talking about how hot it is and even with the windows down and doing seventy it's still hotter than hell. Her hair's blowing in the air all bushed out like a fan. She tells me her name is Celeste and I tell her mine. Then she asks all kinds of questions about me like what do I do and where do I live? When she hears I'm going to join the army in a few years it really impresses her. She's pretty taken with some army people she's met in the past and tells me this long story about a general who had two wives at the same time living in two different countries. After ten minutes we run out of chit-chat and coast along without a word. But then she can't adjust to being too quiet and dreams up a few more questions.

"What town you going to, anyhow?" She finishes passing a line of four cars and gives me a smile. "I'm going into Bainton myself."

"Never been there." I give off a smile to show I'm the friendly type.

"I'm going to a movie."

"Yeah? I've been to movies."

"Want to go to this one? It's good. It's at least fifteen years old but it's still good. I've seen it once already. There's fights in it. You like fights?"

"Sure."

"Then you'll like this one. It's called *On the Waterfront*. I think it's won a couple of awards."

"I don't know." I drag out a big sigh so she thinks the idea is boring. But the fact is I don't have enough money to see no show. "Maybe not."

"Well, think about it. Just as an idea." She smiles with an odd tilt to her head and passes another car fast as she can. "This is a Lincoln, you know."

"I know."

"It's very expensive." And then she sets her fingers onto her shirt and unbuttons the shirt very casual, like she's on her own. "God, that breeze feels good. Here, light us some cigarettes." And she gives me two cigarettes and a lighter.

I light up the smokes and pass one to her. The wind is kicking her blouse all over and her chest is bare and clean and so suntanned she must do this every day. Her nipples are standing up in the wind like dark nuts. For a minute I just stare at them, thinking how good they'd taste, how sweet they'd be in my mouth.

"You want a beer?" She looks at me over the top of her glasses. They've slipped off her nose and you can see that she's got tight bug eyes that take everything in.

"Sure."

"Reach over the back." She puts a hand onto her tit and points to the back seat with her thumb. "They're in the cooler."

I pull out two cans of cold dripping beer and pop the lids open and take a guzzle on one. She takes her beer and rubs the can around her face and over her chest. Then she takes a little swig and props the can between her legs.

We drive on pretty quietly and I start to think that things are going okay. I've got a free ride with booze and cigarettes and a lady who drives with her shirt open. Once in a while I turn my head to look at her chest, pretending to look at the scenery on the left. Everytime I do it she looks right at me and flags out her smile and says something pointless like do I know the time or did I think her tan was okay and did I think this was the hottest day of the year? I poke out some answer or another and turn my head away, figuring she doesn't like my looking at her that way. Eventually we get into Bainton and she asks me about the movie again.

"Nah . . . I can't."

"Why not?" She buttons up her shirt at the first traffic light after a few people in the crosswalk look into the car.

"I don't have the money for it." I mean to tell her something else but the facts slip out accidental.

"No problem, I got lots." She drives around a few blocks and parks in front of a beat up theatre called The Lux that shows old midweek matinees for a few bucks. With the engine shut off she wiggles around in her seat and faces me square and snaps the arms of her sunglasses together. Now I can see her whole face. She's got on eye makeup to make her eyes seem bigger, but it's smudged in the heat and turned into two washed-out circles.

"We'll take some beer for refrigeration . . . and a *special* surprise." She clicks her tongue in her mouth to show that the surprise is a big deal and collects two beer from the cooler and sticks them in her purse.

"Okay."

"Good. See—it's all part of the trip."

Inside she hikes up to the top balcony, to the last row in the corner. She's ahead of me and I can see how tall and skinny she is. At least four inches over me when we finally stand even on the stairs. We sit down and the chairs smell rancid from ages of sweat collected from midday bums and winos that sleep out the one-buck matinees. After my eyes adjust I can make out a few of them way below us, with their damp heads just showing over the seat backs. The odd time you'll see them light up their cigarettes and hear a few bottles roll down the aisles. Then sometimes they'll swear or call out like there's demons in them and they've had too many hard days.

After a while the lights dim and the cartoon starts. We hunker down in the seats and Celeste opens her purse and pulls out a smoke. She lights it up under her hand so you can't see the flame, then leans way back and takes a deep drag and blows out a cloud of sweet grey smoke. There's no mistaking it. It's marijuana. She takes another toke and passes the joint to me and I puff light as I can, so it won't hit me too hard. With grass I have to be careful. The two times I tried it I went straight down the river and over the falls. Had no idea what hit me.

"Come on, Billy, take a good haul. This stuff's got THC *concentrate.*" She takes another drag herself to show me what to do.

"I don't know." Already my head's got a tiny whirlpool starting to bore into the centre of my brain.

"Oh come on—*Billy.*" She says it like some kind of cheap swear word. I take the joint and haul so deep and hard the smoke funnels into my chest like a rollercoaster. It goes down and down until I choke and start coughing like a drowning man. When I cough the smoke comes boring out my nose and mouth. Soon my eyes are watering and I can't hold my head still to see the damn cartoon.

"Oh Billy! Oh Christ, Billy!" She starts laughing and sucking on the joint through two fingers like she's holding some French cigarette. Then she passes it back to me and tries to shush herself up by wrapping her hands over her mouth. But her eyes are still laughing at me, jabbing and taking pokes at my coughing so bad. I take two puffs and hold it in and pass it back and she takes another drag, then butts it out and puts the butt into her purse.

"Pretty good, huh, Billy?" She leans over and wraps her arm through mine. Every time she calls my name she puts a little poison onto it and the whirlpool in my brain starts widening deeper and deeper and her poison sits on the edge, ready to plunge into the centre.

"Let's just watch the show," I tell her. By this time the cartoon's over and they're rolling the coming attraction, a Zorro movie. She leans onto me even more and slumps her ass way across the seat to get down to my height. Then she rummages through her purse for a beer and cracks it open. We sip the beer and finally *On the Waterfront* starts up. This is when Celeste gets excited and presses my arm in and out to show me what a big deal it is for her.

"Just wait until you see Marlon Brando," she says and wraps an arm around my shoulders. "He's got big shoulders. And he's cute as hell—just like you," she giggles.

All this feeling that she's doing is starting to be okay. At first it was like grabbing a bunch of hamburger meat, but now she's stroking more like she cares about *me*. The marijuana whirlpool starts to lighten up in my brain and almost disappears enough for me to really relax. I put my hand onto her thigh and start to squeeze it in and out. For the first time I realize I'm really going to get laid!

Whenever Brando's in the movie she gets specially horny and starts whispering in my ear: "You're my Marlon man, my Marlon man." Then she moves my hand onto the right places and lets me toy around for awhile. Her shorts are the short-short kind, so I just let my fingers do the walking and she begins to squeam all over the seat. When we start kissing I realize how long and narrow her face is. And all of a sudden there's something about kissing her that jerks my head back. It's like whiplash, it's so sudden and painful. Part of me wants to screw her right on the floor. And the other part wants to squeeze her thin little head between the chairs. The whole thing just rips me too far in both directions. My head snaps out of place and my hands pull back and the whirlpool opens up like Niagara Falls. There's just steam and roaring and terror.

"What's wrong?"

"Just shut up," I tell her, grinding my teeth and rubbing my neck where the whiplash is worst.

"But what's wrong?" She's got this worried look and leans back to the other side of the seat.

"Nothing's wrong!" I look into the movie without really watching. It's a good idea to keep one eye fixed on her. If she comes over again I'll have to give her some kinda warning without really smacking her. Don't know what it is about her that got to me. Just all of a sudden my teeth start grinding like I'm going to bite into my own tongue. And then the marijuana goes dead centre into my guts. It's as though too much is happening all at once. Wanting to get laid so bad. Then the marijuana, then the feel of her skinny face pushed against mine. Maybe that's what started the teeth digging around in my jaw. Whatever it is, it never happened before.

After another half hour the storm's closed off enough so I can let down my guard. She hasn't moved any closer to my seat, so maybe it's time to let her know things are okay.

"How 'bout that other beer?"

She looks at me like a cop would and then wipes all the suspicion off her face and smiles. "Sure," she says and snaps the tab open on the can. I suck it down in one long cool swig. The beer reminds me of how hot the air is and how my clothes are wet and stuck to the chair. With the sweat and Celeste starting to close in on me again I don't give much concentration to the show. There's a lot of tough crowd scenes with Brando kicking up a fuss any time somebody gets too sly. Most times he gets the shit kicked out of him and that does a special trick for Celeste.

"Oh-h-h," she says, and holds onto the muscles in my arm. "Let's be good to one another honey. Let's be good."

She runs her hands over me and in a while starts fishing around my pants. That opens the flood gates in my brain just enough for the marijuana to run wild again and I tense up and push back into the seat so hard the chair springs begin squealing.

"Just relax, Marlon honey. Celeste's gonna be good to you." She uses one hand to smooth my pantleg up and down as though she's trying to gentle a big black dog to sleep. "Be good, be good," she says over and over.

I let her do this petting on my leg and it ends up calming me down long enough for the flood gates to close to a trickle. Then I put my arm around her hips and start smoothing them back and forth. This works like a trigger for her and she starts to pant.

"God, Marlon, oh-god-oh-god!" Then she fishes me right out of my pants and pulls her shorts down, hobbles over the seat ahead of us and squats onto me so I'm lost in her skinny wet hips. All I can see is those little cheeks rolling down on me and her long back and the movie screen way below us with lots of noise coming from the speakers because another big fight starts. That's when I feel a tight lid come down onto my face. It's like a coffin closing all the light out. I fight it off at first and concentrate on her back jiggling up and down and the movie scene, but none of it works. What she's doing feels so good and bad at the same time. The closer she gets to me the the more trapped I feel, like I'm being lost inside her, buried and lost forever. Then the coffin closes down tight as a brick grave and the whirlpool spins through me. It's like a big machine in my head, a water machine, a drowning pool with four closing walls. I shut my eyes and see a few numbers clip by but the counting's all gone from me. It's dead and I know I'm getting buried alive.

Finally everything turns quiet. Except for the sound of feet running up the aisle stairs.

"Hey! What in hell's going on up there?" All of a sudden some guy yells at us like a cop and clicks on a flashlight.

"Oh, Jeezus!" Celeste moans out like a bad dream and pumps away furious and raw. But the coffin and flood gates smash together.

"It's cracked. It's cracked! IT'S CRACKED!" The screaming pours out of me and I jump from the chair. Celeste flops forward grabbing at the seat back, but she loses her balance and falls into the next aisle. Her legs start kicking into the air and she tugs at the shorts to get them onto her rump, hollering "Jeeeeezus! Jeeeeezus! Jeeeeezus!" just when the flashlight hits us.

"Stop that damned yelling!" the guy says and I shut right up and zip my pants. Can't see his face because the spotlight's right on my eyes.

"Look at the two of them," he says.

"Yeah. Bunch of sex artists." There's someone else there and when they swing the lamp onto Celeste I see four or five ushers bunched down at the end of the row.

"Okay, you two've gotta go. Get your clothes together and we'll see you out."

"We paid our goddamned money," Celeste spits out, but she's ready to leave. She climbs back to her seat and grabs her purse. "We paid our money and we want it back."

They take us down to the front doors and she haggles with the manager about getting a refund. I'm outside standing in the sun, just happy to be out of The Lux and into a big open space. She and the manager start revving the conversation up to where they're yelling louder and louder and she points me out to the manager and screams "My brother will tell you. C'mere Marlon, and tell this guy!"

I just look at the two of them. She's got her skinny face all red hot and the manager tilts his head and looks puzzled, like he's just spotted me for the first time. It feels like I'm a block away, but they've both got faces that *want me to do something. Anything*.

"Come on, Marlon, tell this A-hole about our money!" The manager's face curls up when she says this and I can tell he's ready to grip that thin neck of hers and snap it in two.

"Come on! Tell him!" and she stamps her foot and the red face goes sheet-white and she starts shaking and pounding the sidewalk with both feet. "Come on, tell him! TELL HIM!"

Then the guy surprises me. He doesn't touch her at all. He just goes through the door and locks it up tight. That's when I realize what to do. I turn around and start down the block past the cream-coloured Lincoln. She starts yelling louder and louder, but I pick up the pace and break into a run. Then I start running like hell, fast as possible and stepping on every sidewalk crack because it's a curse on her: "Step on a crack—break her back." Every step shatters that long skinny spine of hers and my feet hit down extra hard on the curb and gutter cracks. I run and run until my lungs are bursting open and the whirlpool rushes through me till it's drained empty, and everything turns white as though the sun exploded and bleached out all the buildings and cars and people's faces and clothes, and everything's white and exploded and broken and I run and run and run.

And when all the juice in my legs finally spills off I slump down under a tree and think the whole story through. I'd run so hard there's nothing left but the memory of Celeste and her big car and the way she's grown into a legend. At least that's the way I tell it to the boys in the squad. Most of it's stretched out to keep them laughing. But the part about the whirlpool and my teeth grinding so bad is all true. In fact, if anything, I cut the facts about grinding my jaw a bit short. It's the kind of thing you don't tell just anyone. Right?

CHAPTER 5

The military has a way of giving you a family. Not the kind most people think of, with sisters and grannies cooing after you at Christmas, but the kind that pulls you through. The brotherhood. There's something very powerful and true that ties you together and knots the rope tight.

So when I turned twenty-one, I decided I was going to try to make a life of it.

One thing about the army is that everyone in it got lost somewheres along the line. Specially in the all-volunteer army. You can tell right off that half the guys don't know *why* they joined up and the other half don't know *how*. Maybe they got too drunk one night and signed up in the worst part of a hangover next morning. Or maybe their girls dropped them and they went so horny they thought the army would beat the sex right out of their dicks. And for some of them it was either into the army or into jail. But no matter what the past facts might be, every single one of them wants to straighten something out. So to start with, they're the biggest bunch of mixed-up men you'll see.

But at first I start off loving every minute of it. And the hardest drills are the very best. Strange when I think about it, but the tougher they make each exercise, the more of it I want. I'm dying for the roughest there is and that's why Sergeant Rand seems like a god. He pushes until everybody drops. "Hut-two-three-four! Hut-Hut-Hut!" He yells it out, moving us around the training field like a big machine. Everyone kicks their boots into the air and bangs them down so the earth shakes. It's really something—to rattle the whole world in battle march.

After a few weeks it seems like the way all life should be. Everything's figured out beforehand and everyone knows what they're supposed to be doing. It's one step in front of the other, about-face and back you come. Even the crooked twist-ups start fitting in. But there's no room for a lot of mistakes and any guy who doesn't fit drums out the back door in a hurry. Perry and Wilson were gone in the first two months. Nobody knows what happened. One morning they'd just disappeared—by 5:30 reveille they'd vanished. Not a crease in their bunks, not a sheet turned over. And once they're gone you don't ask for reasons. That's what I found out fast.

"Where's Perry and Wilson?" I ask the sarge.

"You speakin' to me?"

"Yes, sir!" My heels kick together so they crack like a pistol.

"Well listen up, Deerborn. You shouldn't be asking about nothing 'less it concerns your nose or mine. Got it?"

"Yes, sir!" I make it snappy so he knows I'm in the picture. Everything's fast and sharp in the military. All the brass want to think they're building the best machine in history. What makes more trouble than anything else is when someone starts to spoil their dream. It's the first thing I learn.

After three months' basic training they shuffle everyone into advanced training groups for another three months: artillery, armour, communications, engineers, infantry—the list goes on forever. First we write some tests with yes-and-no questions: Are you afraid of snakes? Is water heavier than air? Is this your first time out of your home town? Does the sun rise in the west? And there are at least twenty questions about your family: Do you like it when your mother goes on holiday? Is your sister open-hearted? That question really got to me. All I could think of was Celeste and how she's the most open-hearted person you'll ever meet. I put "yes" even though it was a lie, since I don't have a sister. Lied about a few others, too, specially in the personal questions.

Funny thing is that they never ask what you're best at or what you *want* to do. Don't know of one guy who got what he thought he should. It's like they just throw some dice and you take the number that shows. Hoping for the armour corps gets me nowhere and in the end they stick me into the field engineers.

The School of Military Engineering has a special section called Combat Engineers. That's where they unload me, and the truth is it turns out to be the best three months of classroom training in my life. We get all the theory work and a few trial runs and some lab time, and then they split the group up and everyone slips off to different outfits. After graduation I'm sent to a combat engineer regiment with a brand-new uniform on my back and a head full of ideas about high-tech explosives. But the way we hear it from the new combat engineer sarge, the real education is just about to start. Anything we learned about explosives so far is just the first ten letters of the alphabet. That's what he says, anyway.

The new sergeant is named Tilden, a big square man with a blank face and shoulders that look like two-by-sixes. Whenever he talks there's a bite to it, and he's got a way of snapping off your name like a wolf.

"Jamison!"

"Yes, sir."

"Michaels!"

"Yes, sir."

"Deerborn!"

"Yes, sir."

"Wiggins!"

Nothing. Everyone keeps their heads locked dead ahead, but their eyes are shifting around like a hawk's.

"WIGGINS!"

"Yes, sir." A whimper squeaks out behind me and Tilden flattens him down with one fast look.

"Now, most of you boys been picked for two or three good reasons." He's strutting up and down in front of us. We're three lines deep, four to a line. "One thing is, you're all pretty smart. 'Cept none of you ever took the bother to learn. Another thing is that you're supposed to have nerve." He cocks his head a bit and almost smiles. "But that's something we'll find out—won't we?"

The big speech goes on a few more minutes. It's about a cool hand in a hot fire. That's what demolition work wants: cool hands. If you get a bunch of scram-guts when the heat's on, then you're in trouble. The last thing anybody needs is for some egg yolk to pull an ignitor pin early and kill off a dozen men before everything's set. So we're the guys picked to play it cool, and the army is going to fix it so by the time we're through, every inch of jitter is cut out and thrown on the slag heap.

The nickname of our squad is Fire Eyes. It goes back to World War I, when they sent men out into the mustard gas to sap and destroy the German trenches. The gas burnt them so bad they decided to get even, so instead of running away like the first time, they pulled on their masks and went straight into it, asking the Krauts for more, begging for all they had, then blowing the shit right out of their sauerkraut pants.

At least that's the story you hear. Also that once you're in the Fire Eyes you get the tattoo—two big cool blue eyes etched into the skin, two eyes looking through the red flaming window of hell.

After Tilden makes his first big speech everyone wanders into the barracks. If you were flying a helicopter past and looked straight down, you'd see that the barracks is built like a letter H. In the two long sections are the lockers and bunks—enough for a troop of forty men. The four N.C.O.s each have private quarters, one assigned to each corner of the building. In the middle, the centre strip of the H, is a narrow hallway with showers and toilets on one side and laundry and cleaning supplies on the other. There's a few windows, but nothing much else. The whole thing is painted mint green and white inside and out, except the floors. They're coloured a kind of skin-brown.

The Fire Eyes has a few guys who start being your friend right off and a few others that'd sooner push your face in a hole. Jamison, for example, is a face-pusher that no matter how you try to dance away keeps on you like a cat. Most of the guys talk like they're pretty bored, like they'd sooner be off with their girls, but underneath their faces is a wall of fear. Most everybody is putting on the tough-guts act and it's a good idea, because once Jamison sees through it, you're finished. To Jamison the slightest trace of fear is a snake charm. He strikes and rips at you before you've had a chance to think.

"Hey, Knuckle Nose," he says, and his jaw drops down like he's going to laugh.

"Who're you gabbing at, Jamison?" Michaels whirls around and stares him down as good as he can.

"Why, I'm gabbing at you, Knuckle Nose." The jaw grinds away like he's chewing a huge wad of gum. It's as though the jaw is the only thing moving in his body. He's built like a wrestler, wide and stocky, thick in his legs and arms and through the middle of his face. And he has black hair curling out of his shirt—around his throat and the back of his neck and out the arm holes. But standing there, he's as solid and quiet as a brick wall, except for his jaw chewing slow and steady on that gum.

"Then say what you want."

"Damned right I'll say what I want. I always have, Knuckle, and I always will." He throws his jacket onto the bunk and bunches his hands onto his hips. "Point is, Knuckle Nose, that you've got your grub bag on my bunk."

Michaels doesn't say a thing, but looks at him for a good ten seconds. Then he lifts his hand into the air and brushes past the top of his head. Everybody's still got a bean shave, but his is grown in enough so you can see how blond he is. And his eyebrows are blond, too. They're bushy and jump up and down whenever he's talking or making a point about something. But right now those eyebrows are calm and steady, and his big hand sweeps back and forth as though he's wiping some dust from the top of his head. And that one hand makes me realize how big Michaels is, too. Not as stocky as Jamison, but taller and firm and rooted to the ground like a spruce tree. Then Michaels smiles and you can see all his teeth looking just like piano keys, they're so white and square. Just by smiling he's got the upper hand, but then he lays it on even thicker by doing a little song-and-dance around the bunk. "Yes, sir, Mr. Jamison, sir," he says, and he flits around the bunk, sweeping bits of dust away like a nigger maid. "Will that be all, Mr. Jay-me-son, sir?"

Everybody—Williams, Wiggins, Pollock, Sinclair, Tooler, Jackson, Turner, Maxwell, MacEwen, me—the whole squad—starts laughing up a good crock, seeing Michaels curtseying and sticking his finger up to his ass. Meanwhile Jamison's jaw stops grinding away and his head starts nodding back and forth.

"Yeah, there *is*, goddammit!" He yells it good and loud and cuts through all the laughing. Michaels turns and gives him a straight face and a quick wink to me.

"If you or any other guy starts messing up, you'll have some fast accounting to do." He jerks his thumb to point out two other guys who weren't laughing when Michaels did his nigger act.

"What kind of counting is that?" one of the blacks yells out from the back, as though he didn't follow the whole show.

"The worst kind. It'll be a six-inch firecracker up your sphincter." He walks around five or six steps so it looks like he's boss. "And for any Cock Nose too stupid for it, that means your caboose hatch is out of commission." And he kicks Michaels's bag onto the floor and unhinges his jaw again and rolls it round and round.

Then Sergeant Tilden marches in and everybody snaps to attention and we get dressed down because nobody's got their stuff unpacked and their bunks set right.

"Christ," Michaels whispers when the sarge is at the far end of the room, "this Jamison is going to be a touchy bastard."

I nod my head a little to show he's dead right, but I don't say a word.

      □   □   □

After our first regulation stint in the Fire Eyes, a one-day leave comes through and everybody in the squad rolls into town for a binge. Saxonville is about ten miles north of the base, and apart from Fairfield, about forty miles east, it's the only watering hole within an hour's drive. Saxonville doesn't have much attraction to it except three bars and a pool hall and the tattoo parlour that's been scratching the symbol into the squad since they finished the first war. Everybody knows that's what we're going for. But not a word of truth is breathed about it, and to start things off a lot of drinking has to be done.

Michaels drags me and a few others into O'Reilly's, the one bar that has a giant T.V. screen so you can see the football game anywhere in the house. It's the only bar that doesn't have a stripper rolling her tits into your beer, and that seems to please him even better.

"They'd only remind me of Charlene," he says, licking the beer off his lips, "and if I start thinking of Charlene I'm liable to clock any smart bastard who speaks dirty of her."

"Christ, listen to that, will ya." Wiggins jerks his tiny hand at Michaels and sours his face. Next to Michaels, Wiggins looks like a scrub brush. There's nothing to him but a short skinny body and a face that's terrible with ugliness. A line of scars runs from his mouth to the pock marks on his cheeks and chin. But the worst of it shows on his neck and forehead and under his eyes. The scars are red and full of pain and he holds a hand up to hide his face. And the way he holds that hand, as though he's smoking a cigarette, but shaking just at the fingertips—it shows how bad he wants to hide the mess on his face. He wants to see the stripper more than anything else. More than the drinking. More than the tattoo.

"Don't tell me you're *afraid* of big tits," he says.

But Michaels ignores every single word. "Will you look at that!" He swigs down a scotch and chases with a cold beer. "That's old Johnny Unitas doing half-time chit-chat with the players! T.V.'s great for the old-timers, ain't it?"

"Yeah, you're afraid." Wiggins is talking it up to Williams, a blond kid all the way from Florida. His face is pale and thin and sometimes I wonder how he ever passed the physical. The look in his eyes is always distant, as though he's ready to move on, like a leaf catching the wind and tumbling down the road. But the strangest thing about him is he never says a word. Because of that, he's easy to talk to. So whatever Wiggins says is really meant for Michaels. "And I betcha you're *terrified* of wet beavers—yeah, terrified."

"Backyard player, that's how Unitas started." Michaels downs another boilermaker and orders a fresh round from O'Reilly. Then he talks to me as if none of the other guys are there. "Just playing out in the streets with a few pals. Could be you and me, Billy. Out in the streets of Saxonville. You drift downfield fifty yards and I launch a perfect spiral. Then snag it out of the sky and whistle down the yard lines another fifty. And you know what? Old Johnston T. Spokes, chief scout for the 49ers, just happens to be sitting at that window"—he points out the exact chair where Johnston sits on a free Saturday afternoon—"and he sees the whole play right under his nose. That's all it takes, one tight pass and snake-eyes full of luck."

"Dream on, Michaels. While you're talking Billy into the

clouds, me and Williams are going to see some real *touchdowns.*" Wiggins laughs and drinks off the three glasses of whiskey that he'd ordered at once. It's one thing he does better than most. For a skinny guy his size, you wouldn't think he'd hold his booze so well, even at the start of a binge. "Come on, Williams."

But Williams doesn't budge. Wiggins tugs at his elbow a few times, but it's plain Williams has already turned rubbery after two short rums. Since he doesn't talk too much for starters, it's a question whether he's passed out or just forgot to shut his eyes.

"Come on, Williams. Christ, we're gonna miss everything!" He yanks at the elbow until Williams loses balance and slumps onto the floor.

"Leave him rest," Michaels whispers in a low voice that means business. "You're halfway there yourself."

"Aw, bugger your rum."

"Careful, Wiggins."

"Fuck you," he says, and he bounces out of O'Reilly's, barely able to steer his way through the door.

CHAPTER 6

It's about time to round 'em up, Billy." Michaels looks at his watch. There's still ten minutes left in the football game but the 49ers are losing, fifty-one to ten.

"Okay." It doesn't make a difference to me. Mostly I'm sticking around to keep Michaels company. After six or seven scotch-and-beers he looks pretty red-faced and kind of sad. I guess he hates the idea of tattoos.

"Tell you what. You go along with the others. I'll look after Williams here."

"He'll tattoo just as good in his sleep."

"Maybe so." Michaels's red face squeezes tight at the lips and you can tell he's trying to think out a plan. "I'll be along in a sec. Don't you worry about that."

I let him sit as he pleases and after twenty minutes or so some of the squad comes wandering down the street holding one another straight, laughing about the strippers in Suzy-Q's, gogging their tongues out and smacking each other on the shoulders. There's fear riding wild like a horse through each one, but most people would never know it. They'd veer away, thinking, "Those bloody army, they got nothing but fun." But in truth the fun's not even a part of it. The fun is just a disguise.

The name of the tattoo parlour is The Wandering Jew and there's a picture in the window of a snake dancing out of a basket and a little Hindu playing a flute. In the background is a belly-dancing lady wearing no clothes and an old man watching the whole show. It must be the old man who's supposed to be the wandering Jew.

"That's the kinda picture I like." Jamison stops everyone at the front door. "You see that snake there, Wiggins? That's a cobra. And it's gonna bite that Hindu whore right on her tit!"

"She must of deserved it then."

" 'Course she did."

"Then it's nobody's fault but her own." Wiggins is pretty drunk and not so smart as the rest of the Fire Eyes. Everyone thinks they made a mistake on Wiggins's army I.Q. test. But he's not near as drunk as a lot of others. Sinclair is propped between two guys and passed right out. Wiggins keeps lifting his eyelids to show everyone how Sinclair's eyes have rolled up so all you can see is the whites.

"Look at this bugger," he says. "He didn't have more'n five or six and he can't even keep his eyes straight!"

"Let's see." Jamison grabs hold of Sinclair's brush-cut hair and manages to twist his head up into the light. It's a surprise he can pull enough of those short blond hairs into his fingers. But he does, and he jerks the head around fast.

"This man isn't drunk," he looks deep into the eyes like a doctor, "he just passed out from fear."

"Christ. A yellow belly."

"Sinclair? I don't think so." Wiggins braces himself against the door. "Sinclair's pretty tough. He's just had too many."

"Not a chance!" Jamison yells it out like there's no mistake. "Sinclair's a chicken shit who's been complaining the whole of last week. Anyone who's been around him knows it." He walks over to Wiggins and gives him a dark look.

Nobody says a word, so Jamison rambles on about using Sinclair as the number one guinea pig. Just to be sure the tattoo artist is up to snuff. If he does a good job then fine, everyone'll take his turn. If he buggers up the design then the hell with it, we'll get somebody else.

Once everyone steps into the shop it's quiet as a pin. A lot of them are sweating in the face with their eyes darting all over. There's tattoos of everything on the walls: spiders, snakes, bees, swords, guns, naked women of every kind, all the sex parts, anything you could think of.

"Christ, look at that one, will you?" Wiggins points out one tattoo that's fixed high in the corner. "It's a goddam *hard-on!*"

"Yeah, look at the thing."

"It's a *monster.*"

Everyone's eyeing the hard-on, a huge one, larger than life and outlined in blue with a big red tip and two balls dangling below. Right at the thickest part there's a dog collar strapped around it. The collar has pointed studs riveted to the leather and silver colouring that makes it shiny. Underneath is a sign that says: AIMING TO PLEASE.

The tattoo master comes out of the back room and gives a quick look at the squad. Then he singles Jamison out and talks to him. Somehow he knows who the boss is right away.

"You boys're this year's Fire Eyes, huh?"

"Right." Jamison squints his eyes down to two slits. "How'd you know that?"

But the tattoo master doesn't say a word. He smiles like he's seen it all before and pulls on the back of his hair. There's a long ponytail flowing down his spine. It's matted, rusty brown hair that's kind of a surprise because he seems too old to be wearing his hair so long and dirty.

"You boys want to see the design?"

"Sure." Jamison still has his eyes screwed tight.

He disappears into the back room and everyone grows so quiet they've stopped breathing. Only Wiggins and Sinclair are making any noise, and that's from their drunk blubbering and moaning. Wiggins is the worst, because he keeps chomping his lips and grinding his teeth.

"Here it is." He holds the Fire Eyes tattoo over his head so everyone can see it. The eyes are deep ocean-blue with the red coal fire storming behind. There's a big hush as he moves the eyes from side to side and fear pushes into the hearts of them all.

But to me it's a beauty. I can't imagine it being any better than he's made it and I start thinking where I should stick it. Right on my forearm for anyone to see, or a little farther up and more private? Maybe square onto my chest, or high onto one shoulder.

"That's fine," Jamison says, "but we want to see how you get her on before we all sign up."

The tattoo master smiles again and half closes his eyes. "Sonny, I'm the best in the world."

"Maybe. But we want some proof."

The smile is still on his lips and his eyes are lazy as a half moon. Then without turning his head he calls into the back. "Linda. C'mere!"

A minute later Linda steps next to him wearing long black hair and a black lace shirt full of little holes. Everyone's eyes are all over her trying to see through the holes to her skin. The lace shirt is like a dream you want to flesh out so you can touch it.

"The boys want a proof."

Once he says that she doesn't wait a second and starts to unbutton from the top on down. The way her finger plays on each button shows she's done it before. Her eyes are nearly closed and she doesn't give anyone a square look until the shirt's undone. Then she pulls it wide open and lifts her eyes to catch the shock pouring out of everybody's mouth.

It's crazy how they go all limp. They're so taken with the way the tattoo master's drawn her over that their jaws fall slack and they can hardly keep the drool on their lips. Jamison is the worst of them. He tilts his head right down to her chest to take a close look-see. His head bobbles back and forth and then he steps away and scratches his chin, just like the wandering Jew in the picture.

And you can see why they're so hooked. For one thing she's a pure work of art. Not one square inch of white skin's been left to Mother Nature. Every bit has been tattooed, up to the throat. Even her tiny Adam's apple's been made to look like the sun, warm and high above the garden paradise he's painted below. There's butterflies and robins, green vines with roses blooming around a little pasture. Her tits have turned into two small hills with a waterfall pouring off one right onto her stomach. It's been done so well you don't even think to look at her for sex. Not for a minute.

"He's a jane-eous," Wiggins whispers, "a goddam miracle worker. Imagine taking something perfick like that," he says in a voice so low you can barely hear him, "and then makin' it more perfick."

With everyone starting to buzz, Linda buttons her shirt and in one quick step turns around and disappears into the back room. The whole thing is like magic and now the tattoo master stretches his thin smile a little wider. He knows he's got the entire squad hooked and it's just a question of have we got enough money.

"Before we settle on dollars I still want a demonstration." Jamison digs a fifty-dollar bill from his back pocket and pushes it ahead so we can see. "I want you to put a picture on Sinclair here. Good or bad, you get the fifty. And if it's good you get all of us at twenty a throw."

"Forty a throw." He slits his eyes down to nothing.

"Thirty."

"Forty," he says. "I'm an artist."

"All right, forty." Jamison clamps his mouth tight and the fifty dollars passes into a tin tobacco box the tattoo master hides under the counter.

"Which one's Sinclair?" he asks, and Jamison pushes Sinclair forward until he's slumped into the operating chair. He's totally passed out, and Wiggins is buttering up the idea of pinning his tongue to his shirt collar so he don't swallow it.

"Don't usually like working on the unconscious. They could end up suing you good."

"It's all part of the 'nitiation. Ain't nobody gonna sue!" Jamison slaps his legs like he's tired of waiting. "Now let's get to it!"

The tattoo master eyes him lazy as a dog, then squats next to Sinclair. He pulls out a special stool and tucks it under one leg. "Where do you want it? On his forearm?"

"Not a chance." Jamison looks around to us. "I want it right on his ass! Right smack on the cheek!"

"On his ass?"

"You bet."

Next thing you know Jamison has him spread-eagle over the operating chair with pants pulled down to his ankles and his bum starting to pink from Jamison's slapping it over and over, saying, "Right there. That's where it goes. Isn't that right?"

The tattoo master shakes his head a bit, but everyone thinks it's a good joke so he clicks on his tattoo iron and it starts buzzing. The drill head is a little whirring dynamo that sets Jamison looking from face to face. You can tell he's got the Devil in him. All the way into his black shoes.

But just as the drill touches Sinclair's skin the door slams and a voice booms up to the front: "What're you guys gawking at so bad? You look like a pack of wet coyotes."

Michaels has his hat pushed onto the back of his head like he was playing a fast game of snooker and didn't want the hat peak blocking his light.

"Nothing concerning you, Cock Nose." Jamison holds his arms up to fence off Sinclair from any trouble. Then he turns his head to the tattoo master to make sure the drawing's started. "Dammit, get on with it!"

"Watcha hiding, Jamison?" Michaels walks right up to him and plants his face an inch away from Jamison's. They're both sniffing at one another but you can tell Michaels has the upper hand. Somehow he *knows* that Jamison is in with the Devil and no matter what you catch him at there's some bad to it.

"I said get on with it!" he yells, but the tattoo master has the tool clicked off now and he's leaning back on the stool to see what Michaels is up to.

"Sounds like you're in a hurry to tattoo poor Sinclair there. Wonder what *he* has to say about it?"

"Yellow bellies don't have shit to say. You should know that, Cock Nose."

"Well surprise, surprise." He lifts his eyebrows like he's seeing snow in July. "Seems *you* got shit to say."

That's the trigger to set Jamison into a craze. But before he makes a move Michaels does something nobody'd have thought of. Instead of taking a swing he grabs Jamison's arms by the wrists and snaps the wrists down to his knees. It's like two steel cables have tugged him down so he can't do a thing. The wrists and shoulders give a fast crack at the joints and a sore, worried look twists across Jamison's face. "Jesus Christ," he moans and Michaels lets go of the wrists.

"Seems you got a couple of bones out of line, Jamison. I'd have the medics look at your X-rays again." He pulls the peak of his cap down a little lower and walks over to Sinclair and pulls his pants back up. "Thought there'd be a *volunteer* for the first Fire Eyes," he says. "Not this kinda thing with a drunk."

The way he says it puts the shame into everybody and we start sweeping the floor with our eyes. The worst part of being a coward is being found out.

But while all the excuses are whispering like yellow wind, some-

thing comes into me so strong I can't ignore it. The words are rolling up my throat and out my mouth without me telling them yes
or no: "It's just a picture, you know. And a good one, too. Hell,
I'll do it."

"Atta boy, Billy," Michaels is slapping me on the back and adjusting me into the operating chair. "This'll make you the first.
Anybody who goes first is a damn *hero* in my book."

Suddenly Wiggins seems pretty happy about it, too, and when
the tattoo machine gets clicked on again they start watching my
face for any sweat oozing out. But there's no sweat. No fear at all.

"Where you want it?" The tattoo master gives me a cold look,
and for the first time I realize that he doesn't have a mark on him.
Not a trace of tattoo.

"Right here." I roll up my sleeve and show him that I want it on
the biggest part of my arm and I press it tight against my chest to
make it look even bigger.

He asks how big do I want it.

"Big as you can make," I tell him.

Everyone's watching close as they can, trying to feel the little
drill carving out my skin. But it's just a sting. The worst part is
how long it takes.

The tattoo master drills away without ever looking up, drilling
like he's carving a thousand-year-old message onto the stone wall
of a cave. Drilling and drilling until I get the biggest Fire Eyes in
history. From that day on, anybody I've ever met is impressed by
the power of it. And when you stood back from me, looking
down so calmly—the way you always do—even you told me how
beautiful it stands out on my skin.

CHAPTER 7

Word about Michaels and Jamison travels around the base pretty fast. The first sign of trouble is when Corporal Benson, the supplies attendant, pulls Michaels and me to one side the day we're picking up two buckets of whitewash and paint brushes from the maintenance shed. Luke Benson's the oldest man on the base, at least he looks oldest. He's thin and wispy, like a bit of scrub that's grown in the shadow of a pine forest. His face is lean and hard and his eyes have a way of peering out at you like a hungry cat's. But more than anybody else, he knows everything worth knowing on the base. There's times when a tip from Benson means more than a direct order straight from the brass.

"Look," he says, scratching a hand along the side of his face, "I don't want to be seen messing with other people's business—"

Then he doesn't whisper another word. But it's clear he's just waiting for us to ask him to go ahead and mess with as much business as he pleases.

"Sure," Michaels says, lifting the peak of his cap an inch above his hairline. "I don't care to mess with it myself."

"Well, then, you'll understand me when I tell you to keep an eye on Jamison."

"Oh?" Now Michaels lifts the cap right off his head and wipes the sweat from his face with an arm.

"Yeah. Just a word to the wise." He steps right in close so the three of us are standing almost toe to toe. The way he talks is so light and feathery my ears are straining for every breath drifting from his lips. "The enrollment docs show Jamison's a bit of a thug. In high school they booted him out for rearranging the face on his history teacher." He pauses, and a tongue licks out across his dry lips. "A lady teacher."

Michaels doesn't say a word. There's just the three of us there, pressed tight, waiting for something to break.

"What I'd say, based on watching the military for over twenty years, is stay sharp around Jamison. Two young bucks like you just want to let him have his way whenever he's around, then let it all roll off your back. He's the kind that has to run the show. Otherwise he goes wild. He's done it a hundred times."

"That so?" Michaels slips the cap back on and squares the peak with both hands. "You've seen his enrollment docs, huh?"

Benson looks off to the side a second. "Funny thing. You get one of them every five or six years coming through here. Don't know what it is. Some of them are hardly human beings."

"Well, that's too bad," Michaels says, picking up his bucket of whitewash, "cause I don't play lame duck to any jerk loser. The fact is, I think it's the worst thing you can do." Then he hands me my paint bucket and he starts to head over to the barracks. "If I can't walk like a man in this world," he says, shaking his head, "then I'm not going to crawl. There's just no in-between, as far as I'm concerned."

Luke Benson starts to smile. "Okay, boss," he says with a laugh. I guess that some old-timers like to hear a bit of spunk once in a while. Maybe it makes them believe life is still worth getting out of bed for in the morning. "Whatever you say."

Michaels doesn't say another word about it, but you can tell the idea of Jamison is itching under his skin. That's the reason he starts playing his games on me, to throw his mind into a good laugh. And he's got a long time to do it, because we've been assigned to whitewash patrol for a week. The truth is, I'm getting to like it. Working with Michaels is the best set-up I can think of.

Whitewash patrol happens each spring. Everyone gets a turn at slapping a fresh coat of paint on the barracks and supply sheds. I always liked painting, because everything turns so clean and slick. But Michaels hates it and starts talking a storm of nonsense to keep himself from going nutty.

"You know, Billy," he says to me with a long deep breath, "it's just possible that this wall here is not turning the colour we think it is."

It's pretty clear that he says this to get me to go along. So I do, because he's usually okay when you're just talking about nothing. He'll poke little holes in your mind and you fall into them like rabbit traps.

"Then what colour is it if it's not white?"

"No telling what colour," he says.

"You've gone wacky," I tell him. "Plain wacky." We keep slapping the white paint on, and he thinks some more.

"What would you say if everybody else told you this wall was blue?"

"I'd tell 'em it was white."

"And what if they started laughing and saying, 'Oh that goddam Bill, he's as stubborn as dried glue. Imagine him sayin' blue was white. He's a damn slow cart when it gets to hauling sense.' "

I can feel my neck start to bristle. But then I see him wink, so it means he's not really poking at me.

"What about all the colour-blind people?" he says.

"What about them?"

"Well, if they made up the majority then it'd just be a question of more people calling white blue than calling white white."

"Well, they ain't the majority, so they don't." I keep swabbing the paint onto the wall and using the brush so no drip marks run down the edge. He's not as careful as me and his section's full of drips that look like thick white ooze.

"And what about the people who see things that ain't there?" he says and he smiles at me. "The ones with *hal-lu-ci-na-tions!*" He draws this way out like it's a secret word.

"If they see 'em, they're there."

"Don't tell me that if some guy thinks he sees a fox swimming the Atlantic, that it's really happening."

"Nobody'd see something that stupid."

"Maybe not," he says and brushes out more paint, "but there's guys around who'd swear on a six-pack of foreign beer that this blue paint we're using is *white!*" and he starts laughing to himself like this is the funniest idea he's had today. I almost start laughing, too, except when I look into the paint tray— just the way the sun hits, the paint *does* look blue, the way that white ice can look blue when you're out in the winter. For some reason this freezes me up, and I know Michaels has me trapped in one of those rabbit holes.

Then I hear a shushing noise and look around and see Jamison and his two buddies, Maxwell and Tooler, coming along the wall. Neither of them are very big, but Maxwell's got thick arms and has a way of playing with a toothpick in his teeth that makes him look like a tough punk. Tooler's just a jelly roll, bald and fat, a domehead runt always taking punishment from someone. Jamison walks along slowly with his jaws clumping some gum. Then he spits the pink gum out and it lands in my paint tray. There's more of the shushing noise and I see they've got a bag of dust and they're throwing handfuls of it onto the fresh paint job.

"Hey, what the hell's going on?" Michaels slaps his brush into the bucket so hard it splashes white paint all over the ground.

"Oh, just vacuum grits," Jamison says. "The sarge came into the bunk house and saw all this dust and shit near your bunk. *We* had to clean it out."

"Yeah, well knock off spreading it on that paint!" He takes a few steps towards the guy with the vacuum bag, but Jamison holds up his hand like a cop.

"Now, now, let's not get ratchety, Knuckle Nose." He lets this sink in real slow. "All we're doing is returning your shit." Then he rips open the vacuum bag and throws the dirt onto the wall.

Michaels doesn't wind up or anything. He just pokes straight into Jamison's face before you can blink. A gush of blood spits into the air and Jamison jumps onto him. That's when I jump onto Jamison, but the other guys grab me and twist both arms behind my back and lock them tight. Then I start screaming.

But before anybody comes Michaels starts hammering his big fist into Jamison's nose. The face opens in two or three places and Michaels hauls him to the wall and starts mushing his head into the paint and dirt so it looks brown and red and black and white and blue. The two guys let go of me and pull Michaels away before he kills Jamison. They pull him off, but they don't do him no harm because he's turned mad, he's turned crazy with murder in his eyes. All the blood has left his face and hands and arms. His head's white and worried like he can't believe he hit into Jamison so horrible. He starts shaking so bad that he looks feverish and chilled at the same time.

Eventually the M.P.s haul everybody off and we do five days of C.B.— Confined to Barracks. That means extra drill and extra duties after hours. Every time we pass Jamison, he loosens that jaw down but never says a word. His face is puffy with lumps that look like bags of poison eating into his skull.

"I guess you won't be hearing from him again," I tell Michaels when I realize how beat-up Jamison is.

But Michaels doesn't say a word back to me. He puts on a worried look that never leaves his face, like a white sheet stretched over his skin and pulled tight so he can hardly breathe.

□   □   □

Maybe it's because Michaels is such a genius with his hands—being a good fighter is what the army's really all about—or maybe it's because he put the shove into Jamison's face so easy. Whatever the reason, it turns out that Michaels gets to lead the unarmed combat drills. The drill instructor, Sergeant Kebik, is like all the rest of the brass. Stocky and square in the chest, he parades in front of the men like he owns us. And his voice is like all the officers', loud and fast. In fact that's how they all are, not like anything human, just a voice I try to block out the best I can. Because Kebik's the combat trainer he figures he has to scream louder than anyone else, so he yells out the drill routines and Michaels has to show the right techniques. So when Kebik lets loose with "Right reverse punch!" Michaels snaps it so fast you can hear his sleeves slap in the air as his fist bangs into position. Then the squad tries to hit it out just the same. But instead of a lot of sleeves whipping the air, all you hear is a bunch of moaning when somebody's shoulder pops out of joint.

"Now listen up, crapheads," Kebik shakes his head like we're the most miserable puke he's seen. "What you gotta do is twist your wrist through the punch as your fist moves from ready position to full extension." And his fist snaps into the air with a crack. Crack. Crack. Crack. Every time, the fist stops an inch off somebody's nose. Then, *crack!* It's so close to my lips I can feel the heat burning off his knuckles.

"All right now. Michaels! Drill 'em out individually."

"Yes, sir!"

"I don't want to see *one* of these crapheads with their chops withering in the wind for one more day!"

"Yes, sir!" This time we all bark it out.

So Michaels takes each guy off to the side one at a time. Meanwhile we're running laps on the track, pumping squats and pressing knuckle push-ups. With the knuckle push-ups you close your fist tight and dump all your weight onto the first two knuckles. That's what you hit with. Put everything onto those two knuckles and you can split a wooden two-by-four right through the guts. Kebik does it at the end of every drill just to prove the fact. One short jab and that smooth-trimmed board is knocked down to split kindling.

"Deerborn!"

"Yes, sir!"

"Take a round with Michaels."

I jog over to Michaels, and Wiggins slumps his ugly face back to the rest of the squad. Now he's got to run three laps around the track to make up what he missed.

"Okay, buddy, let's see what you got for a fist." Michaels rolls an eye to show me that everything's on the joke but we still have to keep things looking serious.

I stick my hand into the air clumped so tight I can feel the Fire Eyes tattoo rolling on my arm, stretching the skin tight as sheet metal.

"Hmm." His lips pucker like he's surprised by something. "Let's see your hand." And he takes my hand into his and smooths the palm out and shakes it by the wrist a couple of times. "See, you have to keep everything loose. Tighten everything up and you'll exhaust your system five minutes into a good brawl." He keeps shaking that wrist, shaking and shaking until I can feel the looseness rolling up to the tattoo. "The only time you tighten is just when you hit the sucker. Then it's one fast bang. *Wham!* and everything turns to steel, right down to your one-eyed jack."

Once everything's shook down he starts to fit my fingers into place. "Now, the only part of you that's supposed to be always on the ready is your hands. So get 'em nice and tight, just so you know how it feels." Then one at a time he rolls my fingers into a huge fist. Then he locks my hand so tight I can't believe it.

"There. You feel that? Huh?"

"Yeah."

"That's a real Joe Louis mitt you got now. A real Bruce Lee in your gloves."

"Yeah." It's true. I never felt it before. All of a sudden I feel like I could smash down a whole concrete building. Break it right down to rubble. Feels so good I don't want to unroll the fingers, just walk around all day with these two granite rocks on the end of my arms.

"Okay. Now ease off again. You don't want to lock your hands. That could be as bad as before. Ease them in and out so you're ready. And make sure you can lock 'em tight just by thinking about it. What you can do is tighten them up once in a while, you know, when you're sitting on the shitter doing nothing. Do it ten times a day and you'll have it down in a week." Michaels gives a smile, and his white teeth glitter like ivory.

"Now, the big thing is to use those fists properly. That's what Kebik's going on about with this reverse punch. See, you reverse it by having one fist drive into the enemy's head while the other comes back to your waist." His right fist drives into the air in slow motion and at the same time his left comes down to a rest near his pocket. Then the left goes up and the right back. Then the right up, left down. And all of a sudden you can see it. It's a machine. Like car pistons driving up and down in order so nothing's thrown off balance. It's a beautiful thing, a ballet of force and power.

But when I give it a try the machine's disappeared. For one thing the pistons don't know where to stop. Sometimes they fly too high and my whole body falls off centre. Or the two pistons crash together in mid-air and slam the whole works into a stall.

"You're getting her, Billy. Come on now. Little slower. That's it. Good. Hey—you got her, you got her!" Michaels is whispering it at me, but each time it's like a whole stadium cheering me on until finally I hear it myself. SNAP! The slack in my shirt cracks in the air with one tight punch.

"Hey! You got it!" Old Michaels is beside himself with grinning and back-slapping. "Nobody's got it that fast. *Not one dumb suck in the whole squad's even close by a mile!*"

"Yeah?" And I snap another one clean through the sky.

"You bet."

"Hey, next up, guys." It's Tooler jogging across the parade grounds. "Kebik says you got six laps to make up, Billy."

Michaels starts the routine with Tooler and you can see by the miserable look to his eye that Tooler's never going to have no Joe Louis or Bruce Lee sitting in his mitt the way Michaels and I do. Just thinking about it pulls a whole new feel into my head and I can hardly think clear because of it.

By the time I get back to the squad, Kebik's starting the next fighting drill.

"Okay, prunebabies, time to get out your Q-tips." Q-tips is brass-talk for weapons combat. Everybody gets a hardwood stick about five foot long, the size of a carbine rifle, with a fake bayonet at one end. At both ends is a wad of padding covered with pigskin. The padding makes the ends about six inches thick and that's supposed to be the Q-tip part. When you take a close look you can see the pigskin's covered in layers of dried blood. The whole thing's soaked with years of blood, going back to World War I.

"Okay, prunebabies, ring it up here. It's man on man, two at a time."

The squad makes a twenty-foot-wide ring. Each guy fits the head pads over his skull and tightens the chin strap. The pads work like a goaltender's. Lots of leather across the forehead, around the ears and down the cheekbones. Then from the cheekpads it stretches over to guard the nose in two rounded points that stop on each side of the nostrils to let you breathe.

"Now listen up, men. I only want to see three things today." Kebik struts into the centre with his thumbs looped into his belt. "First is making a wide thrust." He grabs a Q-tip by the end and shoves forward so the part that's supposed to be the bayonet is sunk five inches into Wiggins's throat. "Next thing I want to see is defence." He draws the tip back and holds the stick up to block a thrust. "Then from this position I want to see butt jabs." And he whips the stock of the carbine round like a hammer, smashing into Sinclair's ribs. "All right. Those three moves and nothing else. And you keep fighting until one man goes down."

He takes a minute to let the details sink in.

"All right. Fighters in ready position." He singles out Wiggins and Sinclair.

They touch their Q-tips together and start circling.

"Begin."

Each man is like a hawk circling round and around waiting for the kill. Nothing else counts but the way those sticks sway in the air, looping back and forth towards one head, then the other. Wiggins is the tame one, always checking Sinclair's thrusts, then coming right back with a chop to the ribs. A counterpuncher. But everything's just a test, until suddenly Sinclair pulls Wiggins's guard away and plants one right under the throat. Then, fast as light, Wiggins pulls back, smashes the stick down and runs his bayonet straight into Sinclair's guts so hard he drops to the dirt.

"All right, stop!" Kebik calls it just before Sinclair can follow up with a slash across the jugular. "*You grunts are both dead.* Fall out!"

"I said I want to see *de*fence." He grabs a stick from Sinclair and walks around the circle showing everyone the special grip for pure defence—a fist locked onto each end, with the bayonet end sticking forward for protection. "All right. Deerborn, next up. And . . . Jamison."

I take the head pad from Wiggins and tug it over my ears. The hell of it is that the thing's too tight. Somebody's made the face size too small so the chin strap won't cinch proper. Pollock tries to tie her tight, but the strap just won't pull true.

"Come on, Deerborn." Kebik's got to keep the ball rolling.

"It'll be okay, Billy." Pollock finally gets one end of strap barely tucked through the cinch. "Just don't let him touch your head."

Once I turn around, you can see Jamison has been putting on a show for the boys. He's whirling the Q-tip like a baton, twirling it fast between his hands like it's a propeller set to cut straight through me.

"Jamison!" Old Kebik's getting steamed. "I said no fancy bull shit!"

Jamison snaps the stick to a dead halt. Then he takes the point, and just like a goddam Kraut, he points the knife end straight for my belly.

"Okay. Fighters in ready position. Begin."

I lift my Q-tip in the air to start things off fair, but far as Jamison's concerned, touching sticks together before you start a fight is just a bunch of yellow pee in the bowl. Nothing mannish to it at all. Instead, Jamison has spent the time working himself into a killing machine. All the fight's centred in his face, and looking into him you can see the Devil hiding behind the brown pits of his eyes. I grip onto the stick the way Kebik showed—both fists in the defence, with the sharp tip of bayonet just out front. Jamison digs in with a lunge and I tap it to one side. Then he tries another. And another. Each jab digs deeper and you can tell he's fishing for me. Just waiting to pull the line tight. The only chance is to know *when* to hit, then shove it down his throat.

"Come on, Billy. Use the butt!" A half a dozen guys are calling out for me. "Give him a taste of leather!" They might as well be six miles away. Voices calling into a canyon and echoing against the walls.

I twist my eyes from his face and put all the concentration onto that stick of his. He jabs it at my guts, but every time I smack it to the side before he can cut into me. And then, just once, I yank my stick around and plant the butt square into his belly.

"Fuck!"

For a second I glance back to his eyes. The mad dog in him has turned rabid.

Then with one quick jab he cuts under my guard, twists the leather tip around and yanks the stick right out of my hands. It hits the ground and he kicks it away with one foot. Once he's cleared it to the side a dull hush sinks into the ring. Everybody knows I'm a goner. Next he spreads his legs apart and closes in for the kill. His mouth opens into a big O and his lips pull back and forth over his teeth. He switches the stick from hand to hand, balancing the weight of it to find the best angle of death for me. But when the bayonet end shifts forward again, I see it. *I see it*. Impossible, but there it is. A small knot in the wood, a tiny hairline splinter running across the middle of the stick right between his hands.

"You poor Cock Nose," he says and charges straight for my heart.

In one tight snap my fist bangs into the air. CRACK! The first two knuckles break across the wood and send the broken sticks flying from his hands. The pigskin pads flop onto the ground, useless after all those years of war. And the big hush that sank into the fighting ring turns to a stiff chill. Then somebody says "Jesus H. Christ," and the chill turns into two or three guys yelling like they can't believe it, and then all ten of them start jumping all over me, whooping and screaming like they just won the Kentucky Derby.

"You did it, Billy!"

"Knuckled him right out of the ring!"

"Kissed his clock good-*bye*."

And looking back to Jamison is like watching a dark pool of oil swamped in a gutter. His gun and bayonet lie broken at his feet. His black hairy hands are dropped to his side, shaking against the dusty leggings of his fatigues.

CHAPTER 8

It's the chance I've been waiting for, Billy. It's the one time I've even been *close* to getting ahead. You gotta help me."

Wiggins has a way of twisting your arm that I never noticed before. First he gives me the line about me being a hero fighter, then he explains what a great buddy I am, and next he puts it all into one tight ball—without me his dream of being best demolition lead in the squad will vanish into dust.

"See, they need a *team.* It's gotta be a two-man operation or nothing. I either score with you, or I have to pull tight with another slacker." What Wiggins is really saying is nobody can stand the sight of his ugly pimpled face. Somehow he got this big idea that *I can.*

"I don't know." Sergeant Tilden had spent ten minutes on a speech about working with a man you can trust your life to. I was thinking of teaming with Michaels.

"Look. I'm going to hit all the tough stuff. You'll just be my cover man. All you do is stand around looking sharp as a crow."

He smiles like the whole thing's a breeze.

"All right. But only until you get selected as the lead for the squad. Once they know you can do the job, I'm teaming with Michaels. Then they'll have to give you another cover man."

The cover man follows the demolition step by step to make sure nothing's missed. Since every job is a little different, it's important the details are set proper. I don't have to *do* anything, just take care that Wiggins doesn't overlook a fine point. It's a formality that the army uses for back-up purposes.

But the way Sergeant Tilden sees it, the story's just the opposite. "Cover man's the most important part to any operation." He struts around the demolition class, eyeing every man one at a time. "And if there's any accidents on routine jobs like this one coming up, it's the cover man that gets the finger." His thumb reaches into the air, then dives like a kamikaze shot down from ground zero.

"Now, the army isn't in the business of providing you grunts with *reasons* for its operations and orders. But I'm telling you a reason for this operation today." He swings his brick-house shoulders past me and stares into Wiggins's eyes. "First off, you'll be practising charge implementation and detonation. To the pea-brains here, that means you're going to *try* to blow something up. That something is just going to be a pile of old broken rock, but that's no difference to you. The reason I say *try* to blow something up is because some dumb grunt is going to *eat sky*. You know what that means? Means he's gonna blow himself so damned high into the blue he'll be eating those white clouds for eternity. That I can personally guarantee. Happens to one pea-brain at least once every year."

Everybody shifts their eyes around trying to spot the poor sucker who's going down this time.

"Second point is that you're going to be working in pairs. Each Fire Eyes pair is teamed with a Corps of Engineers unit that does the site preparation, drilling, excavation—in fact, they do everything except," he says with a smile, "except for the glory work. That's left for you prima donnas."

He walks down the line of men again and drills into their eyes. You can figure the most important part of the speech is coming next. "Now, why do you men figure we'd start so sudden on a detail like this? Why wouldn't we do charge construction first? Hhmm? Why not demolitions search and destroy first? Huh?" He stops in front of Tooler and presses into his face, looking for an answer. "Why not, soldier?"

Tooler doesn't have the first clue.

"I said *why not, soldier?*"

"Uh . . . because you want to cut the nerves off of us, sir!"

"Nerves?" The way his face prunes, Tilden looks like he just got invited to a gay romance. "Nerves? The Fire Eyes don't have nerves, Tooler. They got *nerve*." And he holds up one finger in front of Tooler's nose. "Just *one* nerve. The nerve for holding an incendiary that could take out your whole family right back to Moses, holding that sucker in one hand and lighting a cigarette off the burning fuse. You got that?"

"Yes, sir!" Tooler clicks his heels together to make it sharp.

Tilden wheels back the other way and rattles the rest of the speech off fast as he can. "The reason you start with a demolition detail like this is to give you a taste of blood. It's that simple. You either like the taste of the beef or you move on to the salad bar. Got it?"

"Yes, sir!" Everybody screams it out in one sharp blast.

"Now when you're working with these engineers, you remember they're full of themselves, too. They happen to think they're the bright boys. Think they're professors. Just like you grunts think you're all the gods of hell. The one thing to keep in mind is to demonstrate your skill under fire. Show them that *one* nerve." And he holds up a single finger again and parades it around like a candle burning in the dark of night.

After two days' training on procedures, they assign two guys to each engineering unit. The story you hear is that the army's decided to put up a new officers' club and that means clearing an acre of bedrock and putting down twenty feet of foundation footings. The area's covered in clouds of grey dust and all the men look like they're wearing grey Johnny Reb fatigues left over from the Civil War.

Operations Lieutenant McNeil is the officer we report to first thing in the morning. He's got a thick blubbering neck and his tie is slacked off the collar. The top button is undone, and it looks like he'd just as soon forget the tie to begin with.

"You boys are Wiggins and Deerborn, right?" He's got a face that's red from hundreds of tiny veins crawling to the surface of his skin. That means he's a drinker and he doesn't care who in the hell we are.

"Yes, sir." Wiggins nods to me and we salute. But McNeil

doesn't watch me too careful and points to some paper forms.

"You filled out the work papers yet?"

"Yes, sir."

"Then you'd better get to it," he says to Wiggins. He itches his big red nose and gives a snort into his hand. "Glenton should have the blast points marked by now. When Murtry's unit has the holes jackhammered, you boys be ready. Right."

Wiggins leads me through the whole engineer unit, talking as he goes along. He's explaining what we have to do, but I'm so busy sucking in what everyone else is up to that I miss most of what he's saying.

"Don't worry about it," he tells me. "We'll just take her step by step."

We walk to the demolition shed and the supply supervisor comes by with a key that's strapped to his belt. He unlocks the door and we step inside. It's the size of a horse stable, with tiny vents fixed in the top—just enough room to keep the breeze blowing through so the place doesn't overheat, but small enough so no drunken grunts can crawl into trouble.

"Now, it's just like they taught us," Wiggins says. "There's three parts in every bomb: the main charge, the detonator and the firing mechanism. In this case the charge is plastic explosives, these are the detonator caps, and the firing mechanisms are these timed fuses." He holds everything up like they're showpieces in a museum. Just looking at them sends a shiver running down my spine. There's something beautiful and magical to it all. I take a deep breath, hold the air in my lungs, then let it go in one long, easy roll.

He loads the explosives into a metal cannister that looks like a fishing tackle box and clips the top down and lifts it by the handle. "Okay, we're set. Any questions so far?"

"Yeah. Why don't we try this other stuff?" All kinds of equipment is hooked onto the walls.

"You joking? Any of this stock goes missing and it'll mean our ass." His arm sweeps around the shed and my eyes follow along, lost in the power of the demolition gear. "Specially stuff like this DM12 and PE4. And look at this: some brand new detonation cord, firing caps, even some of the old plunge detonators."

"You really used all that before?"

"Sure. Pop was a demolition man down in Mexico. Used to

show me his goods all the time." The way he tells it, Wiggins worked two years in mining demolition himself and knows the system pretty good. He'd been cover man for a lead that started drinking and showing up late. Eventually they fired him and put Wiggins into the lead slot. After that they shut the mine down and he came into the army. Figures he's the only guy in the squad with any background in genuine explosives.

After the supply supervisor's counted out what we've got, he locks the door and we head back towards McNeil's office. "Now, first the engineer marks out where he wants the blast set. See those red chalk marks? Those are the points. Then the boys on the pneumatic drills punch twenty-inch holes into the rock. Hear it? You can hear the drills banging into the rock right now.

"Then you and I walk around to each point and set the charge. The fuses are all timed for sixty seconds. Once I tell you the fuse is set, you wave the flag to the horn man. He'll give a blast. That's when we run like hell." He starts laughing and slaps my back. "I'm kidding, really. Hell, we could stroll like we're on the wide streets of Paree and still have time to cover."

When Murtry's gang finishes the drilling, McNeil comes up to us. He gives me a red flag that's attached to a broom stick. "Set two," he says. "Then we'll do two more."

The flagstick is full of red stains that make me think of blood and all the mistakes you can make. But with Wiggins feeling so sunny, I stroll along happy as a lark.

After everyone's clear of the blast zone we walk up to the engineers' points. The drill holes sink into the bedrock so deep you can't see bottom.

"Okay." He sets the box down and blows the dust off the granite. "I like it clean," he says. He shoves some plastics snug into the hole so it fits tight without any adjustment. Next he sinks the detonator onto the explosive and attaches the fuse. "We'll do the next one, then pop the fuses together. Soon as I let them go, you raise the flag and wave it at McNeil."

He starts to set the second blast, but this time it doesn't fit as clean as the first and he has to ram some loose bits of rock free with a long metal rod that's stored in the tackle box.

But the rod sticks fast in the hole and he gives it a curse. A layer of sweat starts to bead onto his forehead. With the red scars on his face it makes him look like the Devil.

Finally he gets the rod free and everything set to go.

"Now, we got the charge ready, the detonator and the fuses, right?" He's speaking like his voice is in a T.V. commercial. It's something he's *supposed* to say and it comes out sounding like a robot. "*Right?*" His eyes flick at me like a whip.

"Right. Charge, detonator, fuse."

"Okay." He closes the box and hunches in a squat next to the first charge. "Wave the flag."

I wave the flag from side to side. It's as though I just conquered a new country and the enemy's flag has finally come down. The wind picks up the red banner and swells it into the air. Then the all-clear horn blasts like a bugle in the first charge of battle.

"Come on, for Christ's sake!" Wiggins is ten feet ahead of me on a dead run. The tackle box is swinging in his hand and he's yelling under his breath. "Both fuses are popped. Come on, Billy, come on!"

I pick up after him and we sprint flat out until we're next to McNeil's shed. Then I turn around and wait for it. It's as though I can see that fuse squeezing down to the last second. And when the blast hits it runs through my feet straight into my brain. There's nothing like the sound and feel of it—the beautiful earthshaking Power that stays with you forever. But none of the other guys pay any attention. Those engineers are slack bastards who don't have a thought for the real truth of war.

"See. It was simple. No problem." Wiggins slaps me on the back and laughs, even though the sweat's still on his forehead from fighting the second charge.

The first set of charges blows the rock into hundreds of fragments. After half an hour, the drilling crew finishes the next site and we go in again.

This time the first hole is fixed and loaded with explosive, but the second hole is too small and won't accept the charge.

"Christ." Wiggins keeps twisting the metal rod to try and find a good angle to mount the second charge.

"I think you need a bigger hole."

"Yeah." He wipes his forehead dry and calls for one of Murtry's men.

"What's wrong?" Murtry comes over himself. "You guys don't know how to stick a snug hole?"

"Snug is one thing, nonexistent is another."

"Back off, grunthead, and we'll see what we can do." He fits his jackhammer into the mark and starts pounding away. The vibrations roll straight through my guts and I have to wince my face up because the noise hits my ears so hard.

"That should do it," he says, and he gives a nod to Wiggins. Then he looks at my feet and sees the first charge planted in the drill hole.

He bends over to look close at the hole and his face turns white near the lips. "Is that the first charge? Christ, don't tell me *that's the first charge!*"

Wiggins is already crouched at the new hole, blowing the dust away. "Sure it is. But the fuse ain't set yet."

"You mean you left the charge exposed while I was drilling?"

"Not exposed really. The thing's sunk in a good foot and a half."

But a foot and half doesn't mean sweet shit to Murtry, and he starts dancing on the spot, mad as a wasp. "Christ, you could of killed us all! Dammit, one little chip of rock flying from this thing could've blown us to Kingdom Come!" He points to the jackhammer as though it's God's own death machine.

"Well we didn't blow to no Kingdom Come, so pipe down and back off."

But Murtry's still hot and he grabs Wiggins by the collar and pulls him away from the drill hole. He's at least six foot tall, and with Wiggins squat on the ground he's got a four-foot advantage. When his arm braces onto Wiggins's shirt, it looks like a crane pulling a blackfly into the air. "Listen boy, you never do that again. You hear me? Not to me or any of my crew. When we come to second-out a hole, you keep the zone safe. It's like you haven't even put your coffee cup down yet. Okay?"

He squeezes on Wiggins's collar, but nothing happens. "*Okay?*"

"All right, okay. For shit sakes!" He wriggles free and gives Murtry a weak look. After he's smoothed his face out and the colour's come back, Murtry waddles to the sheds carrying the jackhammer in one hand.

"Hell. This job'd be all right if you didn't have those jerkoffs to deal with." He whistles across the drill hole again and fixes the charge.

"I hate that kind of thing," he says, and looks the charges over. Then his eyes whip up to me. "Charge, detonator, fuse. Right?"

"Right."

"When a guy wants to muscle you like that I just want to kill him. You know what I mean?" He has a very worried face. "All right, wave the flag!"

I unravel the flag and it takes the full wind again and I wave it back and forth three times. Then the bugle sounds and Wiggins pops the fuses.

"Okay! Let's go."

We set out at a light jog and Wiggins still has a black look stretched across his face. But by the time we're halfway to the work shed he stops and grips my arm. "Jeezus, Billy. I forgot the blast box!" He spins around and sprints back to the drill holes and dynamite.

He's running pretty quick and I figure everything is going to be fine. He snatches the box in one hand and wheels around to finish the distance to McNeil's shed. But after he's turned, the box opens up like the jaws of a dragon and everything fires out. Four sticks of explosives and all the blasting caps and fuses spill into the air and scatter over the ground. Then I find myself racing to meet him. Something is telling me to back off, to escape and leave the dynamite behind. But in a few seconds I'm with him and we gather everything up as careful as we dare and close the box tight and head out on a dead run. The engineers at the shed have put their coffees down by now, and they're staring at us with their mouths unhinged and flapping in the wind. Through it all you can hear McNeil yelling: "Get down! Get down!"

When the blast hits we're about thirty yards from the drill holes. We crack onto the ground and cover up. The shock from the explosion washes over us like a huge wave and rolls through every muscle and crashes past me. The noise sounds like a scream echoing in a cave for days on end. When the dust finally stops showering down I look to Wiggins. He's lying still as a stone.

"Get him up, get him up!" McNeil's hollering all kinds of orders, and it makes me realize how bad the drinking has spoiled his nerve. The worst thing is to panic under fire. He rolls Wiggins onto his back, bends over and takes a pulse at his throat and slaps his sorry face two or three times.

But all that happens is a little cloud of dust dances into the air every time he slaps at him. Like a haze of fine powder that someone's blown into the wind. It's funny, the way it catches the breeze and never lands again. And that's when *you* start singing. Just like you always do to calm me down when things get rough. One of those soft lullabies, sung so soft it's like the wind itself. *Hush, hush, hush-a-bye, bye.*

CHAPTER 9

I'm at least half as lucky as you. If not luckier. Just fell asleep on the job. You know? There I was, cozy as could be, lying face down and all snuggled in for a nap. I thought, hell, this seems like a good chance to make up for lost dark time."

"Dark time" is Wiggins's way of saying "sleep." He had about five minutes' dark time when his eyes popped open under the red nose of McNeil, just as he's shrieking out orders about ambulances and surgery.

"I'd sooner have a coffee," Wiggins tells him, and shoves up onto his elbows. A few guys help him back to the shacks, but he manages to walk the last ten feet on his own.

When the ambulance arrives McNeil insists on X-rays for both of us. And as we're leaving he looks me in the eye. "Until you learn the basics, Deerborn, I'm having you reassigned to another lead man. Just remember — you're lucky to still be alive."

It's true. But the way the facts sort out I get four rolls of lucky dice in that one week. First one, of course, is pulling myself out of that blast without so much as a scratch. Wiggins ends up with a lot of bruising where the rock fragments hit down on him and a headache that comes and goes for a couple of months. And for a while he complains of broken ribs, but they never showed up on the X-rays and the complaint only comes when it's time to sweep the barracks or scrub-brush the floor. But nothing touched me, and that lucky charm sits right above my shoulder bright as a star for the next few days, and everybody seems to take notice.

"Hey, Lucky Bill," MacEwen says one night when he's got a handful of poker cards and the pot's loaded with a hundred bucks. "Come on over here and just kiss the next card I draw, willya?"

"Yeah. And you can kiss my ass," Jamison says. So far, he's been winning.

"Sooner have Mr. Lucky kiss my cards than your ass. 'Less your ass has the queen of diamonds sitting up the bung hole."

Everyone laughs up a crock about Jamison's ass. And to make that bugger all the worse of a joke, I go over to MacEwen and, just as he says, kiss the next card that draws to his hand.

"Deal it face up," he says to Pollock.

Pollock frowns and shakes his head and then deals the card face up. Next thing you know, there's a queen of diamonds smiling dead-centre into MacEwen's eye.

Nobody can believe it.

"Misdeal!" Jamison yells, and he slams his cards onto the table.

"Up yours! That was a fair draw, as good as the rest," MacEwen says, "just as good as when you were winning."

That was my second lucky strike. They go on for days about that red queen. You'd think it was the game of the year and in the end, who knows how the whole argument wraps up? But the main point is all the guys start treating me special. They all get a look to their eye that doesn't know just how to measure the truth.

Except Michaels. He figures it's all part of my mind.

"You see, some people have these *visions*," he explains to anyone who'll listen. And after a day or two he starts thinking we should test out my vision at the racetrack.

"Thought it'd be kind of special for my girl, Charlene, too," he says with that grin of his. "She loves riding. Don't know much about horses, though." He gives me a wink once, and then again. Then he laughs. "But she does appreciate the look of a well-trained specimen."

Michaels likes to run on with his stories and I like to sit back and listen. It's like having an older brother who lies under the bedcovers with you and just talks the night out, telling you all the truth in the world. Never had a brother myself, but Michaels makes up for the missing part.

"You probably got a touch of horse sense yourself, don't you?" He lifts a hand and waves off a fly buzzing near his forehead. "I mean, weren't you brought up in the countryside somewhere? Thought I'd heard that."

Only time I remember being in the countryside is on trips in the car or on hitchhikes, when I'd spend the night on some roadside. And the fact is, that always felt pretty good. Out under the stars, the coyotes hooting at the moon. You get the feel in your blood that that's where you really belong.

"Sure," I tell him.

"Yeah?" He looks me over real close like some idea has just sprung into his brain. "You got a feeling for horse*flesh*, too?"

"Uh-huh." That's a lie. Horses are too big to really like very much.

"Well, hell. I think I've got an idea that could pull us out of the treadmill, old buddy. Tell you what we're going to do."

And he starts to spell out this new idea like a big dream that's drawn in technicolour. But you know, the more he talks it out the more my ears shut down for thinking about horses and the way their round eyes keep looking at me, one at a time. Long time ago some smart trainer figured that's the dangerous part to horses and invented blinkers to stop the horse from going crazy while he was on the run. Scares me just to think on it.

◻   ◻   ◻

"Here's the keys. Just make sure you keep the revs below the red zone on the tachometer."

I can't believe it. Michaels is handing me the keys to a miracle. A white Camaro kept in showroom condition for at least six years. The miracle isn't that she's in mint shape, or that she's such a hot machine. The miracle part is that Michaels has kept something this hot under covers for so long without any of the guys knowing.

But instead of fussing I slip into the driver's seat, dump the clutch under my foot, then start the ignition. One twist and she turns over perfect. Fast and low and all in one kick: vvvrrroooooom.

"Okay, big buddy, just head her down 99 to the bus depot outside Fairfield. Then I'm going to introduce you to the Queen of Hearts." Fairfield's the biggest town around, and the one place that's got a full-scale horse track.

The Queen of Hearts is Charlene. Michaels twists his feet under the dash and props his head onto the neckrest. The way he's playing it, I'm the chauffeur and he's the rich tycoon off to pick up the Queen from her royal visit to the outbacks. The idea is that the three of us make a quick break from the depot to the racetrack, meet up with the boys, then burn down the town for the next three days.

In fact, everyone's got the same plan, and for the last two weeks, whenever two or three guys get together, all you hear is them singing out the troop song:

> We are the Fire Eyes
> Number one
> Pillage the village
> and fuck everyone.
> We are the Fire Eyes
> Number two
> Burn down the town
> then get screwed . . .

The song goes on forever and every verse counts up one, two, three, four and it always works into a rhyme that has something to do with sex or death or both sex and death together. But for now everyone's stuck on verse two and how we're going to burn down the town.

No matter who's planning what, I make the best of shoving the Camaro down the highway any way you please. And when I slap her into overdrive it's like a jet hitting through the skies. That car doesn't move, it *dreams*. And the only fear that snakes into the cockpit comes when we cross into Fairfield itself. That's when the radar patrols can hit without warning. But Michaels has a little beeper, a Fuzz Buster, that fits into the cigarette lighter. Once the Fuzz Buster lets out a squeak I pop her down to thirty and cruise into town cool as a cat.

"Park her out front." He looks around the back of the depot for the bus. When he spots it rolling down the street he looks back and winks. "See you in ten minutes," he says. "We'll be saying hello for a little while."

Fine with me. I watch him walk over to the line of buses, watch him walking proud but very free, and begin thinking that whoever this Charlene is, she should hold him tight and never let go. Then I start playing all the tricks the car has to offer: Crank the heat up, then the air conditioner, then the A.M., then the F.M., and finally the tape deck, which plays the one and only tape Michaels has, called *The Best of Willie Nelson*.

Willie's a pretty good singer. A little on the throaty side, but I guess that's why the girls like him so much. A few songs into the tape, I look up and there's Michaels strolling across the parking lot with a blond angel attached to his arm.

"This's Charlene," he says. "Charlene, meet Billy Deerborn, the best soldier in the history of the Fire Eyes."

"Pleasure," she says and pushes her little hand towards me. She lets me shake the tips of her fingers and then draws the wrist back. The two of them huddle into the back seat and Michaels wraps his arm around her head so she's got a headrest. Then he gives her one whopping kiss that lasts so long she has to start screaming to get free for a breath of air.

"Youuuuuuuu-eee!" He yelps a huge cry of joy and slaps me on the shoulder. "To the races, Jeeves." He plants another smooch on her jaw. "And crank up that stereo. Willie Nelson churns Charlene to cream."

"Oh, you. . . ." She slaps his chest, but he gives her another wet kiss anyhow.

When it comes to chests, Charlene's got a set of B-52s. She's wearing a white blouse that buttons right to the middle of her breasts. Except in her case the last two buttons have come un-popped from the pressure of skin rolling under the cotton fabric. They're like Niagara Falls, just tumbling out of her clothes from ripeness. Some fruit just falls into your lap, and in Michaels's case, he's taking full advantage.

I adjust the rearview mirror to keep an eye on things in the back seat. Then I set the Camaro into second gear and drift down the street almost at an idle. Willie's starting a new song, a song about missing his girl at the railroad station and how Willie'd been counting on it so long through so many nights but now this next night is going to be the longest night of all.

Michaels looks over the seat with a big smile and slaps me on the arm again. "Guess Willie Nelson has it pretty tough, doesn't he?"

"Yeah."

"Well, let's make some winnings today and go celebrate on his behalf, then."

By the time we pull into Fairfield Downs, Michaels has this idea set out where we win all this cash and go buy all the Willie Nelson records in town and then make a long-distance call to Texas to explain how his records have sold out and now he can cheer up. "That poor bugger's got nothing but troubles, if you believe his singing."

"But he's *so* sexy," Charlene says, dipping her head to get out of the back seat. "Remember when we saw him last year and he had everyone in tears?" She buttons her blouse the best she can and fluffs her hair two or three times with both hands.

"Great, if you think crying is sexy." Michaels slips one arm over each of our shoulders as we walk towards the entry gate. "Hope you brought your cheque book, honey, cause old Billy here has an eye for horseflesh. Don'tcha, Billy?"

Everything feels so warm and sunny I couldn't say no to a thing. With Michaels wrapping me under his arm so snug and Charlene smiling so friendly at me and the sky opening a deep blue colour above the track—it all seems too beautiful and delicate to disturb. This one moment's like a special artist's vase that nobody can touch. There's a little sticker on the side of it that says Do Not Touch.

"Sure," I tell her. "Horses are in my blood." And for a second I get this dizzy feeling of all these horses galloping around inside my veins.

Michaels pays our way and we swing through the turnstile and head up to Section G. The place's set up so that there's one huge mass of seats rising on one side of the track. Every fifty feet there's an aisle that climbs to the top of the grandstand, where dozens of kids are running wild. At the bottom, the beer counter and privies and betting stalls are set underneath a long concrete wall that has a roof made of red shingles. There's lineups everywhere, and a shiver runs down my back just thinking of everyone so crammed together.

"Fellas, I'd like you to meet Charlene," Michaels says when we reach Section G. "Charlene, this's the boys."

"Hi, everybody," she says and wiggles down the row to our seats.

They can't believe how wonderful she is, they're falling over themselves so hard to say hello to her. Even the guys with girls of their own—MacEwen, Jackson and Sinclair—their tongues are gagging down their throats with bright comments about what a swell day it is and ain't the racetrack a good place to make a few bucks.

Once we're settled in, Michaels skims through the daily racing form, looking for the best clues on the betting odds. "Now, look. See, it's the Daily Double that has the best payouts on the long shots. Now, what you have to do is hike down to the pre-track stables and scout the winners. The long shots are set that way because nobody's figuring they've got a broadside chance to score. Likely that's true. But what you gotta do is measure that against your intuition." He taps the side of his head with two fingers. "Now, take the track book and this pen"—he pulls a Bic out of his pocket and hands it to me—"and just stroll past the ponies very casually. And when nobody's giving you the eye, give 'em the first degree."

"Good luck, Billy," Charlene says, and she lays a big kiss on my cheek.

"Weee-uuu." Wiggins and Sinclair pipe out a slick wolf whistle to show what a hot deal it is that I got wet lips from Charlene.

"Yaaaahoooo!" Everybody's back-slapping and drinking beer and rolling their daily racing forms into horns so they can make more noise than the next guy.

Once I get down to the beer lineups I push through the crowds to the end of the grandstand. Sitting in Section G, I can see where the stables are set up past the track. The closer I get to them the more I can see track police and race officials wearing striped shirts and a few jockeys who're dressed in shiny clothes and peaked caps. Most of them look like they belong in a circus, but the more I see, the more this feeling creeps into my stomach of how they want to win so bad. Their faces are twisted, and the look of winning is so fixed in their eyes I can tell they'd almost kill to win.

But I play it just the way Michaels said. Stroll up to the stables until I can smell those horses and their manure steaming on the floor. The way they've got the stables set is almost the same as the barracks, and for a second I figure the army did the designs on the whole operation. There's one long building and in the middle is an alley that runs between two rows of stalls. Each stall is like a bunk lined up against the outside wall. But instead of a plain wall there's a window, and each horse can stick his head out the window to see what's going on. In the middle alley there's a four-foot wood gate to every stall, and the trainer can load in the hay or scrub the horse down and whatever else they have to do to keep those ponies happy enough to run for a living. On every gate there's a slot where the horse's name is written onto a white card, and below that another slot that says Race #6 or Race #2. At the end are some special stalls branded Race #7 and Race #8. They're also marked Daily Double.

That's when I realize that no matter how much I want him to believe in me, there's nothing I can do to help Michaels win the Daily Double. So I reach in my pocket, unfold the racing form, close both eyes and stab two fingers onto the list that shows the ponies running the Daily Double. Then I look down to see what horses my fingers hit on. And there they are: Crestar and Mister One. There're the winners. Yeah. They're the ones. And it keeps rolling over and over through my head, *they're the ones, they're the ones,* until the sound of it gets to be a freight train screaming in my brain.

CHAPTER 10

... Fourteen-fifty, fifteen hundred, *and* five bucks for the pleasure!" Michaels opens his mouth with his biggest grin yet. The last five minutes he's been counting out my winnings fifty dollars at a time, just so I know how big we really hit it. But the real miracle, the part that makes this the third lucky time in my life, is the fact that he bet an extra fifty bucks *in my name*. With all the excitement of the Daily Double and eight races one after another, I'd forgot to put even one nickel onto any pony at all. But Michaels had figured that and went ahead as a surprise for me. What I keep wondering is if Crestar and Mister One had lost. Would he have told me about throwing this last fifty at two losing horses just because he believed so deep in me? That's the kind of answer you never know.

"Now let's go *party!*"

"Anything you say, sweetie!" Charlene has her arm wrapped tight around his waist and the pressure of them locked tight together is pushing her breasts out of her shirt again. Every time I look over she rolls her eyes like she's sorry that I don't have a sweetheart to press onto me. And when I think about it, the truth of how lonely I'm feeling comes all the harder. Especially seeing the two of them so close in love.

"How 'bout you, Billy? Where do we go first?" Michaels screws his eyes into two nutty-looking glass bulbs like I'm supposed to be seeing the future. "Got any hot *leads?* Some kind of *intuitions?*"

"Nope." I open the door to the Camaro. "Nothing."

We get into the car, this time with Michaels driving, me in the back and Charlene at his side. First we go buy some fancy street clothes. Next we rent an even fancier apartment-hotel suite and book it for three days. Never heard of it before, but the Pacific Hotel's set up just like an apartment building, and we get a place with a kitchen and livingroom, two bedrooms, and sofas, beds, refrigerator and all the rest, right down to the knives, forks and spoons. Only missing piece to the formula is a sack of cold beer, two all-dressed pizzas and a fifth of scotch, but Michaels tends to that two seconds after he's signed his name to the register.

Once we get into the apartment the two lovebirds start looking sheepish as hell, and the next thing you hear is one of the bedroom doors clicking shut and then a whole lot of muffled panting and groaning. I head over to the window to get a good look at the city. You can see the whole place spread out for miles—buildings, bridges, cars, and police sirens screaming up the streets. When the pizzas come I pay the bill off, stick one in the oven and finish the other off with a slug of Heineken beer. By nine o'clock I figure there's no sense in waiting for Michaels and Charlene to finish up their marathon, even though they've got my new threads in there. So I grab the keys to the Camaro and strike off on my own, looking for a good bar that's got some fun to it.

A couple of miles down the road I find what is probably the closest thing to a Broadway burlesque: a Main Street bar the boys are always talking about called The Cascade. It's got a set of stairs leading from the street to a second-floor show bar. At the sidewalk you can look up and see all the lights flashing and from time to time a stripper'll be dancing and peel off a glove and then move away from the window so none of the street kids get too wired.

When I'm inside I pick a table with a view of the dancers and anyone who comes into the place. They've got a spread of customers: businessmen in suits who suck on their drinks through plastic straws, army guys who drink scotch in a gulp and chase it with a beer the way Michaels does, women dressed to show off their goods who drink fruit juice and gins from tall glasses half-filled with crushed ice. Then there's the shadow people who come looking for something to beg or steal, you never know which. They might lean on the bar and watch the girls or maybe they'll sit down and tell you how hot they are and how much money they make on cards or selling dope. Then there's three guys who look like Italians, dressed in dark suits, and they wander behind the bar or into the back room where the girls change. At the same time a few whores come up and sit with the army grunts or businessmen who are drinking too much—the girls know with them they can turn a trick without having to flat-back for it. And mixed up with them all are the dress-ups and theatre people or maybe some guys with beards who talk so you can't follow them, or the ones with dark glasses and yellow skin who sit and shake their heads to the strip music. They stay in the same chairs all night and never take off their glasses.

I spend a lot of time thinking where I fit in and finally decide that I don't fit at all. But after about two hours this lady sits down and tells me that she's just like me and I'm like her. That's why she picked me out and how she's so sure I'd buy her a drink. She tells me that *after* I buy her a gin and lime on crushed ice.

"You're very different from what they get here."

"Oh, yeah?" I'm feeling warm to her at first because she's got guts to just start in talking like this.

"Yeah." She gives me a smile that shows her teeth, small and rounded where they should be flat and square. Somehow it seems really lady-like to have those teeth. "What's your name?" she asks with another smile.

Maybe I tell her a little too quiet because she throws it back and laughs. "Well, my name's Renee, Billy. Renee Stark."

I hold my beer up to toast her and she clinks her glass against mine. "Nice meeting you," I say, taking a good slug on my beer. I really don't know *what* to tell her, even though she's set her eyes square on my face. It's like I could say anything at all and it would do, but every time I open my mouth to say something, nothing comes out.

"Hey," she says after a minute, "isn't that from the Fire Eyes?"

Her hand reaches to my shirt sleeve and she fingers the I.D. badge sewn across the shoulder.

"Yeah. You heard of them?"

She laughs a little and looks around the room. "Sure. You hear of them from time to time, with the base being so close."

"Oh." There's a dead spot drifted between the two of us and she keeps sweeping her eyes around the room and then back to me. Every time she turns her head I look her over and size her up. She's dressed in green corduroy pants and a white and green striped blouse that's tucked into her pants. Her body's square and lean and very tight looking. There's nothing fancy about her, nothing put on and haughty or anything fake to worry about—no hiding behind a lot of makeup like the strippers all do.

Maybe she's trying to figure out what to say, too, because all of a sudden she swings around in her chair and pulls a pack of smokes from her purse. "You want a cigarette?" she asks, passing one over.

"Okay." It's a menthol, which I hate, but I take it anyway.

She strikes a match and lights mine, then strikes another for her own. That's when I get a look at her eyes for the first time. Maybe it's the dark room and all the candlelight that makes the reflection so sharp, but just the way she holds the match up to her lips I can see the flame dancing in her eyes, flickering there in the green, green watery eyes that she has, and for a second it looks like fire glowing on the surface of a lake hidden in the forest—a lake lost in the wilderness, somewhere way up north that only a few people have ever been lucky enough to see.

Then the music blasts into another bluesy jazz number and a new set of strippers gets ready for the next act.

"Look," she says, blowing a stream of smoke into the air, "I feel like getting out of here for some air. How 'bout you?"

"Sure. You want to take a drive?"

"Got a car?"

"Yeah."

"Well," she says with that smile she used the first time, "let's go for a ride."

We drive around town for a time, across the freeway and then back down the main strip. She's real quiet most of the time, so I hog it down the ramps when there's no cars around to try and loosen her up a little. When she asks where I'm staying, I tell her about the apartment and ask if she wants to see it. She says okay, and I park right in front of the building.

We go into the lobby and up the elevator to the ninth floor. The building's got ten floors and it has two elevators. Once we're in the apartment she walks from window to window, looking down onto the city.

While she's getting used to the place I scout around for Michaels and Charlene. From the way things are sprawled out, you can tell the two of them had one helluva reunion. Their bedroom looks like a party ripped through everything. Sheets rolled onto the floor in a clump, clothes dumped onto the chairs, even Michaels's three-hundred-dollar wardrobe spilling out of the store boxes. The all-dressed pizza's been eaten and the box tossed next to the garbage. On the kitchen table is a note written in a woman's writing that says how they missed me and went out for a drink and will see me later. I just sit and look at that note a couple of times, wondering where they've gone. The worst part is trying to figure whether I miss them or not. Or maybe it's just Michaels. But if there's going to be any hot times with this Renee Stark, it's probably best that they've taken a hike.

I crack open two beer, stroll back into the livingroom and hand her one that I've poured into a glass. She's sitting on the sofa with her legs crossed, pumping the top leg up and down to some music playing in her brain.

"Drown your sorrows," she says, and holds up a glass for me to toast.

I clink glasses with her and sit in the chair without talking. I can feel little shivers running up and down my back and some heat coming into my face. Somehow Renee's got me worked up so I'm watching every step I make. It's like I have to be perfect for her. Maybe *more perfect* than I know how to be. Anyhow, I can't say much of anything, but it doesn't seem to bother her. She walks to the window and looks out to the city lights again.

"Some people would say all those lights are pretty," she says. "Like it's some kind of sparkling jewel." She takes another sip of beer and lets it sit on the back of her tongue before swallowing. "But when you think about it, it's madness. It'll kill us, you know. The plutonium will end everything."

I look at her and she cocks her head to have a good look at me.

She's different—I can tell she's different by that one look in her green eyes. And by the way she talks.

"How'd you end up in that bar?" I ask her.

She breathes a deep sigh and moves from the window to the radio set. "I was . . . lonely."

"Tonight?"

She's whipping the radio dial back and forth. "Does this play any music?"

"Yeah." Then I press her. "Tonight?"

"Any jazz?"

"I guess. Hey—was it tonight?"

"What?"

"That you got lonely."

"No," she says, looking directly into my eyes, smiling. "Not just tonight."

Then I start to feel talkative and run on about the Fire Eyes and the horse races and how I won so much money for everyone today without doing anything more than picking two names off a sheet of paper. Renee seems pretty struck by the idea of me winning so big for everybody at the track and nods her head and drinks off the rest of her beer in a gulp. She does it in a mannish way, with her head thrown back and without looking around for approval. When I take the time to see it I realize there's a number of mannish parts to her. No makeup, for one thing. And her body is flat and square and wider at the top than at the hips. Her hair is cleaner and shinier than a man's, but it's short and there's no fuss been put into making it curly or dyed blond. Her face is clear and the nose and mouth and eyes are in the right proportions, but somehow it hasn't made her beautiful. Her eyes tell me how smart she is. Smarter than me, but if she doesn't push it around, maybe it's the kind of smartness I can live with.

We fall into a silence that we don't have to punch holes into with empty talk. She's rubbing her foot along the carpet, and I wonder where she comes from and all the things I don't know about her.

CHAPTER 11

We end up talking the whole night through. Not talking about anything special, but just on and on, tripping from thought to thought until Michaels and Charlene stumble through the door, drunk and surprised at me having my own girl, and then they tumble into bed laughing their heads off about something. I take a quick shower and change into my new store-bought clothes and drive Renee home in Michaels's car.

She invites me in for a coffee and puts out two clay mugs and sets a match to the gas stove. "I know it's a lousy part of town." She puts the match to her lips and blows it out in one quick breath. "But the people are friendly. Chinese."

"Really?"

"Uh-huh." She brings out a plastic tray loaded with cream and white sugar cubes. Everything's stored in the refrigerator and ready to go. "Here you are," she says, as though it's just for me.

"I guess your rent's good then."

"Not bad. Three-sixty a month." She sips on her coffee without adding cream or sugar. "But I'm thinking of moving in a month or two."

"For a change?"

"No. To be closer to the university."

"You go to university?"

"No," and she smiles like it's the last place you'd find her. "It's just closer to my friends."

"Oh."

Then she walks to the record player and puts on an L.P. and shuffles around the apartment, straightening out her things. Every time she's not looking at me I give her the once over. Her tight corduroy pants cling to her legs and stretch around her thin hips. Her shirt's pulled tight and you can tell she's got a muscular build, but more like a swimmer than a wrestler. Everything about her is lean and stretched tight. There's nothing wasted, no extras to slow her down. Her breasts are small and you wouldn't think to look at them again and again.

"It's been a week since I cleaned up," she says, and comes back to the table for another sip of coffee. "Sometimes I can't stand it."

"I don't mind," I give her a shrug with my shoulders.

This makes her smile a little, and her mouth rolls up at the ends. "Yeah? I guess I'm the one who minds," and she walks to the bedroom and begins to tuck in the sheets. Instead of a regular bed she has a foam mattress laid on the floor. And there are pillows in the livingroom dumped together to serve as chairs. Everything is laid out simple and without a lot of money behind it. There's a few polaroid pictures tacked to the bedroom wall and some newspaper clippings glued to the wallpaper in clusters. The curtains on the windows are the kind that come with the place. Only the rugs on the floor have any newness. They're lambskins, thick and shaggy and clean white next to the dull grey floor tiles.

"What're those news clippings about?" I ask, pointing to them.

"Those?" and she goes to have a look for herself, as though there's a secret kept inside each one. "They're all about the . . . the revolution," she smiles. "Sandinistas, Palestinians, A.N.C. The whole history."

"Thought you didn't like soldiering."

"No, I didn't say that." She gets back to dusting and straightening. "I don't like *revenge*. But the military definitely has its—" she digs for the right word, "its advantages."

When she's done cleaning she flips a new record onto the player and sits down to finish the coffee.

"Do you like Miles Davis?" she asks, "trumpet and all that?"

"I don't know. Don't think I've ever listened to him."

"This is Davis right now." She pulls out a cigarette and holds it like a man, stuck down to her knuckles. Davis is playing a long-winded piece that sounds like two trains running through the night, and we sit there listening to the loneliness for a good half hour. When the record's over she lets the machine click off automatic and turns to face me. "You mind if I ask you some personal questions?"

The way her face is stuck over the table means she wants to do some close asking. The music is still playing inside my ears; the low, tired Miles Davis trumpet calling over the swamps at night. The idea of questions drifts past me.

She goes on fast without an answer: "Because it seems to me I already know a few things about you."

"You mean about me picking the Daily Double?"

"That and other things, too. Maybe you don't want to talk about it. Some people don't." She lights up another cigarette and gives me one. It's a menthol again, but I smoke it anyway.

"You already told me a few things. And then I've guessed most of it," she says. She lets a silence string between the two of us like a spider's web. Something inside me starts to prickle and tremble along my back. Suddenly I get the feeling that if I don't get out right now then I'll never be able to leave. It's either right now or never. And forever hold your peace.

"The way I see it," she breathes out the menthol smoke like a dragon, "is that you're right on your own."

"Nothing hidden about that," and I glance into her eyes and she holds on with a look like no one ever has. Like a fish hook slipped down my throat to the belly and just starting to pull tight.

"But with you there's never been anyone else," she says, even faster now. "There's never been a woman of any kind. Like you never even had a mother."

That hits into my throat and grabs on so I can't swallow. After five or six tries I manage a little gulp, but I can't talk back to her. Then she lets that silence spin between us so the longer I wait to say something, the better answer I've got to give. After a while all I can think of is the noise of the Chinese on the streets.

"Goddammit, it's noisy out there!" I jump to the window and pull it closed so it hits with a slam.

She looks at me and keeps her eyes glued to mine. She doesn't do anything about me slamming the window. It's as though it didn't even happen. Then I stare down at her. For once I'm back in control.

"I don't like getting squeezed," I tell her. "I don't like getting squeezed for an answer."

Then she surprises me. Instead of all her fast-talking machine-gunnery, she just closes it down completely. She pours another cup of coffee as though this is just a T.V. show where nothing serious can happen. Just the way she pours it with her lady-limp wrist sets aside the big storm inside me and turns things around so she can do the talking. But when she does talk it comes out tender and gentle like a Miles Davis lullaby. There's a softness to her I hadn't seen before. Something new and beautiful you wouldn't guess at.

"What *do* you like, then?" Her voice is so low and tender you can hardly hear it.

"I don't know."

"Maybe I can help you find out," and she smiles a half-smile. You could hang onto her lips the way they offer so much warmth, and I start to believe that she *can* help me.

"Maybe."

She puts her coffee down and stubs out the menthol cigarette and takes hold of my hand. There's no sex to the way her fingers rest on mine, but it still shoot pins and needles across my arm and into my heart.

"But you've got to give a little if you're going to get."

I don't say a word. Then she lets go of my hand and spreads her fingers flat onto the table.

"I mean, look at it this way, Billy. Look where I'm living." Her hand lifts from the table and sweeps around the room to show you she thinks it's a dump. "And you know what I do for a living?"

"Nope." I figure the best idea is to keep her going as long as she needs it.

"Keyboard operator for First City Electric. Keyboard, *grade three,* that is. Eight hours a day in front of a V.D.T., screwing my eyes up and probably my whole damn reproductive system with eighty-seven other women — *not one man,* mind you—for a total of $428 gross, every two weeks. Ten days off a year with a Christmas bonus, *if* the company does well, *if* it makes the transition to nuclear, which it's been planning for the three years I've been dragging myself in there."

She's standing up now, walking around the room looking down

at me, telling her story louder then quieter then louder again. That old machine gun's revved up again, firing all over the place. Sometimes it's as though she's trying to explain that the whole thing's my fault. Then she takes a little break and drags on her cigarette a couple of times. "So what I'm saying is that, you know, I don't have a helluva lot to give myself. But at least I know that I'm never going to have a thing in life unless I can dig into myself and pull out this . . . this kind of *gift*."

"Who're you going to give it to?"

"Humanity!" she says like it's as obvious as the grass is green. "The people." And she points to the batch of news stories glued to the wall above her foam-mattress bed.

I don't have much idea what her gift is, but you get the feeling that there probably is something inside her that's pretty special, once she gets to making it. Maybe it's like the polaroid photographs on her wall, and her special gift is to be a developer who turns beautiful pictures out from a roll of plain brown film. Maybe she's a transformer.

We slip into another blank spot in the conversation. And every time I start to think about driving off, she does some tiny thing to give the idea that she doesn't mind me staying on. Asking what record would I like to hear next, or fixing a pair of lettuce-and-tomato sandwiches. And the longer she keeps me around the more I can feel that hook in my belly tighten and squeeze. The funny thing is, I don't know who's reeling in the fishing line. Is it her, or me, or somebody sitting way up in the sky pulling the strings of fate? Then I start thinking about myself and why she'd even bothered talking to me.

"Why'd you get started in with me?"

"Why?"

"Yeah."

She rolls her eyebrows up as though she can't figure it either. "Lonely, I guess."

"But you're not lonely now?"

"Can't you tell?" She gives me a deep look from her eyes that means a lot more than I can figure out. But instead of explaining anything we just keep looking at one another until something inside me has to push for more facts.

She rests her head on her hand. "There's something to you. I don't know what . . . your looks. Maybe your eyes. Something

that says you'll *do* anything. That makes you the right material."
Then her hand drops from her face and her head tilts a little to the
right and she smiles. "Besides, you're very cute."

All of a sudden I realize that she's opened me right up. Slipped
into my guts with her words and her looks and the way she has of
moving her hands and arms so gentle and sure. And now that she's
telling me the clear truth I realize she's cutting a bit too close to the
bone, and all I want her to do is back off a minute so I can get a
hold on my thoughts.

"So why'd you go to that bar, anyway?" I ask her.

She looks up to the ceiling and stretches back in the chair.
"Well, I hadn't really seen anyone for about two weeks. So I went
downtown, had a drink at Sweet Virginia's and didn't see anyone
worth talking to. Then I went over to The Cascade. Next I saw
you sitting in the corner and noticed the Fire Eyes badge on your
shirt. And looking at you, I thought, yeah, a Fire Eyes is the right
material to work with."

"What's that mean? The right material."

"I don't know. I just had to figure out a good line to pick you
up." Then she looks at me and smiles. "By the way, you were
very easy to pick up, you know."

The way she tells it makes me laugh.

"Besides, that badge reminded me of my father." She looks at a
little slick of grease swimming on top of her coffee and stirs it with
a fingernail. "Except he was a *real* creep. But I always felt sorry
for him. He was in it, too. In the Fire Eyes for fifteen, twenty
years."

□   □   □

When you think about it—wherever you were hiding away at the
time — it may seem that meeting Renee shouldn't be counted as
the fourth piece of luck at all. But the way I see it, she's the only
one that can make something really important happen. My first
guess about her proves to be right on the money: she's a transformer. Somebody who can switch a plain ordinary life, like my
own, into something that finally has a centre to it. A centre of
gravity that will pull me home no matter how hard or how long I
fall. So meeting Renee isn't just the fourth straight piece of luck in
my life. *It's the best.*

And the fact is, it takes me three weeks of mulling the idea over before I figure that the fish hook pulling inside my stomach isn't really a fish hook after all. It's that centre of gravity telling me to pour my guts out to this woman, this Renee with her thin soft face and dark green suffering eyes. She's got a huge emptiness that somebody should fill up before she gets too lost and lonely to survive when the time comes for *her* to fall fast and far.

One way to start filling up that hole is to find out the truth behind her old man. She didn't really tell me any details beyond his name, but in the Fire Eyes even a first name is enough to start nosing into some history. So when the time's right I warm up to old Luke Benson, the supplies corporal who's been here practically forever and knows everything. He's always telling you how many months to go before his pension kicks in and he can push on to easy street. Normally, a guy can retire with full pension anywhere from age thirty-seven on, depending on when he started up. But in Luke's case everybody figures he's close to sixty, because of the way his face is creased and lined so bad.

When I ask him about Nathan Stark, you can see Benson's eyes flinch as if I found a new code word for the belly of hell. "Sheeitt," he says in a low whisper. "Where'd you hear about him from?"

"Just came up the other day."

"Yeah? When you were talking about the Devil's ass, huh?"

"Something like that."

"You know what we used to say about Starky?" He's still whispering, but not so hushed as before. "He was *stark raving mad*. I even heard he *killed* his old lady. And drove his own daughter crazy as a loon."

"Yeah?" Funny. Renee never said anything about her mother. "What happened to him?"

He looks around to make sure nobody like Tooler's spying on us. "Ate sky." This time he looks over the top of the supplies shed to the grey clouds closing in from the north. "By somebody's good graces he got blown away one day by a training mine."

"You mean it was live?"

"Live enough to put old Starky down. It just takes two-bits' worth of model paint to make a live one look like a trainer."

Hard to believe. It's like Renee's old man had the same Devil to him that Jamison carries around. And he'd probably still be here if somebody hadn't seen to it.

"Happens every once in a while. Fire Eyes is like that. Different than any other unit in the army. Same with the Russkies and Chinese, too. 'Tracts the kind of fella who just don't have no sense for decent living. Fighting dirty's one thing. But living dirty's another. Eventually nobody can take it any more and they figure a way to snuff you out. Either that or the bad get *so bad* they make it right to the top. Like Hitler and Stalin."

CHAPTER 12

Ever since we won the horse races, Michaels has caught wind of what he calls *the take*. Says it's all over the base. Right from guys like Luke Benson playing bookie for the brass all the way up to the top C.O. There's talk of hookers being brought into the officers' mess and poker games running with stakes up to a thousand bucks a night. Somehow Michaels gets the word from two or three guys who're really supposed to know the inside track. Says the whole damn base may be on the take. Maybe even worse.

But the truth is that Michaels has been growing moony over the last couple of weeks. Since the last leave, he can't think of much more than Charlene. And believe it or not, all his mooning got him into a little trouble on the side. One day he was gazing into space, thinking about her instead of paying close enough attention to Tilden. So when Tilden barks out Michaels's name there's just a quiet lull in the barracks. I give him a quick pinch in the ass to try and shake all the daydreaming out of his head, but he doesn't even flinch. So Tilden lays on a week of extra detail. Scrubbing floors, cleaning the urinals, dusting down the drainpipes. Just exactly what Michaels hates most about the military. And I think that's what's really turned him sour. The fact that any time of day you can be screwed just for sticking your brain up in a cloud for a few seconds when you think nobody's watching.

But right now he doesn't really want to let all that bad juice sour him. Starting tomorrow we're up for another seventy-two-hour leave. And two weeks after that we all hit the half-year mark of active duty, and that means getting leave on a regular basis. Michaels is even talking about marrying Charlene and having her move up to an apartment in Fairfield instead of renting the hotel we used last time. "The way I see it, Billy, a girl like Charlene only comes around once a lifetime."

"I guess that's true," I tell him, and I believe it. Never met a girl like her anywhere. Specially with a chest like hers.

I head back to my bunk and slip a hand under the pillow and pull out the postcard that came in the mail today. Just holding that card is enough to make me shake a little. I can't think of the time when anybody sent me a letter, except as a kid when the group home parents would set up a deal with Welfare to have someone send each of us a letter from Santa Claus at Christmas. But this card isn't from some big-heart trying to soften up all the punks in the world. On the front there's a picture of this atomic bomb blasting into the atmosphere with a huge mushroom cloud shooting its bag of poison into the sky. At the bottom of the card the artist has written: "One nuclear bomb can ruin your whole day." On the other side is a note from Renee. "Just want to thank you for driving me home. If you're not planning anything next leave, give me a call or drop by. Coffee's always hot." Then she signed it Renee Stark.

The handwriting's smooth and clear, like she's practised it for so many years it comes natural as breathing to her. But it's tiny and shrunk down so it only takes up a little space at the top. Probably started out with some story she wanted to write down for me but then gave up after those first three lines. Funny how a woman thinks it through.

I look at that bomb sizzling on the cover again and just let my eyes drift into the middle of it. Pretty soon I've slipped right into dead centre of that cloud, riding a wild current of air like a slip-stream breeze into the whirling fire storm. And there at my side with her arms wrapped tight around me is Renee whispering something over and over. And no matter how hard I try to make out what she's saying, I can't take my concentration from that fire, with its ball of smoke rolling up to heaven.

☐   ☐   ☐

"You sure about spending your leave with her?" Michaels pulls the Camaro up to the curb in front of the Chinatown apartment and looks around like he can't believe anybody'd *live* here. "Not that I mean you shouldn't. Hell, that Renee of yours is one smart lady." He scratches an eyebrow with a finger. "What I mean is that if you wanted, you could bunk in with Charlene and me again."

I look into the lobby of her building. The front door's open, inviting. "Don't think so," I tell him. "On the telephone she said I could stay the whole weekend."

"Yeah. Well, you're gonna miss one helluva party." But he smiles so you can tell he's poking at me. "Mind, you'll probably have a time or two of your own."

"Sure."

I climb out of the car, and as he drives off he yells out something about giving him a call, but I can't really hear him over the buzz of traffic. I step into the building, then down the hall to her apartment. And just as I'm about to knock, the door pops open and there she is.

"Hi."

Funny seeing her again. I'd forgotten how she looked. In fact, all I could really remember was that she looked okay, but seeing her now so suddenly is like having the glass on a picture rubbed clean. Everything so fresh and real, somehow better than I pictured, lying on the bunk night after night.

"Why don't you drop your bag off. Dump it in the bedroom. I'm just going down the street for some groceries."

For some reason my voice just isn't coming through at all. I got all kinds of ideas and hellos to get out, but they're sleeping in the middle of my throat.

"Put everything in the bedroom," she says, and she leads the way down the hall to her room. "On the chair here." Then she gives me a big smile to show how it's okay for me to be coming by like this.

"Thanks," I tell her. What I'm thanking her for is a big question, but she doesn't seem to make a fuss over it.

"Sure. Hell, you've got to stay somewhere on furlough. No point in paying a hundred dollars for some sleazebag hotel bed."

"Yeah."

"Come on," she says. "Let's get some food. I'll show you the neighbourhood. It's quite a slice of life here, you know. A real kick in the ass." She's grabbing her keys and wallet and shopping list—talking away the whole time.

She leads the way down the street, and every place we go she knows the names of the cashiers and store owners like she's been buying from them for years. Then we head down to the open market and she picks out some fresh vegetables and the curly noodles they have. She gets some fruits and meat and special Chinese vitamins. I hike into a liquor store when I see one and get two French red wines and some menthol smokes for her, and Camels for myself. Then she buys some bread and long black stick candles.

"Want a newspaper?" she asks.

"No."

"Okay." But she folds one up anyway and sticks it in the top of her shopping bag. "I like to keep up," she says. "Or *pretend* to keep up."

When we're back in the apartment she unloads everything onto the kitchen table, then locks the front door and slips the chain across.

"Always like to lock up," she says. "Not that I'm worried about the neighbours. Just everybody else. You know, the creeps and pervs."

Locking that door's like sealing a secret pact. It's clear that she isn't worried about me charging at her. For the first time I get the idea that she's actually trying to warm up to me, trying to ease everything into a loose and casual manner between the two of us. And the look in her eye after she's got that door secure goes a long way to saying it all.

"Why don't you slip out of those army clothes into something for the weekend?" she says, disappearing into the kitchen. "I cleaned out a space in the cupboard to hang them up. On the right side. Use the hangers if you like."

I take it just the way she says and stroll down to the bedroom. She's changed things since the last time I was here. The bed's been raised off the floor and set onto a bedframe with wood head and foot boards. And the bookcase has been moved to the other side of the room next to a chair she's brought in and set beside the window. The newspaper stories are still glued to the wall, except now there's twice as many. And stuck to one wall are a dozen new black-and-white polaroid photographs of different people.

I strip off the uniform and slip into the clothes Charlene picked out on our shopping blitz. All the time I'm wondering what's going on, because it feels like I'm moving in somehow, especially with the uniform gone. I feel like somebody's stretched a new piece of skin over my body and I've turned into a whole new person.

When I finish changing I walk into the bathroom to check myself in the mirror. From there I can hear her in the kitchen, stirring some food around in a frying pan.

"Put on a record. Anything you like. Hell, I've got 'em all," she calls out, and she sticks her head through the door to see where I am. "The stereo's in the livingroom."

I sort through the albums which are mostly old Fifties records; records with Elvis Presley and Buddy Holly and the Shirelles and the Ames Brothers. She's got hundreds of them lined against the wall under the stereo and T.V. Finally I find one I recognize: Willie Dixon, an old black singer who always has a sad but true way of singing.

After the Chinese meal and the first bottle of wine she's feeling like a good talk. The black candles are lit and the other lights turned low so it's hard to see the edge of the room.

"I could get to like this." She smiles as though she's too shy to bring it up. "You're not the kind who's trying to force anything onto me. No grand ideas about yourself or your ambition unfolding in the future."

"I got some ideas."

"But nothing stupid. Nothing so crazy that it's really an empty dream. And a waste of time." Her lips turn flat at the corners of her mouth.

"How do you mean?"

"Look. A lot of men have this *thing* about who they are. Most of them are so much in love with themselves they've got no idea about the rest of the world."

"You think so?"

"Yeah. And women. There's one lady on my shift, Susan. It's

so *typical*, what's happening to her. First some good-looking pongo happens by one lonely night, they see eye to eye over a few drinks and the next thing you know the whole world drops from under her feet while he strings her a line about love, fidelity and a little bungalow filled with babies."

"Uh-huh?"

"Yeah."

She's come to a pause so I figure I should fill in with a point of interest.

"So where's this bungalow of theirs?"

"In her fucking head." She looks at me like there's no worse place for a bungalow in the world. "The whole dream's in her head. Except for the baby part. *That's in her belly.*"

"Wow." This pongo guy sounds like a real hole. "He dumped her?"

"Who knows? He just disappeared. That way he has the option of coming back on board any time with some new mind-fucking charade. It's so fucking *typical.*"

The way she tells the story you can tell it must have been as bad for her at one time. Not even Jamison uses that many *fuck*s in his stories.

All her talking gets me rolling inside. Being with this Renee is digging deeper and deeper. Then I get this picture coming to life in my mind, a picture Wiggins has posted on the inside of his locker. Some close-up centrefold shot with nothing showing except what he calls the Big C.

She passes the second bottle over to me and we start drinking with no glasses, passing it back and forth like two winos slumped into a back alley. After a while it feels like the perfect way to be drinking and she starts laughing and puts on another record. The whole time there's no talking between us, just that wandering bottle. Instead of talking she's started looking into me with her crystal eyes, deep green eyes that remind me of tall grass you see in a field on a spring day. Green and liquid, like the dew just came fresh from the cool night air.

Then one time when I'm passing the bottle back to her she slips her hand on top of mine. Instead of taking the bottle she just lets it rest there. And looking into my eyes she says, "You *are* different, you know."

There's a million ways to figure what she's meaning. But instead of trying to figure it, I just look back to her and say "I know," and leave it at that. The way she's pressing things is starting to bristle up an edge in me. I wonder if I'm going to make it with her the way Michaels does with Charlene, if I've got the guts for it, the way of making a woman turn in your hand, especially *this one,* who doesn't want a man taking advantage like that pongo. And thinking about it, with all the booze swilling through my brain I realize that *I just don't know* what kind of loving she'll find inside me.

Then a Presley record clicks onto the turntable, and she lights up with a smile and begins singing along. She knows all the words and the beat and exactly where the guitar parts come and the singing stops. She slugs off another gulp of wine and dances around the room like she has Romeo in her arms and she can't get enough of him.

"Come on, Billy, dance." She lifts me off the chair and pushes me through the livingroom. I can't dance a step but it makes no difference. She dolls her arms across my shoulders and I start rubbing her back slow and easy and she sways through every song like there's nothing prettier than Elvis singing about warm nights near the water.

We waltz around the room for about five songs and then stumble over to the kitchen table. She drinks back some more wine and looks at me with her head pushed to one side. And looking straight into me she says, "Hello," just once the way you'd say it to a kitten or a newborn pup, like you're giving them a greeting on making it into the world. Then without saying another word she leads me into the bedroom, to the bed, and takes her shirt off. Then she kisses both my hands and puts them onto her breasts. I kick off my new crocodile shoes, but she tends to everything else. In a few minutes she has us both naked and moving our fingers across warm soft skin. Then we lie down and I shut my eyes and drift with the motions of her hands and her lips on me. She does it very, very slow and smooths all the tired, lonely edges from my body. Every time something inside me starts to jump up she's right there, smoothing down the nervous muscles and planting a kiss where there's never been kisses before. After a long time she's smoothed out every tension that I have. My breathing slows to nothing and I open my eyes and see her kneeling beside me smiling like she knew she could do it, and see, didn't I like that after all?

That's when I lay her onto the bed and massage her a little and then climb onto her. She moans like I've hurt her so I stop, but she coaxes me to keep going. After that there's no stopping at all.

Then everything floods back into my head, all the misery and loneliness, all the time I've spent on nothing at all. I start crying, small tears, five or six of them that burn along my cheeks and fall onto her face.

"Oh Christ," I say when I realize I'm spilling tears onto her. I brush them off with a finger but it doesn't get rid of them.

"That's all right," she says, and kisses me on the lips. Then she brushes my hair back with her fingers a few times and whispers into my ear. "Let it go," she says, "just let it go."

□   □   □

"Oh, Jeezus. I've had too much." She burps a huge long burp and grips the side of the mattress. "Christ, Billy, this never happens to me. I swear it."

After the love-making I must've drifted into sleep. But it looks like Renee managed to get her nightgown on and then tried to make it to the washroom but realized she couldn't take another step from the bed and had to wake me with her swearing and burping.

But swearing doesn't help at all. Her head drops flat onto the pillow and her tongue rolls from her mouth. I grip her under the shoulders and haul the rest of her onto the mattress. She flops down with a thud and I drag her legs out straight and unwrap her arms. The tough part is trying to come up with a position that would be comfortable for a woman. In the beginning I've got her on her stomach, but I start to worry she might smother in the pillow. So I roll her onto her back. Her arms look so twisted that it takes five minutes to find the best position for them. Finally I just fold them together as though she's a corpse in a coffin.

Once she's out I decide to pull on my pants and nose through the place. It may seem a little crazy to you, and I can just hear you telling me to calm down, like you always do, but something about Renee is driving me wild. It's the fact that I don't know anything about how she *lives*. It's not what she could *tell* me that would set things easy. It's getting to know the *feel* of who she really is. It's sitting in her chairs and touching her clothes that'll show the truth. Getting right inside the way she sees and touches the world.

First I look at the records. They're all lined up in order from A to Z. Mostly rock 'n' roll from the Fifties, old blues records and then a lot of modern jazz. In total she's probably got over a thousand albums. It would take months to listen to all of them.

Then I go through the kitchen cupboards. There's some dry foods and canned fruits and vegetables. In one section there's all kinds of pills and vitamins in small brown plastic bottles. Vitamins C, A, B-complex, rutin, lecithin and others. She's got more of them in the refrigerator. One cupboard is stacked up with newspapers, and when you flick through you can see she buys them once a day without a miss. There's not a trace of booze or empty bottles, and I give her credit that she probably *doesn't* drink too much and tonight's a big mistake.

The bathroom is full of lady-stuff: woman's razors, tampons, jars of cream and spray cans. And it all has a musty smell that's trapped because there's no window or vent to let the gases escape. Next to the vanity there's a massager and a set of plastic attachments. When it's clicked on it's silent except for a light hum that comes from all the vibration. I let it drift over my face and put it to my tongue and teeth. Makes my teeth sting so I can't stand it.

Her drawers are messed up without any of the thought that's gone into tidying her books and records. Top drawer has socks and underwear and bras mixed together. Middle drawer has shirts, sweaters, jeans, shorts and extra socks. Bottom drawer has winter clothes, a few folded jackets and even more socks. Under the sweaters is a clump of maybe fifty letters that have been mailed to her, all of them in Chinatown.

I take one letter out and read it:

Renee,

After the last meeting I considered your proposal. If you think that action is to be carried on the frame of revolutionary ideals, you are correct. But if you think action should be mounted on the basis of the ideals of one or two cells then you are inspiring factionalism. Unity is the premier ideal. Unity of class, thought and action.

I am passing this along because the thought occurred to me after you'd left. I'd say it to you personally, but it's often weeks between seeing you and by that time I might not be inclined to put it to you.

Until next time.
In Unity,
S.

A few other long letters are from some friend in Alberta and another friend travelling in Europe. Then there is one letter written in a slant that I can barely make out:

Dear Renee,

This is not for your heart or your brain. It's for your cunt. When you come it is something to see. There is animal in you. Maybe it's the Devil. My back is sore where you scratched me and your teeth marks are still in my arm. After you it took five days before I could get it up again. I didn't even want to jerk off. I don't know if it was good or bad. But it was a hell of a sight seeing you get off. Maybe one day you'll see it too. I just wrote down your address as I left, hope you don't mind.

Suffer Unto Me,
Farrell.

After that letter I stuff them all away under the sweaters and go for another sip of wine. That guy Farrell is a hog for being straightforward. Seems like the type who would just show up at a woman's door and expect the world to stop. It's like he's waiting out in the street right now. Looking through the window, picking his own sweet time to make a move.

When I'm too tired to think any more I pull off my clothes and hit the sack. But soon as I touch the mattress Renee comes to and rolls her head onto my shoulder and starts feeling across my chest and legs. When I push her hand away she wakes up.

"Oh, hell," she says, and folds her hand over her forehead. "Christ, I'm gonna be sick." Then the hand drops to her mouth to hold back the vomit that's creeping up her throat. "Oh, Jeezus," she moans.

I don't lift a finger to help her, and she crawls into the can and props herself over the toilet. After most of the barfing is finished she starts swearing because the vomit's on her nightgown. When she can't peel it off she starts begging for help.

"What for?" I yell. "I'm trying to sleep."

Then I hear her fall over and some more barfing. When I figure she's suffered enough I go to her and pull off the stained nightie. Once she's naked she has another attack and leans over the toilet bowl to let loose. That Chinese dinner makes a helluva mess. I flush it for her and she gasps for air.

"Thanks," she says. She looks up at me pitiful and damp in the face. All that sickness has worked up a body sweat. Then I notice a long red scar on her leg that cuts a good five inches across her thigh to the knee.

"What's that from?"

"My father." She breathes a deep sigh from her nose. It's the first clean breath since I woke her.

"Your father?"

"Yeah . . . the bastard." She's still hunched over the bowl but propped onto her knees now instead of lying on her side. Then some more vomiting comes but it's only the dry heaves. By now her stomach's empty and she needs to relax. I hand her a wet face cloth and she wipes up. I stick the clothes in the bathtub and turn the taps so the stink will be buried underwater. Then I put her to bed and rub her stomach so the muscles can shrink down. After a while I don't feel as much spite for her but I still want to know about this guy Farrell and when he's due back.

"*Who is he?*" Her face sours up and she pushes my hand away. "Christ! You read through my mail?"

"Yeah. When'll he be coming back?"

She locks onto my eyes, almost looking straight through me. "You want to get *that* close?"

"What do you mean?" I shrug my shoulders and get back to rubbing her stomach.

"I mean so you know everything about me?"

"I don't know." I just keep rubbing.

"And I know *everything* about you?" She's got these questions loaded up with something. It's as though it's the biggest thing she could ask me. She grabs my hand so I can't rub anymore and squeezes tight.

"Sure," I tell her. "Why not?"

"Yes?"

"Yes."

"Then don't ever be a bastard to me, Billy."

"Who's Farrell?"

She looks at me hard as a rock. "He's a bastard who raped me. Then he thought it was a joke to send me that letter. I kept it for evidence. In case I ever take him to court."

My hand starts rubbing her stomach again and slips down to the scar on her leg. But instead of telling about how her father caused the operation she puts my fingers onto her sex and tells me to rub there. Then she slides on top of me and we do it again, this time slow and careful so she won't get sick if we rush it. When it's over I think about the fact I've done it two times in one day. *Two times.* But she's thinking other things and whispers dead into my ear:

"Don't ever be a bastard to me, Billy. Not ever. I just couldn't take it again."

It's funny her saying it to me that way. Like I was in on her problems the first time. But none of it's my fault, and there's no way I'm going to take any blame. So when she whispers her warnings to me, it's just warm air blowing past my skin. She never knows I can only half hear it.

CHAPTER 13

In the morning there's a hell of a pounding at the door. It's a tough, hard pounding, the kind that Sergeant Tilden would make, the kind of pounding somebody makes when they think they own the world.

"Damn it." Renee stumbles out of bed, holding her hand to her face. She grabs the wall to get her balance, then slings a robe over her shoulders and ties it at the waist. At first I slink down into the covers. But then I muddle over the idea of that bastard Farrell and how he's come back to get Renee. So I jump into my pants and shoes and get ready for a fight.

"Oh, Jeezus," she says when the pounding comes again. "I'm coming." Her face is white because the blood is too weak to run uphill into her head. Everything is slow about her. You can tell she's not used to drinking and being hungover.

"I'll get it," and I jog down the hall and hold my hand up to her so she'll stay put.

"Who's there?" I check the chain on the door and crack it open.

"I've got something for Renee." He's a tall thin guy with blond hair and wire glasses. I think about Farrell and the kind of power

he has. Then I look at this one again. Could it be Farrell? He's taller than I am but a good thirty pounds lighter. I could have him on
the floor in one move. He has a suitcase with him and he looks
over his shoulder like a twitch has crimped his neck.

"Is Renee there?" he asks again.

"Who's asking?"

"Steven."

Then Renee grabs my shoulder and slips the chain free. "Hurry
up," she says, and he glides in like a cat and walks down the hall to
the livingroom. It's clear that he knows the apartment layout.

I follow them past the kitchen, but at the livingroom door she
puts a hand on my chest and whispers low as possible. "Not now,
there's trouble. I'll explain to you in five minutes when Steven's
gone. Just wait in the bedroom, okay?"

He has the suitcase set on the floor and looks at me through the
wire glasses. There's no expression attached to his face and for that
reason you know he's dangerous. Maybe not now. But in a cold,
thoughtful way he's as dangerous as they come.

"You sure?"

"Yes. I'll be five minutes. That's all. Just wait, okay?"

Then she closes the door and I head to the bedroom. I light up a
Camel cigarette and let my thoughts drift with the smoke. After
it's out I can hear her opening the livingroom door and the two of
them walking down the hallway. There's a "good-bye" and she
comes back to me.

"I feel awful," she says, holding onto her face again. She lies
down beside me and pulls my arm around her. "Don't let me
drink like that again, Billy. It's too much for me."

"You should drink some juice. Maybe take some pills."

"Yeah." She walks to the kitchen and brings me a glass of
orange juice. She has a jug of it and drinks straight from the bottle.
"I never drink like that," she says between gulps of juice. "Jeezus,
what a mistake. It really throws me off."

Later on she cooks some scrambled eggs and toast and coffee.
When everything's settled in her stomach and it looks like she'll be
able to keep it down, the colour comes back into her face and she's
able to stop biting onto her lips. It's a habit she has that she probably doesn't know about: biting her lower lip and pulling it over
her bottom teeth into her mouth. When she's finished washing
dishes I ask her about Steven and his suitcase.

"Steven?" She smokes a cigarette and pauses as though she only wants to tell me so much. "He's just a . . . worker. Nobody important. In most ways."

"In *what* way, then?"

"In no special way. I mean it."

"Then how come he knows the apartment so well?"

She looks at me with a deep green look and comes to where I'm sitting. "Don't do this, Billy, okay? We just met and it feels pretty good right now. If you push it too hard you'll push it right out of our hands and we'll lose one another. Don't you see?"

I don't see. But with her leaning against my shoulder and her little breasts pressed into my arm it doesn't matter. None of my questions disappear, only the need to know right away.

"Then tell me about the scar on your leg." I want her to tell me *something*.

Anything to fill in the spaces in her life. It's because she knows more about me than I do about her that I have to have the spaces filled in.

"It's so boring."

"Tell me anyhow."

She kisses me around my ear and tries to draw my mind off.

"Tell me."

"Oh, shit. Really it's nothing." She pulls away from me and goes to her chair and sips the coffee. You can see she's thinking about it. Her eyes move to the wall and her teeth pull at the lower lip.

"I thought you said your father did it."

"Yeah. When I was twelve."

"What'd you do to him?"

"To him? Nothing. He did it to me. He did it to everyone." She lights up another cigarette and draws the blue smoke deep into her lungs. "He was a bastard, too." The smoke pours across the table from her nose.

"What do you mean?"

"Well, from the start he was pretty firm. No one was allowed to get out of line. Especially my mother. We always had to stay quiet and serve him his dinner and whiskeys. Thought he was entitled to it. He worked all week in the army and since he paid the bills he wanted some weekend service to go with it. 'Who pays the piper plays the tune,' he'd say—even though it was a bloody misquote.

"When he got drunk it was even worse. And it always lasted the whole bloody weekend. Booze turned him into a big fucking stupid bear. He'd maul my mother. He'd have her on the floor pushing her from one paw to the other. As a kid I'd hide under my bed with a collection of dolls and blankets and dried bread. I'd have a chair pushed under the door handle. It was crazy, really. I'd pretend I could hide in my bedroom forever; I had everything I'd need. And outside in the livingroom he'd be beating her. Never like a boxer standing up straight. God, he was too drunk for standing. They were always on the floor hitting the tables and chairs.

"Then one day I guess I was too old to hide under the bed any more. Something happened to give me the guts to try and do something about it. Maybe she was screaming. Usually she never screamed, but maybe this time she did. I don't know. The important thing was that I went out there and saw what was happening. He was on top of her with his pants down. It was scary, I thought, because his ass was hairy and I guess it surprised me. I never guessed *what* his ass looked like. Maybe I just supposed it would be white and smooth. But it wasn't. It was like an animal's, and that made it very easy to hate him.

"I went into the kitchen looking for a knife. It's terrible when I think of it now. If I *had* found a knife everything would be different. But I didn't. I was in a daze, I guess, so instead of a knife I got a cast-iron frying pan from the sink. It was still wet with suds. I remember thinking, what if I drop it? God, what if it slips out of my hand? Finally I just went and did it. I held it over him meaning to bring it down onto his head. But instead of his head it hit his shoulder. It hurt him, you could hear him moan, but all it did was make him turn over and grab me by the ankle.

"My mother started screaming 'Renee, Renee,' but it was as though she was scolding me for being out of bed. I realized then that she actually *liked* what was happening and *I* was the one who was being crazy. Then my father gripped me so hard I started to cry. He pulled me down and I hit the coffee table. Then he pulled my nightie up as though he was going to spank me. But instead of spanking me he used the frying pan. He hit around my legs again and again until he broke the femur and I started screaming, too."

A few tears start coming down her cheek.

"Then what happened?" Now that she's started I figure she

might as well go straight into the details. That way she'll only have to do it once.

"They took me to the hospital. It was a compound fracture, so they had to cut the leg open and set pins in the bones to line them up. And I broke two ribs when he pulled me down onto the coffee table. But the ribs were nothing. With my leg in traction I didn't move for months."

The tears are streaming down her face now, and she wipes them away with the back of her hand. All of a sudden she starts giggling and the giggling turns into laughter and then she's laughing through all the tears. "But you know what? Lying flat on my back like that gave me something to do. *That's* when I started reading. By the end of it all I could read a book a day. Cover to cover."

"Then what happened?"

She looks at me with her eyelids half-closed. Then she scratches her chin with the tip of one finger. "Once I could walk again they sent me to a fucking shrink. Can you believe it?" Her eyelids are wide open now. "Twice a week to start, then once a week for a year and then group therapy for another three years until I could get the hell out of there. They kept telling me I was manic-depressive."

Just the way she's telling it brings that whole world back home to me. Doctors and nurses and one-way mirrors. Everybody making a million dollars picking into your brain. "Tried to get you to tell a lot of stuff you didn't know, huh?"

"Oh I knew what they wanted, all right." She hauls on her cigarette, tapping a book of matches against the table. "What they wanted was adolescent hysteria. There's nothing juicier to them than young girls trying to get it on with daddy. Jeezus. What a bunch of perverts."

She's sitting there thinking the story through with all the terror of it slipping back and forth like a slow muddy tide caught in a back harbour. One small tear comes out of her eye, and she brushes it away.

"So then what happened?"

She shrugs as though nothing more could happen. "They moved me into Uncle Frank's house. I guess my mother was pretty pissed about my father. And it took years for me to be able to look at him again. In fact I only saw him twice more. Then a few years ago he died during some training routine. Nobody ever told the whole story about that one."

"And that was it?"

"Yeah. He died and that was the end." She rubs a hand across her face and looks off to the wall. "Then I finished high school and got a job and an apartment. Ten years later and here I am!" She flings her arms into the air as though it's a big surprise. Then she smiles, her face red and wet from the crying, and she says: "That's it."

"And you never heard what happened to him in the Fire Eyes?" If she doesn't know the truth, it's probably best to save her any more misery. The fact that somebody put him down like a dog wouldn't solve a thing.

"No. All I want to do is forget him."

"Yeah? Like Farrell?"

A serious look comes into her face. "Why do you keep dragging that creep into the conversation?"

"I don't know."

"Shit."

But no matter what she says, her father and Farrell and Steven wander in and out of my brain for the rest of the day. The first two don't have faces, so they all take on the look of Steven with his suitcase and blond hair and his cold dangerous eyes. It's only when she comes to me and holds on tight that they really disappear. Later in the afternoon, when her hangover is finished, she opens her blouse and starts singing to an Everly Brothers record. It's beautiful to watch her sing, like her voice is right on the album, and she's shirtless with her head thrown back and her nipples tight and pointing straight at me. It's the kind of thing you'd want to take a picture of. It makes all the other men vanish like ghosts.

And taking pictures is something that Renee does pretty well. She's got a little polaroid camera and takes a few snaps of me sitting on the chair. After each picture the film rolls out the bottom of the camera and you can watch it develop right in your hand. Then she gets me taking a few shots of her dancing shirtless around the room. One or two come out pretty well, and she tells me to keep them for when I'm sitting on the bunk all lonely at night. But I figure keeping shots like that around is like setting a piece of raw bait for sharks like Jamison and Tooler. They'd be onto shots like that in no time.

"Then how about giving me a little beefcake," she says smiling coy like a fox. "You know, just one or two torso shots. Huh, honey?" All of a sudden she's turned playful. Even put on a little French whore's accent.

"No way."

"Ah, come on, sweetness." And she slinks up to me, draping herself over the edge of the chair so I'm looking straight into her chest. Then she starts rubbing mine and undoing the buttons one at a time, purring away in her French-kitten voice. "Mmmmm. What delicious shoulders you have."

"Sure." It's all play-acting, the way Michaels might do with some wacky trick.

"And what gorgeous rib lines." Now she's got the camera clicking away. As soon as one picture slips out of the bottom, she's taking another and another. Pretty soon the whole roll of film's been shot.

"Hey, come on. Let's have a look." She puts the camera aside and leads me into the bedroom and spreads the pictures out on the sheets.

"See what a sexy bod you've got."

"I do?"

"Yes!" She starts laughing and running her fingers over the pictures of my chest. "I know women who would *kill* for an opportunity like this." And she lolls her tongue along my skin until it starts tickling and gets me all hot and tight. And again she takes care of all the love-making, letting me lie back while she does all the play. And the whole time she's saying, "This is how I *love* it. *This way. This is the way.*"

And it works like a dream. I don't have to worry about pleasing her, and she keeps rubbing her fingers across my chest, smoothing all the roughness away like she did before. After ten or fifteen minutes I realize that I could really stick with her.

□   □   □

By ten o'clock she's beginning to feel lazy and we lie together on her mattress. She complains about her job at the electric company and how she has to get up for work at six in the morning and what a shit it is that we'll have to say good-bye.

"But just for a little while," I tell her.

"How long is that?"

"How long would you like it?"

She smiles like there's ideas hidden in the back of her mind. "It can work two or three ways," she says and lights up her last cigarette of the day.

"What do you mean?"

"Well ... we can either have a short but deliciously *intense*"—she pauses and fits a deep kiss to my mouth—"affair that sweeps us away, but completely destroys us." She has a glow in her eyes that doesn't show any tiredness at all. "Or we could wait a while and show a little patience. We could split up for two months and get together again and see if there was still *something* between us." Her face turns cold like a machine that doesn't care if you live or die. "Or we could have an *arrangement*." She dangles this idea out like it's her favourite.

"What's your idea of an arrangement?"

"Oh, something that's there. Something that's always safe and you can count on. It could be Saturday nights. You see, every Saturday night we'd get together. Have dinner maybe and do whatever we wanted together. Saturdays would be entirely for us. Sacred. And the rest of the week we go our own ways and live our own lives without any interference."

"Sounds like a little holiday."

"Yeah," she laughs, "except it would be every week."

"Except I don't get leave every week."

"Oh. Well, I guess you'd have to quit, then."

"What for? I'd lose everything."

"*Everything?*" Then she stubs out the cigarette and runs a hand over my face. "Sounds like you're afraid of losing the little you've got. When you get hold of something, you don't want to let it go, do you?"

"What's wrong with that?"

"Well, if you don't let go then you'll never know if I'm here because you're holding so tight, or if it's because *I* want to be here."

I take my arm from her and sit up and lean against the head board. "If you want to be let go, then tell me right away. But don't toy with me like a fish. Don't lead me up the line and then throw me free."

She puts on a look I've never seen before. It goes right inside me and fills me up with warmth and the feeling of life. "I won't," she says, "I won't." And she pulls me beside her and wraps my arms around her and keeps whispering, "I won't, I won't," over and over and after ten or fifteen minutes falls into a strange murmuring sleep.

When she's been down for a solid hour I unravel my arms and pull the covers over her shoulders. She has a way of sleeping that makes the rest of the world evaporate. There's not the slightest line of care to her face. And her breathing's so soft and low you can hardly tell it exists. I keep staring at her so long that I realize I've never watched anyone sleeping before. It's the kind of thing you'd normally pass by and forget about. But with Renee it's like having a chance to watch yourself sleeping, which is something you'd never see and if you could you'd probably study it for hours. I keep thinking, yes, that's the way I want to sleep. So carefree and not a thought to anything.

After a while she rolls onto her stomach, and I get up and wander into the livingroom. I nose around a little and finally find the bag hidden on a back shelf in the closet. The two of them hid Steven's suitcase pretty carelessly. When you want to hide something you should do it so *no one* will find it. Never.

I pull it out by the handle and lie it flat on the floor. It's heavy-duty, all right. All the sides have wood linings and steel corners to sturdy the edges. The two clips that lock the suitcase together have combination locks. The locks are barrel spindles that click around to show one number in every digit space. There's four spaces on each lock so you can read any number up to 9999 on both of them. One is set at 6703 and the other at 2109.

I try to click her open just the way she lies. Nothing happens, so I turn all the numbers a few spaces together, thinking maybe Steven never tumbled the combination after he locked it. Nothing happens.

Next I squat down on the floor and set one lock to 0000. Then I move the numbers to 0001 and try to pop the clasp. Nothing. Then I try 0002. Nothing. I keep turning the numbers over and over, trying each one separate. At first it seems slow, almost endless, and it reminds me of all the counting I used to do and how mindless that was, too.

But once I get into it everything drifts free. Only my fingers have any brains and they're doing all the thinking each time they turn a number and try to open the lock. Then a light humming comes to mind. It's a lady's light singing, just like the negroes when they were slaves. It goes on and on, sweet and never-ending.

Finally I get lucky. Even before I try the clasp I can feel the way one row of numbers fit together and seem to click. The number reads 7935. I push a finger against the tab and it springs open with a loud *snap* that sets my heart pounding.

The next part should be easy. I spin the other lock to 7935 and try the release. Again nothing. Then I try 7936 and it pops free with another *snap*.

Once the suitcase opens I can't believe my eyes. It's like being right back at the base. I can see Tilden and Michaels and Wiggins and even Jamison. Everyone is sitting around polishing their guns and bragging about how shiny the metal is and how perfect all the gun parts snap together, like God must've invented each one of them. It's all in the suitcase. Guns of every kind. Everything in small arms, pistols mostly. There's Colts and a Walther P38 and two SIG210s. Altogether there's eight handguns and clips of ammunition to fit each make. A real gold mine of death.

But before I can close the whole thing down I hear a shuffling at the door.

"Christ, you're a sneaky bastard!"

I can't say a word. When you're caught red-handed all you can do is smile.

"When it comes to men," she says, "I always get some bastard who doesn't know where to stop."

CHAPTER 14

The army runs everything backwards.

First we start out blowing two or three charges a day. Next we've got to take a banger to pieces one step at a time, breaking it down so we can clear a demolition site from any hazard. Then they teach the art of bomb construction, turning our fingers into machines—splicing wires to fuses to detonators — so we can build a knock-out punch from nothing but a handful of household chemicals and old wire stripped from telephone lines. It's a miracle, really. The way they teach us to make a banger from just about nothing at all. And I'm right there every step of the way. There's never been a thing in the world that held me to such strict attention as demolition training.

But even though I love every minute, I have to admit they do it all backwards. In the first place, we should start off learning about explosives by building them up, then learn the disarming routines, and finally study the fine points of using them. But of course the brass don't think it through. They've got to shove it down our mouths dessert first.

The way Sergeant Tilden tells it, we should be able to make anti-personnel weapons out of the quicksands and slime of yellow commie guts. "And once you got the first one killed," he says, strutting through the class with his barrel chest jutting ahead of him like a Sherman tank, "then you cut his nuts off, hollow them out and load 'em up with nitro for the next commie bastard." Then a funny thing happens. Old Tilden starts smiling. It's strange, because nobody's seen him get even close to a laugh before. But believe it or not, he's got a set of nuts strung together by a fuse line that he starts passing around the room. I take a close look at them and start whistling over the tiny blow hole on the top of each one. Somebody's drilled an opening just big enough to load them with nitro and plug the hole up with a two-minute fuse line.

"Jeezus," Wiggins says, testing the weight of the nuts with his fingers, "do you think they're really *balls?*"

"I don't know." I never seen pure balls before but they don't look a bit like I would've guessed. These things look more like apricot pits than communist nuts. Then I figure Tilden's pulling a real joke on everybody. I look up and there he is, smiling away like an alley cat.

"Course they are," Tooler's just about drooling when he gets ahold of them. "Anybody *knows* they are at first glance." If Tooler thinks they're the real thing, it's a safe bet they're not.

Real or not, Sergeant Tilden straightens his smile out and pushes on with his lecture about bomb construction. First he starts filling the blackboard with diagrams, then he gets his slide projector going, and finally he sets a bunch of math equations onto the blackboard for everybody to memorize. The whole thing's like two hours of high school. There's not one guy that hasn't been left behind after the first ten minutes. But Tilden figures he's a real professor and shoves on regardless. It's all *x to the fourth power and add the inverse of g.* There's not a man in the room that hasn't twice counted the number of flies buzzing across the rafters before Tilden finishes the first special drawing on the board. But worst of all is Wiggins. He starts squirming in his seat like spiders have nested in his crotch.

"Hey, Billy," he says, whispering under the back of his hand, "you heard about the girls coming onto the base this Friday?"

I don't even turn my head. Tilden catches anyone making a squeak and it means three hours of double duty somewhere on the base.

"I heard they got a real *selection*," he says.

I twist my head around, squeezing my lips tight so he can see I ain't interested in three hours of trouble just for his damn dream of a whore. But you can tell by the look on his sore, pimpled face that nothing could count more to him in the whole world.

"I heard there's going to be one of everything. Blond, brunette and red-headed."

Tilden snaps around from the blackboard, digging his eyes straight into our section. The man's like a hawk. Nobody can figure how he got so sharp. His eyes drift over us like a judge would do, measuring you for the worst sentence he could lay down. Then he turns back to his equations slow and easy, like nothing ever happened.

Wiggins copies a few more numbers into his book and then starts squeaming around again. "I got dibs on the blond," he says in a whisper so low I can hardly make him out. "Jamison says I got *first come*."

"Jamison?"

Tilden whips around, cocking his arm as he turns, then rifles his chalk dead centre of the room. It fires straight from where he stands—in a line so fast and sudden you can barely see it coming. Then it cuts into my eye so hard I have to cover up with a hand to stop the tears from streaming onto the floor.

"Deerborn!" He screams it out. "What the hell are you and Wiggins hollering about up there?"

"Nothing, sir!" Wiggins snaps to attention. But I can't do a thing. One hand's still covering the eye where that chalk's bit in.

"Nothing, huh, Private?" he pushes over to the end of our row of chairs. "I'll show you about *nothing*, mister."

Finally my eye starts to clear and I take the hand away without too much shame for any tears falling off my face. I can see the piece of yellow chalk that's landed at my feet. A little bullet the size of a thumbnail.

"The two of you report for three hours of B and B at 1900. And that doesn't stand for bed and breakfast or fancy liqueurs or Brigitte Bardot," he says. Then he turns back to the lesson and keeps right on with his drawing on the blackboard.

What B and B *does* stand for is Betterment and Beautification. And Betterment and Beautification is nothing more than a lot of fancy talk for breaking your back scrubbing some muddy corner on the base. But instead of seeing to the detail personally, Tilden turns us over to Luke Benson after we've shovelled down some burgers in the messhall. Benson rolls his eyes like he doesn't really want to give me the toughest punishment, but he knows it's got to be three hours of cleaning up the camp or else he'll be hearing from the brass himself. So he takes us over to his operations office, leading me by the elbow, whispering new ideas about using my lucky streak and getting a tip on this week's Daily Double. The whole thing has left me flat, so I tell him just to give us the chores and forget everything else until I can make it over to the barracks and fall into bed without wanting to kill Wiggins for being such an asswipe.

□   □   □

The next evening Michaels and I are having a smoke next to the barracks. He's been dreaming more about cutting free of the army and taking early retirement. Maybe move in with his girl and forget all the B.S. the military grinds into your nose. After three hours of B and B with Wiggins I'd been thinking the exact same idea. But instead of telling Michaels how I was planning the same move, he snaps my chest with his hand and twists his shoulders so his back is faced away from the barracks doors. I turn my head around just in time to see Tooler's shining dome glide out the door into the moonlight. He sees us right away and pushes over for a chin wag.

"Say, you guys interested in purchasing any medical supplies?"

"Medical supplies?"

"Sure." Tooler edges between the two of us and starts to roll his shoulders like he's the most important guy in the world. "You know, what they call *pro-fill-antics*," he says with a sick smile. "For tomorrow night."

"You're playing host for Jamison, are you? Or has he just got you looking after the important details like the come bags?" Michaels can hardly stand breathing the same air as Tooler. The way he says *come bags* shows he thinks Tooler's the worst one of all.

"Nothing to do with Jamison," he says, sliding a hand into his back pocket. "It's just a little venture I'm running to get everyone fully supplied for party time. That's all."

"Forget it. Besides, why aren't creeps like you using standard issue?"

"Cause *these* are *tailor-made*." He pulls a little pouch from his pocket and opens it up to show five or six plastic packages. On each one there's a sign reading: *Leisure Condoms*. "See, they're lubricated," he says, pointing to the fine print. "We take the best, then tailor one special for your pleasure. Already had three requests for ticklers attached to the ends." He nudges his elbow into my ribs and drops his voice a bit. "That drives 'em wild!"

"Sure." Michaels can't stand it no longer. "Look, I'm going to head in," he says. "I'll see you later." And he rubs both hands over his face and walks into the barracks.

"What about you, Billy? How 'bout a tailor-made for your honey?" Then he fishes into his shirt pocket for a special sample. "This one's designed for Wiggins." He holds out the little balloon between two pudgy fingers and you can see where rubber bands have been attached to the end. "Also had this specially *lubricated*." The way he smiles means he's done some real oil work to the lubrications.

"How much?" I ask him out of curiosity.

"Twenty bucks." His eyes light up like he's sure of another sale.

"Forget it," I tell him. "I wouldn't use the thing if it was a gift from Brigitte Bardot herself." And thinking that's a pretty sweet way to leave him, I plant a kiss on my hand and rub it into the shining skin of his dome. "Not even if it was from Marilyn Monroe."

□   □   □

Friday night at midnight most of the guys hang around the mess after happy hour. But tonight especially, the whole troop wants to have a look at the girls that Jamison has stowed in through the back gates. He's been bragging about having a stable of three, but when you get to counting them, there's a total of five girls, and each one of them turns out to be pretty good-looking. Sneaking some broads onto the base is the kind of thing that goes on all the time. But on this one night, it's not what happens to them that's important—it's what Tooler does, and how everything that happens to him and me and Michaels stems from his crazy lubricated tickler condoms.

"Just pay your entry fee," Jamison says, slapping the palm of his hand, "and take your pick. First come's two hundred. Sloppy second's one-fifty and everything after that's one-twenty-five."

Nobody can believe it. Jamison has them all lined up looking like prom queens. There's one blond, a red-head, one Chinese girl and the two others are sexy-looking brunettes. They're lounging around, trying to look comfortable on the wood chairs or leaning on the walls. The fact is, it's impossible to look like a Playboy Bunny in the messhall, but they've done their best to make it the sweetest place the whole base has seen in the seven months we've been on board. In the back, Jamison has set up five little rooms using curtains and some mattresses stolen from the barracks. Everything's designed so professional, it's hard to believe he did it all on his own.

"Tooler! Just remember to give me a call when you get word from Lieutenant Reems. Immediately." Jamison has four other men set outside the building to handle any danger. Inside, everything's dimmed to candlelight and there's a waltz record playing on the jukebox. It seems like all forty guys in the troop are there. But that shouldn't cause concern because as far as the brass know, it's regular movie night and they expect a lot of men stuck in the mess making a fuss and knocking back too much booze.

"Okay." Tooler's sitting at the telephone waiting for his special signals coming over the line. He's also got his box of safes set up for display. Two or three guys are turning over their cash already.

"God. Look at that, willya!" Wiggins can hardly keep his tongue rolled up in his mouth. The minute he saw the blond I could see his pants starting to strain at the starch. "And look at the hungry red mouth on the bitch!"

A new waltz comes across the speakers, and he shuffles up to the blond and they start dancing slow as possible across the room. After about two minutes he's guided her towards the stall at the back. Jamison comes by, takes his cash, and Wiggins and the blond slip onto the cot and pull the curtain tight.

Once two or three of the bedrooms are closed you can feel the room start to vibrate from heat pouring off the guys. There's got to be fifty of them milling around, drinking beer and whiskey, rolling their hips to the sound of the music, smacking their lips waiting for the right timing to make a move. And the way Tooler's smiling, you can tell he sold out all his condoms in the first twenty minutes.

"Nope. I had most of the selling done yesterday," he says when MacEwen starts asking him about it. "I just finished with the extras right now." Then the telephone rings and he has to run to the desk and handle any alarms that are coming through.

And just as I'm buying a second beer at the canteen I start hearing this muffled scream coming from Wiggins's bedroom. At first it's a panting noise, then a moaning, and then it breaks into a full-blown screaming fit.

"Aaaahh!" Wiggins comes roaring out of his cubbyhole with his shirt and pants dangling from one hand and his face blazing with pain. "KEEriiist!" he says once the air rushes back into his lungs. "Where the fuck's Tooler?"

All the partying has come to a halt and everyone's looking at Wiggins running towards Tooler at the phone desk. "What the hell did you do to me? Eh? What the shit *is this*?" He drops his clothes and grabs Tooler's throat in one hand. The specialized condom is gripped tight in the other. Now he starts pushing that safe closer and closer to Tooler's mouth.

A few guys are starting to laugh. The two of them are spitting away at one another, Tooler sputtering and trying to smile like it's all a big joke, his domehead turning redder and redder and Wiggins stripped down to nothing, wagging that condom with its rubber tickler under Tooler's nose.

"It's a *joke*," he says, once he can pry the fingers away from his neck. "Hey, come on, everybody. *It's a goddam joke*."

"Joke?" Now Wiggins is using both hands to hold onto his pecker. All of a sudden some pains streak into him and he's doubling over.

"Yeah. You wanted it lubricated, didn't you?" He waves his hands and shrugs his shoulders a couple of times. "Hell, what's wrong with a little extra kick?"

"Extra kick?"

"Sure," Tooler says, "with a touch of acid. Just to pepper things up, Cock Nose."

"Cock Nose?"

Nobody ever says *Cock Nose* except Jamison. So when he hears Tooler using his favourite expression he boots over to the table fast as he can. Or maybe it's because Tooler and Wiggins are starting to square off for a bullfight and Jamison doesn't want any spats to spoil his show.

"What the hell?" he says when he sees how bad Wiggins is doubled up. "You guys are gonna drive me crazy with this damn arguing. Now what's going on?" He's talking to Tooler mostly. At this point, all Wiggins can do is moan and clutch onto his pecker.

"I got him under control," Tooler says, inching closer to Wiggins. "This suck just can't take a joke. That's all."

"Joke?" Michaels lifts Wiggins by the armpits and drags him towards the door. "This your idea of a joke, Jamison? I don't think the boys relish the idea of having their dicks rotted off by your right-hand man, here."

Once Jamison sees bodies leaving the messhall, he doesn't need any more explanations. It's like having every man stealing a hundred bucks right out of his pockets. And instead of laying out a big speech to Tooler, he walks over to him, cinches his head under his arm and pulls it tight into an armlock.

"AAAAHHhh!" Tooler falls limp as a worm.

"Don't you ever screw up when you're working for me," he says, wheeling him around to the back of the table. Then he turns to face the mess so everyone can see what he's going to do. "Not ever." And he rolls his free hand into a fist so the middle knuckles of his first two fingers are jutting forward. Then he spits once onto Tooler's pink scalp and etches a big X into the skin. The way his knuckle grinds over the skin is enough to make most of the guys want to puke. Tooler lets out another scream, but it doesn't do a thing to set him free. And when the X has been carved as hard as possible it stands out like a white scar across the top of his head.

Then something happens that I would never of guessed. First it starts with Sinclair and Pollock. The two of them walk over to the jukebox as casual as they please. And with one snap of the wrist Pollock unhooks the power cord, and all the sweet waltzing tunes come to a halt. Then they join up with Michaels and Wiggins and slip out of the mess, banging the door behind them. Next it's Williams, Jackson and Turner heading out three at a time and slamming that door for all it's worth. Then Maxwell and MacEwen. One at a time or in twos or threes, the whole troop clears the decks until there's nobody left in the hall except Jamison and

Tooler, the five whores and me. Jamison isn't saying a word. It's like the shock is too big for him to even breathe.

"Well, girls, I guess we just booked off the night for free," says the blond.

"Shit. I don't think so, honey." And the Chinese girl wiggles over to Jamison. "The boss here said four hundred guaranteed. Isn't that right?"

But instead of talking about overhead expenses, Jamison looks Tooler in the face, screwing his eyes up so all the black light glares through his skull. "You're a marked man, Tooler. Your fucking days are numbered."

At that point I head for the door, too. Whatever's been holding me back just suddenly springs free. But the sound of my feet tripping over the floor twists Jamison around, and he takes notice of me for the first time.

"What the hell are you doing here?" he says. The way his eyes are blinking you can tell the Devil's running in full control.

"Just watching," I tell him. "You know—collecting evidence." And just to let him figure I got more Power in one hand than all the men in the troop put together, I bang that door behind me so hard that the glass pops free from the window and shatters into a hundred pieces on the floor. Shatters so damn loud it even makes *me* jump.

CHAPTER 15

Y̦ou men wanted a war? Now you're going to get it." Tilden
struts past us, looking each man in the eye as he goes. He's got our
squad lined up shoulder to shoulder the width of the classroom.
For the last half hour he's been building up to a portrait of technicolour hell. But the funny part is, he doesn't seem to be liking it.
Most times Tilden's a hawk for a good fight, specially when the
unit's suited up with the kind of explosives he's talking about. But
this time you can see how his eyes have gone soft in the middle, as
though he's kissing half of us good-bye.

"Tomorrow at 0900 hours we'll be pushing off for three days of
manoeuvres." He gets to the end of the lineup, clicks his feet into
an about-face and strolls back the other way. "There's going to be
just us and support personnel on this operation. And you
gruntheads are going to be cracking a path through forty-five
miles of mountain terrain. *Forty-five*," he says, shaking his head
like even he can't believe it. "There's six abandoned railway
trestles that need to be brought down right away. Before they kill
anyone else. We'll do four the first day, then one each day after."

Now the facts are starting to set in. Just the way the guys start sucking the air into their lungs a little quicker with a little more panic—it all tells you how close that angel of death is singing in their ears. It's one thing to clear out a few miles of rubble a day. But old railway bridges are something else again. Tilden says four hunters fell to the canyon floor when a few rotten railway ties tumbled loose under their feet. The poor buggers dropped a hundred yards onto the rock. So now the cops call us in to take the track out. And just to make the whole operation like a true war, the brass have got us dressed in battle gear, complete with gasmasks and rubber gloves.

"We'll be sweating like hogs," Michaels says once the convoy starts rolling down the highway. "Ain't no way you can get through a day in these duds without losing twenty per cent of your entire body weight through perspiration alone."

"Yeah." MacEwen rubs his backside with both hands. Sitting in the troop transports eight hours straight can ruin your spine for good. "And chances are two to one you'll lose another forty per cent shitting bricks while some creep like Tooler buggers up the firing sequence."

The firing sequence is the plan Sergeant Tilden figured would take us through the whole shooting match in three days. The idea is to blow down the first bridge fast as possible. Then we check any problem spots and clear them with secondary charges. Now, the only way to work the system right is if each banger team blows their charges on the key structural points at one time. Once the first pair of guys sets the first charge they climb down from the trestle, run up the far side of the ravine and wait for the others. Then the next team runs up to the rendezvous and so on, until the first trestle is completely wired and fused. The key to the operation is to time the detonations so they all hit in one huge blast. That way none of the timbers can snag on a section that hasn't blown free. To do that right, every team has a remote-radio detonator set on the same frequency for each banger. The trick there is to make sure nobody screws up the frequency setting. And that's why MacEwen's worried about Tooler and Sinclair and a few of the other guys whose memories were never so hot.

"Specially when they got their heads wrapped in latex." Michaels holds up his gasmask and points out the little eyeholes they cut into the rubber. "You'd figure they'd give you a little more viewing room than these damned bug-eyes."

"Yeah." Pollock gives a sigh and looks at his own mask. He's been looking at the floor the entire trip. The truck ride has knocked any talking right out of his mouth. Same goes for most of the squad.

"Guess they don't want you breathing in any country air." Michaels is the only guy who doesn't mind the rough road, and he keeps trying to brighten everybody up with a few jokes. "Might turn you into a mountain man, Pollock."

"Yeah?"

"Uh-huh."

"Shit."

Once the truck rolls to a stop everyone can see what kind of job lies ahead. A dozen other guys are already in place setting up base camp. And a thousand yards to the rear is a ravine that leads off to some foothills, stretching out like bear claws in the wilderness. Behind them is a wall of mountains that looks like it shoved straight up from the earth. Grey and cold and perfect. So high and cliffed that you wonder how a railway got even half way up their stone face.

Tilden troops us over to a tent barracks, and after we get bunked in and finish dinner he runs over the final details of the mission. The whole operation's keyed to kick in at 0800 hours. That means we head up the first ravine at 0600 and plant the first trestle so it's ready to pop at 0800 on the nose. Then we cut along the track two or three miles until we hit the second bridge.

That night, thinking through the fine points builds into a wild dream that starts rippling through my brain. Lying there on my bunk, I can't think of a thing except the sound those bombs are going to make rolling through the hills and echoing off that huge mountain wall. My head fills so full of the earth shaking and pounding that hours go by with nothing but that storm of Power pumping through my veins. And the whole time there's a tiny voice whispering in the back of my ear, whispering in a song like Renee singing her sweet lullaby blues. Then I draw up a picture of her face floating like a cloud in the night sky. And the cloud sails past the way she might do: seeing the earth below her, knowing all the parts of what's going on and figuring the details of how the world ticks along its lonely trail through space. But inside that perfection there's all the misery she's had to face, and that thick wall of pain that someone's got to smash away. And looking at that black wall, I can see the exact place to set the perfect charge, a small crack along the stone, a tiny crevice that I can open up with one quick bang. Then just as I'm blowing a bit of dust off the charge, my feet start trembling, then shaking harder and harder until I can't keep my concentration. It rattles right along my back and into my hands until the whole thing drops at my feet and explodes into a million pieces of eternity.

"Billy. Come on, buddy. We got to get rolling."

The shaking's rising into my chest, running along my arms.

"Hey. Wake up, dream boy." Michaels. It's Michaels. He's sitting next to me in his fatigues lighting his first smoke of the day. After the last demolition trials I was ordered to team with Michaels instead of Wiggins. Since then Michaels has gotten the habit of having his first smoke while he's perched on the side of my bunk. "You expect to team with me, then you better keep your head out of those dream clouds with that girl of yours."

"Sure," I tell him, and I slip my legs over the bunk into my boots. But while I'm pulling the laces tight I try to figure how he saw Renee's face drifting in that cloud. Must be that Michaels has gotten to know me so well. Or I've been dreaming too loud, maybe even talking right out of my sleep. Anyway, he saw into the centre of it—the fact he flashes me a quick wink shows it all. The kind of wink he uses whenever he figures I'm having some kind of *vision*. Sometimes I think he knows about everything going on inside me. He might even know the truth about you. That at times like this you're never too far away and always ready to hand out some piece of advice. That's why he thinks I'm weird. At least that's what he says.

The next half hour we grub up and get kitted with all the demolition gear. Tilden put the alert out at five in the morning, and one by one each guy woke the next, quiet as can be. He wants to slip out of the camp without the base personnel knowing. That way the squad scores more points for being sharp and on their toes.

"Okay!" Once we're out of earshot of the camp, Tilden starts barking out orders. Everyone's dressed in full combat gear and the sweat's starting to build on each face. But nobody's got it worse than Tilden. His shirt is already starting to stain from the sweat pouring off his chest. "From this point on, nobody loses sight of his buddy. You got that?"

Everybody sidles up to his team member and gives him the nod.

"Now, look. I don't need to tell you about how much rock and lumber we're going to be pushing outta here today. It's a helluva lot and you all know it. But we can do this thing right if everybody follows the plan and hits the firing sequence the way you've been trained. I want the first run to pop at 0800. That means we meet up at area B at 0730. You got that on your maps?"

Michaels checks our map. A few guys snap out "Yes, sir," but most of the teams are sitting pretty quiet. Nobody's looking anyone direct in the eye.

"Okay. Mark time." Tilden holds his watch just under his eyes to make sure he's reading the figures right. Then he counts off the seconds until it reaches 0600 hours. "Time 0600," he says, and looks at us all.

Everyone snaps the winder tight on his watch. So far, the machine is set to go right on target.

"All right. Pair off down the line. Every team to hit their designated point on the first bridge. Remember, team one hits point one. Team two hits point two. Right down the line. I'll be pulling up the rear behind all of you. You got any trouble on your plug, you stay on the point and let me know. You got that?"

A few guys mumble out an answer.

"*You got that!*"

"Yes, sir!"

"What?"

"*Yes, sir!*" And we bark it out so loud the ravine picks up the echo and fires it back to the camp to wake the lazy grunts that're still dreaming their midnight women.

"All right. Remember you're *the Fire Eyes*. And good luck." He looks over the squad one last time. "Now *go.*"

We head up the ravine in pairs. After five minutes the tracks come into view and we walk up the line and around a bend on a rising grade. The railway tracks are rusted along the top, and some of the bolts have slipped free where the ties have rotted through. And along the tracks are millions of coal stones that must have fallen from the coal freighters that pushed through the mountains over the years. Around the next turn the tracks run through an old tunnel. An avalanche has covered most of the entrance, but there's enough room for one man to slip through at a time. Michaels heads in, then me. Inside it's pitch black.

"Okay, here's the light." Tilden hands his flashlight ahead and squeezes into the tunnel. Then everybody follows in line and we push ahead. The track runs in a long left turn. Then a slip of light dances against the tunnel wall and everybody starts laughing. It's funny, at first it was like we were dipping into the belly of hell, but with the sunlight up ahead, suddenly it's like a Sunday picnic.

Then we reach the mouth of the tunnel. The track stretches straight ahead over the first trestle. Beneath the bridge is a low, grassy dip that falls off maybe fifty yards. From the bottom a hill climbs up to the far side. There's a lot of broken rock on ahead, mostly loose shale, but nothing we can't climb.

Tilden pulls out a diagram of the bridge and reviews all the spots we're supposed to hit. "Okay. You men know your points. Let's wire in and meet at area B by 0730."

Michaels and I are team four, and our point's set on the bottom of the hill. That's where the key supports are anchored. Tilden wants the main truss levelled. That means setting two charges. One at the base and the other about ten feet up. The idea is to pop both charges at once. That way, you knock the bottom out and the whole thing falls on top of itself.

"Okay, let's do it one at a time." Michaels sets his pack down and digs out two separate charges. "We'll set the first one here and the other at the top of the beam." He hands me the digging tools and marker flags. Then he waves a hand in front of my eyes, like he's taken up hypnotism or some damned thing and he has to check his patient's reflexes.

"Hey. Billy boy. Wakey-wakey. It's six fifty-two in the morning. Let's get a shine in those eyes of yours."

"Sure." I guess I'd been daydreaming about the way the wood trestle is going to shatter in a million pieces. Anyhow, I clean out the setting for the first charge, he plugs it, checks the fuse, and I set the marker flag.

"Check that one, willya." It's routine procedure for the second man to check that everything's set right.

"Looks good," I tell him, making sure the flag's in place and won't blow off in a gust. The flag's important cause you don't want anyone running by kicking the fuse off before you're set. Everybody's been trained to jump past any red markers. Even in full stride they show you how to pull your leg to one side if you realize you're going to smack onto a banger in the last second.

"Okay." He checks the coding on the radio remote. "That's got her. Now for number two."

This time both of us straddle up the beam to the first Y-joint. I feel around for a good spot to set the plastic, clean it a few times with a flat file, then blow the dust away so Michaels can place the explosive.

"Good." He sets everything true, I check and flag it, then he checks the coding again. "Okay. Everything set?"

"Yeah."

"Okay. Let's go."

We climb off the trestle and push up the far side of the hill. It takes maybe thirty minutes to set those charges, and during that time five teams have skipped past us, moving up to the rendezvous at area B. The team working the other side of the bridge base jogs up the broken rock ahead of us and slips off their packs. By the time we roll up to the rendezvous the rest of the squad looks drained, their faces a dirty grey.

"Hey, fellas, everything ready to trip?"

"Button up, Michaels." Tilden comes over with his hand held square in front of him. "Just check your gear so we can pop the trestle."

"Sure." He strips his backpack off and rests it against a boulder. "No problem."

"Okay. Wiggins, Wilson. Let's set them up and run 'em." Tilden takes the detonator to a little flat clearing and sets it on the ground. "Everybody gather around. I want you all to watch this carefully."

The squad hunches down so everyone can see over Tilden's shoulder as he goes to work. "Now this time *I'm* going to hit it. But next run I'm not going to be around to do it for you. Everything will run like clockwork." He's checking the setting and codes on the detonator to make sure it's perfect. "Just remember to check your emplacements on the next trestle. After the next bridge, I'll be breaking you into three groups. Two teams to stay behind with me to do the clean-up detail. The other two to push ahead and take out a couple of bridges on your own." He looks around to all of us to dig this last point in as deep as possible. "Got it?

"All right," he says, checking his watch, "it's 0800." Then, looking over his shoulder to fix our attention, he hits the detonator. In one instant flash the valley fills with clouds of dust and light, then crashes down into nothingness with a huge explosion that blasts out louder and louder, echoing harder on the mountain walls until the banging starts ripping so long and loud it rumbles through my feet straight into the centre of my soul. And finally the whole world is vibrating with the smash of all the beams and steel rails crashing into hell at one time. It reaches a peak that must have been the way the old composers heard it when they wrote the last two minutes of their war symphonies.

"Okay." Tilden stands up once the show's finished ringing in everybody's ears. "That's what demolition's all about," he says with a laugh. And the way he laughs—the *first time he has laughed*—shows how the Power rolls through his blood, too.

Once the dust clears, everybody edges up to the track and peers into the pit below. What's left of that old bridge is just one hell of a mess of twisted, broken metal and rotten ties and beams. A lot of it's still settling, kicking up a few rocks and shrubs that roll a few feet down the hill. Then a bit of shale starts shifting and falling away from the bank, and a few guys pull back closer to firm ground.

"Now, I need two teams to come back with me for assessment and secondary blasting." Tilden walks back from the bank and loads the detonator into his pack.

Everyone stands around wondering whether they should volunteer. Nobody comes forward.

"All right. Wiggins and Williams. Maxwell and Turner. The rest of you head out to the next bridge."

"Yes, sir!" Half the squad yell it out together. Michaels picks up his backpack and checks to make sure our gear is all in place.

"Good. Now one final word. After the next trestle we're going to suit up for gas. That means everyone's going to be sealed in tight. If you want to enjoy the country air, then suck back as much as you can now. Got it?"

A couple of guys nod their heads to show they're ready for it. But most of them slump their shoulders and start fingering through their packs.

"All right." Tilden just frowns and seems to forget that nobody's barking back a "Yes, sir" every time he snaps out another order. Then he nods his head as if to say "Yeah, I hate this bloody detail too, dammit." But instead of saying it, he picks up his voice again. "Push on and good luck. I'll be coming up the line behind all of you, so you better be looking sharp. And remember, *you're the Fire Eyes.*"

CHAPTER 16

Come on, let's go!"

Once Michaels realizes we're going to hit the next bridge without Tilden, he's first man to head up the hill. If you run it by the book, we're supposed to be the fourth team going up the line, but that doesn't mean nuts to him now.

"Tilden's buggered off, hasn't he? So who cares?" he says to Pollock. "Billy and me have a taste for getting the job done ahead of schedule, then taking a holiday. Therefore, Commodore, we're pulling rank. See you in Paree." And he hauls the second backpack onto my shoulders and cuts into the woods before I get the harness cinched tight.

But getting up to the next bridge isn't so easy. Another avalanche has covered the rail line and we have to hike around the slide, away from the tracks, and then come back in towards them at the next trestle. The fact is, there's avalanches all over the mountain, and the worst risk is from part of the mountain driving us over the edge.

Once he's in the woods, Michaels scouts up a path and starts whistling down to me. After a hundred yards the trail leads to a sheer rock bluff, and I manage to catch up with him. It takes two men to unload the packs and pass them along hand-to-hand. Now we're both working up a good sweat, pushing the packs up onto the ridge and hauling them along by the straps. When Michaels pulls the last pack to safety, I swing onto the top of the ridge beside him. From this point on, the mountain trail levels off.

"Another mile or so," he says, looking at the map. "Then the next bridge is just off to the right a stretch."

And just as he's tracing his finger over the map, a new explosion rolls up the canyon. In the distance a puff of smoke drifts above the tree line. Then the echo starts shaking through the air. *Boom, boom, boom.*

"Must be Tilden and the boys doing the clean-up committee. Come on, let's get to the next trestle before anyone even gets started."

We jog up the trail until Michaels catches sight of the tracks again. The old rails curve along to the right, then we cross a gentle rise and the next bridge comes into view. This bridge isn't as long as the first, but it's higher and crosses a stream that washes over a mass of broken rock two hundred feet below. A rough trail winds along the ravine down to the stream, a switchback that slips from one end of the valley to the other, weaving back and forth from the bridge itself. The path is lined with shrubs, so it's impossible to see anyone coming or going, and we drop along the cliff edge, half-blind, until we hit bottom.

Once we get to the base, we slip our packs free and match the technical diagrams to the bridge itself. Michaels points out the centre beam, then walks over to it and slaps it a few times, as though it was a prime flank on a thoroughbred racehorse.

"Guess this is our baby," he says, but I don't say a thing back. To me everything's business from here on in. First I climb ten feet up to the Y-joint on the main truss. Then I dig out a fix with the files again, jump down and let Michaels climb up with the plug. He sets everything straight and I spot-check from the ground. Far as I can tell, he's got everything perfect. Once he checks the codes he jumps down and wipes the sweat from his forehead.

Another explosion punches up the mountain, then a second one right on its tail. *Boom, boom.* And the echoes trip over one another, rumbling along the cliffs and ravines.

"Jeezus. Those guys are working double time." He scratches

his ear with a finger and looks back towards the first bridge.

"Maybe Jamison and Sinclair screwed up their charges," he says with a laugh. "Trust them to bugger it up."

And speaking their names out loud like that works a piece of magic. Along the switchback trail a few bushes start slapping in the air. Then you can hear the sound of their feet scuffing over the rock and brush.

"Well, well, if it ain't the four saints," Michaels says, toying with his backpack. He starts bobbing his hand up and down like a majorette in a parade, so they can keep pace. Jackson, Tooler, Sinclair and Jamison all in a row. "Off to the races, huh, fellas?"

"Sure." Jackson's leading the way. Nobody's saying much of anything except Jamison, whose face is dripping sweat onto his chest and the back of his shoulders.

"Think your point's just up at the far end of the bridge there," Michaels says.

"Just mind your own, Cock Nose. And make sure you set your banger straight so we don't have to tidy up after you." Funny hearing him say it like that. His back turned away, lugging up the trail, sweating like a bull, and all you can hear is his thick voice dribbling out more garbage. I watch them mule down the line to the end of the trestle. The whole time I'm thinking, what if his pack of bangers tripped off right in the middle of nowheres? Just strolling along and suddenly *ppffft*—one of the detonators sparks and the whole show blows straight into the clouds. Eating sky. Jamison in this case. And the whole time that's all I see. Every step he takes is one more inch into oblivion.

"Come on, buddy. You gotta ream six inches out with that piercing pike."

Michaels hands me the tools and I drill into the rock where the key truss is anchored. This time the rock doesn't have any breach at all and I have to dig and hammer out the granite for a good fifteen minutes before there's room enough to fit the second plug. While I'm setting up, a few more explosions roll up the canyon. Michaels says that's got to be the last of the clean-up series and we're only going to have a few spare minutes to get ready for the next set. Then the rest of the squad drag themselves along the trail and start working their points on the bridge.

"That's everybody except the sarge and his group," I tell him.

"Yeah. Well, they'll be tailgating all day doing the secondaries.

141

Besides, old Tilden knows the ropes. Know what I mean?"

"Sure." But something starts telling me that things are getting tricky. Like an invisible hand that slices past you and leaves a shadow on your face. It's a warning that something's coming, that somewhere along the line there'll be hell to pay.

When we reach the next rendezvous, everybody sets their backpacks down and MacEwen pops the detonator like Tilden did on the first run. The explosions rip up the tracks towards us, then all the steel rails and lumber fall away in the emptiness. No matter how many times you hear it, the Power's fresh and raw and comes over you like a tidal wave of glory. You can see everybody, the special way they smile just on the corner of the lips, a little tuck on the edge of the mouth that tells the whole story. Each one of them saying, "Dammit if that isn't better than any woman, sweeter than any honey candy you could ever taste. And *I got it all*. Right in my hand."

Because Tilden isn't around, everybody plays it slack for a good fifteen minutes. But then MacEwen grabs me by the arm and hushes everybody up.

"Hey, it's Tilden." Nobody can believe he snuck up on us so fast. Below him Wiggins, Williams, Maxwell and Turner are scrambling up the hill around the rubble from the last blast. Tilden's got his backpack slung off one shoulder and he reaches in for his special field gear. "Now, look," he says holding the mask up in the air. "I want everybody to gather around for last-minute instructions. Wiggins, Williams, Maxwell, Turner and me are going to be placing the rest of the clean-up secondaries. Looks like this last bridge went okay. Apart from one or two sloppy spots on the first one, we're pushing along on schedule.

"For the rest of the day we're going to break into three groups. Like I said, my group'll do the clean-up. Then Jamison, Tooler, Jackson and Sinclair form the second group. The rest of you," he waves over in our direction, "are group three."

He looks everyone over a minute, trying to size the whole situation up in two or three minutes. "Now look, the next two bridges are both small, maybe fifty feet each. But both of them are dangerous. You've all seen the landslides around here. There hasn't been anybody to shore up these ridges in twenty years. So anything can trip you up. Even too much yapping. That's why I'm breaking you into two groups. And why we're going to suit up for

gas here and get that detail over with on day one. I don't mind
losing three or four of you," he says, with that cat's smile of his,
"but all twelve of you would put me right out of a job." You can
see he thinks this is supposed to be a big joke, but nobody's
laughing.

"Now Michaels, your group takes the first bridge down the
line. Jamison, you take the second. After the first trestle's down,
we'll meet halfway between them and pitch camp on level ground
somewhere. So once the first one's gone, Michaels's team scouts
the campsite while Jamison blows the second trestle." Then he
pauses and looks everyone over careful, eye to eye. "Apart from
that there's one last catch . . . these things." He wipes off his gasmask and holds it up for inspection. "The brass want every man
checked out on gas warfare routines. So you've got to be fully
suited at all times. I catch any man out of gear, and I'll blow you
out the army's wet ass."

"Yeah? Well how the hell they gonna know?" Jamison says,
picking some dust off the eyeholes in his mask. "I mean, we're the
goddam *lead* to this operation."

Tilden looks at him cold as steel and shakes his head. "We've
got it under control, Jamison. Don't you worry. All right. Any
questions?"

Nobody says a word. Mostly we're busy taking out the anti-gas
gear and trying it on. When a bunch of shale breaks off the ridge
and whistles into the canyon, everybody starts to hustle.

"Okay. Good luck. Stay sharp. I'll be along to surprise you."
Tilden slips his mask over his head and pulls on the anti-gas gear.
Gloves, boots and a one-piece suit that zips up the front. Then he
shoulders his pack and heads down the trail.

"Holy Sweet Mary. This's going to be one hell of a costume
party." Michaels gets his gear on and checks to make sure I'm
zipped tight. "Let's go," he says.

But once I'm sealed in I can barely hear a thing. Everything's
wrapped too tight on me. The first thing I notice is that my
breathing is too loud. It's like I'm breathing into a long empty
funnel and the echo of my lungs keeps rolling back into my ears.
And the face mask is pressed so hard onto my cheeks that the
skin's squeezed against the rubber. I twist my head around to see
how the others are doing and just then I realize that there's no give

to the shoulders. They got me sealed in and all set to lie down in a grave. And thinking about it, my teeth start grinding back and forth. The whole time all I can think about is peeling the damn suit off and running up the hills, free as a wild deer.

"Come on, Billy," Michaels says, giving me a nudge on the shoulder. "Don't worry about that suit of yours. I'll do the lead work. Just stay as close as you can."

When we see the next trestle, I realize how tough it's going to be to set any bangers with all the anti-gas gear stuck to my skin. For one thing, I can't use my fingers the way they're made to work. And trying to see anyone through the bug-eyes they give you is impossible. Every time I need to check with Michaels I have to turn my body all the way round, then yell so loud it starts to make my head deaf. But the worst part's the sweating. All the water dripping down my legs into the rubber boots. It's just crazy. And the feel of being all stuck and sweaty on my skin drives an itch all over my body. But there's no way to get in and scratch. There's just the slow roll of sweat, the echoing of my lungs, the grinding teeth. And in the back of it there you are, whispering: *Get out of it, Billy, get out soon. Get out before it's too late.*

"Just dig it the best you can," Michaels says, seeing how I've slowed down. "I'll do the rest."

I finish up the Y-joint position, pull the tools away and watch him check the codes for the charge. Then we climb down to the next point and lay it all in again. Everything's starting to turn hazy on me. There's no talking at all, only fingers and arms whispering to one another in the bubble suit, while my ears strain for the sick sound of an avalanche coming off the ridge.

When both charges are set, the two of us lay off and wait for Jamison's group to push past us. Finally they break through the brush, four guys spaced about fifty feet apart, carrying their packs like they were loaded with scrap-iron weights. Two of them, Jackson and Tooler, have pulled their masks off. Their faces are turned white and spit's drooling off Tooler's chin.

"Better keep those masks on," Michaels says as they drag past us.

But they don't say a thing. Then a few feet ahead, they slip the masks back on and just keep pushing forward like a train of dying horses.

Then the next blast hits in from Tilden's secondary charges. A minute later MacEwen and Pollock, the two other guys in our group, climb down from the upper trestle.

"That's it," MacEwen says through the mask. It's just about impossible to hear him through all that gear. "Let her rip."

"Okay. Why don't you two push ahead and scout the campsite. Billy and me will handle the heavy metal." The two of them walk on while we set up the next blast.

Once we've cleared the zone, Michaels pops the detonator. This time the bangers hit in two waves. The first one runs through me something awful. But the second showers down a hundred fragments of rock and dust and dead leaves, showers so bad a layer of dust covers the bug-eyes on my mask so I can't see a thing. I try to wipe them clean with my fingers but the gloves are such a mess of mud and crap themselves they just smudge the eyeholes all the worse. At this point I figure I'm about to turn crazy. It's like a bee's been slapping against my nose so long I can't ignore it a second more. But when I go to swat it I realize I'm up against a hornet's nest and a whole cloud of yellow jackets is ripping right up my nostrils straight for the brain.

I rip the mask off and snort as much air into my lungs as I can.

"Put that mask back on!" Michaels starts yelling straight into my face. "And get it on tight!"

But I don't say a damn thing. Just slap that mask against my leg and let it drop to the ground.

Then Michaels is next to me trying to pull the rubber mask back onto my head any way he can. That's when the craziness goes wild. I give him a crack across the head that sends him rolling onto the dirt. Then all I can hear is him yelling "Jeezus, Jeezus, Jeezus," over and over. When I finally get some sense to me I crawl over to him to find out what's going on. At first I can't believe what I'm seeing, but there it is: his bug-eyes have got spats of blood on the insides of the glass and he can't see a damned thing either. He tucks his thumbs under the rubber seal at the throat and peels the headgear off real slow.

"Lord Jeezus," he says when he's got his head free, "I never should've shown you that damned reverse punch." He's got his nose pinched between two fingers trying to stop the flow of blood. "Goddammit!" he yells, but any yelling just makes the blood gush all the more. The frame of the gasmask must've cut him pretty deep.

I dig some cotton batting out of the pack and hand it over. Once he's got it pressed into his nose and the bleeding stops to a trickle, I start to feel a little easier. Never meant to lay a punch onto his face, but that damned bug-eyed mask had to go. There was just no other way. God himself couldn't keep it on me.

"Sorry," I tell him. That's saying a lot. I've never told anyone I was *sorry* for anything.

"Ah, shit."

"Here. You can wear my mask if you want." I rip off another strip of cotton and wipe the dust off the eyeholes. "I ain't wearing that thing again."

"You're crazy."

"I don't give a crap."

"You don't, huh? Well you know something, Billy Deerborn? Huh? I don't think I give a crap either!"

And he starts laughing until the nose pops open on him again and he realizes he better stop making his jokes before he ends up leaving a quart of blood behind. So he twists the cotton further up both nostrils and leans against his backpack. But just as he starts to relax, his hand starts shaking from a whole lot more belly laughter.

"Ah-ha! I can't believe it!" He wipes a hand across his eyes to hold back the laughing tears. "Here we are out on goddam gas-warfare manoeuvres and you strip us nude as a cue ball. And on top of that, you lay a honker on my nose! You know something, Billy?"

I settle down beside him and ease into my backpack, too. "Nope," I tell him, "what's that?"

"Well, I'll tell you," he says, slipping an arm across my shoulder and patting me nice and easy on the back. "There's nobody—absolutely not one soul in this world—that's ever laid a finger on this beautiful little nose of mine."

"Yeah?" At first I figure he's going to be madder than hell with me. But the way he snugs me under his arm is so warm and easy feeling that I don't care what he does. Everything just feels so sunny and clear all of a sudden.

"Yeah. And you know something else?" He adjusts the twists

of cotton in his nose again. "You're lucky I'm not going to tear a strip ten inches off your ass!" And he smiles those beautiful piano-key teeth of his and starts laughing again. Then he gets me laughing, and pretty soon we're both rolling on the ground, so lost in the craziness of me laying a honker on his nose that we both forget about the gasmasks and all the slides that might be coming down above us. It may seem ridiculous, but for one second I feel like wrapping myself up in Michaels's arms and just holding onto him forever.

But pretty soon Michaels heaves on his backpack and shakes all the dirt off his leggings. Then he grabs both masks and sticks them into my pack. There's no time for fooling around—we gotta get out of here, fast.

"Better keep these just in case Tilden sneaks up on us again," he says. "Come on, let's go."

But we don't walk more than fifty feet when we hear some chunks of shale slipping loose behind us. It's like a ghost rattling so cold and lonely you can just barely hear the shaking of it in your ears.

Both of us turn around and for the first time I can actually *see* a wall of rock cracking free of the mountain and crashing into the guts of the valley.

"Tilden said they could be dangerous," Michaels says, waving off some of the dust flying into the air. "But that was just a hundred yards off our ass!"

"Yeah." The whole idea makes me shake. And instead of talking about details we push down the rail tracks, walking quiet as possible. The best strategy is to keep your ears open and walk soft. But before we get too far, there's a huge explosion ahead of us, mixed with the sound of another avalanche. Around the next bend, a cloud of dust billows into the air and an echo of hell rips through the mountains.

"What was that?"

"I don't know."

But it doesn't take much to figure it out. There's only one way you'd get a blast like that—one of the boys up ahead triggered a huge avalanche with a tripped detonator. All kinds of rock and bush and tree limbs are dropping from the sky like an April rainstorm. And once the dust starts to clear you can see what a mess of things that blast made. Looks like the legs got pulled right out from under the whole ridge and it just tumbled down.

"Come on, let's go!"

Michaels drops his pack and heads up the line towards the explosion site. It takes me a few minutes to get up any speed and by the time I reach him he's come to a stop next to some rock that's piled into a new hill of broken stone and steel and railway ties. He's got his back to me, yelling at the top of his voice into the crater that's been shovelled off the ridge and rolled into the gully below.

"What the hell are you doing?" He's waving his arms and throwing rocks down into the pit. "Hey! Leave that man alone!"

I pull myself up to the last rock and look down. Then the next thing I'm thinking is what a hell of a mistake. Should've stayed at the bottom of the rocks and let Michaels handle everything on his own. Should've stayed at the bottom of the damned mountain. Should've stayed out of the goddam army.

In the centre of the pit are two guys who've been ripped to pieces. Not just arms pulled off and a head yanked to one side, the way they show it in movies. These guys have their guts spewed onto the rock and all their insides strung across ten feet of broken granite. Intestines running like wet sheets tossed out a window. Liver flopped onto the dust. Raw stomach slopped down beside it. Both of them still wearing their masks. No telling who they are. Then off to the right is another man pinned under a large rock who hasn't been gutted as bad. His arms and legs are still shaking a bit, shaking the last memories of life from his brains. There's not a shred of hope for any of them. Then behind him, there's another man climbing out of the pit, dancing from rock to rock as best he can. A few times he tumbles backwards when the toeholds crumble under his feet. Then he digs in again, desperate to scramble out of that nightmare.

"Jeezus! Stop there, you bastard!" Michaels goes into a fit about that guy climbing out of the hole and starts chasing after him. "Billy, we got to get him!"

But I'm not moving an inch. All the muscle in my legs has lost spirit. It's hard enough to keep looking into that pit of death without puking up. But Michaels is running like a new life was born under his skin. He jogs from rock to rock, skimming into the pit and letting the loose beams slide under his feet, catching a foothold once or twice until he hits bottom. Then he cuts past the three bodies and starts up the far side. This time the rock drags him down as it slips free, and two of the dead men start rolling backwards to the bottom. Michaels reaches out with a hand and grabs the runaway by the chest and pulls him in tight.

That's when the real scrapping starts. Michaels tries to rip the gasmask from his face, but that opens his belly to one hell of a smash in the guts. Michaels falls back a step and then grabs on again. You can tell by the look in his face that's he's not taking any more crap. Everything's set for a counterpunch. Just waiting. And when a fist comes ripping toward his balls, Michaels blocks with his left and lands a reverse punch square into the guy's chest. That's it. One punch and it's all over. But on the way down, he plants a hammer fist onto the collar bone. *Whap!* His sleeve slaps tight in the air, just as the fist cuts across the bone.

"Come on down here, Billy," he calls across the slide and waves his arms to get me on the hustle. "I want to tie this guy down with some of that cotton stripping."

I dig my heels into the broken shale and rotted wood and try to slip down the rock without taking too many steps. By the time I reach the two of them, Michaels is hunched over the other man trying to peel his gasmask away.

"What's going on?"

"Just get me two feet of cotton strips cut." His nose is bleeding again and he keeps wiping the blood away with one hand. Then he wipes the hand onto his leggings.

"Sure." I pull the cotton out of my pocket and cut it down just the way he says.

"Now, let's see if we can guess who this bag of dirt really is."

With one last yank he pulls the mask away. And there he is. Face white as a ghost, gasping for a fresh suck of air. Jamison.

"What the hell are you doing?" Only his lips are moving. The teeth are gritting together so tight you can't see his tongue. "Three dead men aren't good enough for you, Michaels? Or you want to kill me, too?"

"You're the one doing the slaughter." Michaels cinches Jamison's hands together in front of his stomach. "You goddam murdered that man under the rock. Saw you with my own eyes."

"You're *crazy!* It was a fucking avalanche triggered by Jackson, for Christsakes!"

"Sure." Then Michaels turns to me. "Go see who that poor bugger is."

And without thinking I head over to the corpse pinned under the rock, just the way I'm told. But the closer I come, the more the nerve drains out of my legs. I get about three yards from the body and all my forward motion disappears.

"Pull his mask off!"

I inch up to him and start looking at my fingers. And all of a sudden a voice begins whispering through my head and I start wriggling those fingers back and forth, trying to flex some life into them. *One. Two. Three-four-five* . . . I bend down to the gasmask and hook my fingers under the throat seal and pull it free. It's Tooler. His head's gone blue, even that bald clean skull of his turned blue as the great rolling sea.

"It's Tooler!" I yell out.

But the sound of my voice drowns in the rattling of two more rocks tumbling past us down the crater walls. This time they roll to an easy stop fifty yards away. And watching them slip across the shale, I start counting a whole army of stones sliding along behind them. *One. Two. Three-four-five. Try to keep your ass alive.* . . .

CHAPTER 17

Lying on Renee's foam mattress is like floating in a different universe. All the thousand shadows of the army roll through the fog with me lying there, watching them marching past, watching myself walking down that wild broken mountain out of the bush and climbing back into the personnel carriers. And before that there was Tilden cursing us out, telling Michaels he was going to break him so far down the line he couldn't make it as Senior Sixer in the Boy Scouts. Then he unroped Jamison and ordered the two of us to hustle down to the base camp, commandeer a stretcher and haul those three corpses out of that crater of death. Wouldn't listen to any of Michaels's ideas about murder. Damned avalanche had done it all. Anybody could tell it was the avalanche. That, and the fact Jackson tripped his banger off by accident.

But Renee's mattress doesn't have a hint of landslides. No smoke or dust plugging up your nostrils, no rot creeping onto the back of your tongue from the smell of Sinclair's and Jackson's intestines leaking through the body bags on the way down the mountain. None of that. And to shove it out of my head I keep rolling my head on her pillow, pushing my nose into the linen, knifing up any smell of her I can find so it'll skin off the puke from my system. There's one or two little pockets of sweetness right on the corner of the bed, beautiful little islands of it, and when I find the best way to lie I just stretch out with my nose pressed to the smell of her sleeping head and wait for her to come home. Just wait there. Maybe two or three hours.

Then all of a sudden she's at the door. Standing in the hall with an armload of groceries. Her face clear, the short brown hair straight along the sides of her head. At first there's no feeling in her face at all. Then it comes slow, a little smile that shows her bottom teeth, then her eyes blink and she says, "Hi."

"Hi," I tell her. Then, "I came through the bedroom window."

"Yeah?" She walks over to the window and locks it tight. "Guess I should have given you a key. I didn't realize I was going to be this late. Had to run a second on-line batch through the V.D.T. You know, compulsory overtime."

"That's okay," I tell her. "I had lots of time to think. Drove in on my own and did some thinking then, too."

"Oh?" She's been expecting me. Everything's cleaned up in the apartment and there's extra food in the shopping bag. Even a carton of Lucky cigarettes. On a day's notice she's done pretty good. "I saw Michaels's car outside. He here, too?"

"No. He just leant it to me during leave." I start thinking about what happened to Charlene, how her mother came down with stomach troubles and she rushed out of town before she could tell him personally. Then Michaels figured he'd stay in camp on his own for the seventy-two hours. Otherwise he'd just get drunk and miserable. "Said he wouldn't be needing it."

"Oh." She dumps the package on the floor and sits beside me on the bed. Not touching at first. Her fingers two or three inches away from my arm.

"Went pretty bad, huh?"

"Yeah."

"Couple of guys hurt?"

"Three of 'em. Dead."

She shakes her head and looks off to the newspaper clippings. One whole wall is completely covered with them. "Shit." She just whispers it under her breath and then takes hold of my hand and strokes the palm, running her thumb back and forth, again and again.

"Want to tell me what happened?"

"I better not." Fact is I don't think I can. There's something too frightening about letting the story loose.

"Okay." Her thumb slows and slows but doesn't give up a stroke. And she gentles the raw nerve away in my hand and her medicine starts to run up my arm into my chest and then all over my body. After a while my heart's tuned to the beat of her fingers working on my hand, rolling gently back and forth so peaceful and kind that I don't have to do any of the work, nothing but the breathing and resting. Renee does it all for me. And when she's got the edges totally played out of my body the story starts to come a step at a time, right from the moment our feet stepped off the truck until the time I cracked open her bedroom window and climbed onto the bed.

By the end of it she's laughing at the idea of me opening the window and all her Chinese neighbours wondering what the hell is going on with that white woman and her man. All of them singing away and pointing their chopsticks at my ass scuttling through the wall. She even gets me laughing a bit and then wraps her arms around my shoulders and says she's glad I'm back.

"You are?"

"God, yes. Are you kidding? A hunk like you? My lover? You're beautiful!"

"*How* beautiful?"

"This beautiful," she says and curls beside me and kisses me. "And *this* beautiful," she unbuttons my shirt, "and *this* beautiful," she kisses my chest and pulls my nipples with her teeth.

"That doesn't do anything to a man, does it?"

"Not much."

"It does to a woman. It goes right around her ribs into her spine." She rises from the mattress and strips her blouse off. "See. They stand up when you just look at them." Her nipples come out into two dark points. She targets them right at me and jiggles them a bit. "Now, let's find the perfect music." She walks into the livingroom and pulls out a Billie Holiday record. It's full of deep-felt songs, and Renee starts humming along with them. She lies next to me again and rests her head on my shoulder and twists my hair with her fingers.

"You know what I really like, Billy?"

I don't say a word. Just let her ramble.

"The fact that you don't force anything on me. I mean, sexually. You know? Nobody else has ever been like that. This may sound crazy, but sometimes I feel like a man's supposed to feel. Taking control and everything. What I mean—what I mean *exactly*, is that I love it."

I just let the idea drift, then give her a thought of my own. Somehow she's got the power to drag me out of the black of night straight into the eye of a full golden moon. "Do you remember talking about all the ways you'd like to have it? Where you had this plan one, where it's just for the sex and this other plan, plan two, where it'd be on Saturdays only?"

"Yeah. Sure." She sits up on her elbows and pushes her tits onto my chest. "Sure. Did you like that? God, I thought about all three. Except instead of Saturday nights, I want it every night."

"Me, too."

She starts laughing and that sets me laughing with her. Her fingers start running all over me, poking me in the ribs, tickling under my chin. We're like kids in a sandbox with no sense of time or hunger. It's just summer and warm and there's nothing to do but laugh and play.

"With all three," she says, "we'll have every kind of love there is: love and sex and happiness and the freedom of no strings attached."

"Sounds like a dream."

She sits up again and looks me straight in the eye. Then she sighs and gives me a big kiss. "It *is* a dream, Billy. Don't ever let us wake up."

After we have the love and sex we fall into a deep sleep and I start a real dream, the first good one I've had in years. It's the kind where everything is so clear you can touch it and the story makes perfect sense. It begins with her and me living together in a big old house. She always has her shirt off, which is her favourite way of teasing me, and she's baking cakes while I'm busy fixing the light switches. For some reason all the lights have gone bad at once so I'm fixing them one at a time. When I've got the last light ready to go she calls me over to her. She's so brown and wonderful-looking, specially in the half-light of our house. Somehow she knows how to wear a smile so it hits right into your heart. "Look, Billy," she says, "look what I made. It's just for us because I love you so much." I go to throw the last light switch so I can see what she's made me. But that's where it ends. That's when the knocking starts to pound at the door. It gets louder and louder until her cakes disappear and then *she* disappears and I'm left groping around trying to find the light.

"I'll get it," she says.

I wake up and realize the dream's over. And there *is* someone knocking at the door and Renee's got her robe wrapped tight around her and she flicks on the hall light. The glare of the lamp stings my eyes so I have to squint them closed.

There's some whispering and heavy footsteps coming down the hall. I can't find my pants so I wrap a sheet around me and lean against the bedroom door.

"Make sure you come on Friday night." It's a man's voice whispering like he's in a coffin. "At eight."

It's Steven. He's wearing exactly the same clothes as before: blue jeans and a yellow shirt and brown corduroy jacket. None of the clothes seem to fit. He's thin like an old stick and the clothes fall limp from him. Only the wire glasses seem to be right. The glasses tell you he's got brains and that he's a cold thinker, the kind who can plan ten steps in advance. He's got the suitcase with him. The one with the guns. His hand grips onto it like it weighs too much for him and he shifts it from arm to arm.

"What the hell do you think you're doing?" I yell it out, then step into the hall to show myself. "It's three in the goddam morning!"

He spots me and you can see his eyes wild as deer's. He takes a fast glance at Renee, nods to her and darts out the door without another word.

She closes the door tight and comes up to my nose. "And what the hell do you think *you're* doing?"

I look right into her eyes and she holds me steady. "Trying to keep the place safe!"

"Safe?" She reaches into her pocket and pulls out a cigarette and lights it. "Well, *safe* is not yelling at *my* friends in *my* apartment."

"Yeah? Well, *safe* is getting rid of some skinny madman with a suitcase full of guns."

"Oh, Jeezus," she says, and she sits down on the floor and leans against the wall. After a minute of watching her smoking I sit down beside her. Then she looks at me again.

"You know when you found those guns? I didn't say anything to you. Right?"

"I know."

She starts picking at the skin around her thumbnail. "So, I didn't say anything because I didn't want you to know anything."

"Well, that plan of yours worked pretty smart—I don't know anything except that that guy Steven is dangerous."

That starts her laughing. She holds up the back of her cigarette hand to her mouth to try and trap the giggling. "Oh, God," she says through her fingers, "Steven is as harmless as they come. He's more harmless than, than—" She can't think of anything harmless enough.

"Than a deer," I tell her.

"Yes. More than a deer."

She nods her head like she's ashamed of how I treated him and smokes lazy, with big blue plumes of smoke pouring from her mouth. I think about Steven the deer and how hungry a deer can get in the winter, how it can start feeding on the tree branches and bark and after a long time how it will kill a whole forest.

"Look," she says, butting the cigarette into an ashtray. "We have to have a talk."

"Fine."

"A *long* talk." And she lifts herself off the floor and saunters into the kitchen and sets the kettle up to make some coffee. "There's things about me that you need to know about. And if we're going to stay involved, then automatically, *you're involved.*"

"Let it out." It's about time, I figure. Things have been running too loose too long without her squaring up to me. Damned weapons arsenal in the closet and that machine, Steven, creeping through her place every time I'm around. Just the look on his face makes me want to twist his mouth shut in my hands.

"Okay. Remember I told you about my job, right?" She sits down opposite me at the kitchen table and passes a coffee my way with a pack of smokes. The two of us light up and I wrap the bedsheet tight around my chest. "And I told you that they were going to install a new power network. A *nuclear* power line."

"Yeah."

"Well, look. They're not even having any public hearings on the procedures. I mean, they're going in there like they have in every other situation *to make a fucking buck on plutonium!* As though there wasn't enough of it infecting us all right now. Did you know that since 1945 over thirteen hundred so-called underground atomic bombs have been detonated? And over three *trillion* atoms of plutonium have been released into the atmosphere. Each one of them cancerous. And they'll continue infecting people for another twenty-four thousand years. Did you know that?" She's starting to get wound up again. At times she'll carry her voice so high, you wonder how she's going to get down off the peak.

"It's the government," I tell her. The government doesn't mean a thing to me, but the way she's talking it's like she wants somebody to sit up and argue the details with her. "Besides, nobody *can do* a damn thing about it."

"Shit. You *believe* that?"

"No. But the way you're talking made it seem like *you want somebody to believe it.*"

That shuts her down. Never said anything that could turn her words off before. But somehow that one line brings the whole thing to a halt. She takes a deep drag on her menthol and opens her lips just enough to let the smoke drain out. The way she does it, with her eyes half-closed, looks sexy, like some of the girls you see in skin magazines.

"Okay. Skip the rationale." She sips the coffee slowly, like she's thinking about letting all the secrets out at once. "Look, I'm involved with some other people in a group. We're going to close the power station down. In fact, we're going to close the whole company down."

"How you going to do that?"

"Blow it up."

"What?"

"The whole thing. Within the next two months."

She means it. At first I think about giving her a little laugh, but then I notice how the bones in her face have turned to iron ridges and the shape of her mouth has gone hard. Then I figure she's never meant anything so serious in her life before. Not even when she was looking for a knife to stick into Nat Stark's back.

"That's a big job."

"Yeah."

"Specially if you want to get away with it."

"Not if we've got the right *talent.*"

"You need the right equipment, too," I tell her. And I start to think of all the supplies she'll need that she doesn't even know about. The fuses and detonators, all the jewels of demolition that make it run like a Swiss watch. "You can't knock out a steel-and-concrete bunker with a few sticks of T.N.T. you find in some backyard demolition shed."

"I know. We've got that end under control." She looks into my eyes to show she's holding something back. Another damn secret.

"But we don't have the talent."

"You don't?"

"Not yet, anyhow. But maybe we'll get it today. Maybe right now." One hand reaches over and pulls the sheet from my chest.

"Yeah?"

"Uh-huh. I think maybe it's you, Billy," and she rubs her hand along my shoulder.

And all of a sudden everything fits right into place. The Fire Eyes, demolitions, all those months of training in the army, and now Renee. And with her hands skirting across my skin, it's like an extra heart pumping in my chest. And I can just see having all the demolition parts set out on the table, and how it runs my whole body raw with the Power of it. And the more I think about it, the more I realize how that rush of the heart is like being with Renee, having her kiss along my skin and work her mouth so wild on me. Then I figure how to put together an assembly lab right here in her apartment. And how I'm going to turn myself over to her as I'm setting the wires in place with the timed fuses and dynamite. That'd be beauty like no one ever had. Nobody in the squad could come close to it. Even Wiggins with his first-time screw, or MacEwen with his royal flush poker hands, or Jamison himself, with his fix for the Devil. None of them come even close to it.

Then she takes me in her mouth and swallows me.

CHAPTER 18

This's where you can set up."

She opens the door to the storage room and I have a look inside. It's bigger than I thought. And when she clicks on the overhead lamp you can see that it runs a good ten feet over to a covered window. The ceiling's sloped at an angle because the room tunnels under an outside stairway that climbs to the second-floor apartments. In fact, if it weren't for the crooked ceiling you could almost use this as another bedroom. She's got the place loaded with old clothes and suitcases and boxes of books and records that nobody needs any more. And the room is probably crawling with spiders and bugs of all kinds, and there's yards of cobwebs strung across the ceiling and over the window.

"I'll start cleaning it out and you can get organized on what you need."

"Sure." I butt out the Lucky I've been sucking on and sit down at the kitchen table and finish up a breakfast of ham and eggs and start making the supplies list. If that power station's going down in one punch, she'll need a helluva lot of gear. Including a good remote detonator like the army carries. But there's no way she could get ahold of those. Old Luke Benson guards them like his own babies.

"All right," I call out when the list's wrapped up. "This is what you need."

"What *you* need," she says, slipping a box of old newspapers under the kitchen table. "Let's see."

She reads it over carefully. "Hmm. Most of this you can get down at the hardware store."

"I know. But the *real* hardware you can't pick up in any store."

"Leave that to me."

"I'm talking about those remote detonators."

"Fine," she says, grabbing a broom to clean all the cobwebs out of the room. "You'll have them. In fact I'm getting them this afternoon." And she leans over to kiss me on top of my head and touches one hand under my chin like I'm her little boy. Her five-year-old kid.

"This afternoon? That's moving pretty fast, isn't it?"

"I told you we had to. Now look. I'm going to slip out for probably five or six hours. It'll take that long to complete the pick-up. When I'm gone, I want you to set up the lab to suit yourself." The *lab* is her way of turning demolitions into a scientific experiment of some kind. And in some ways she's right. "Demolition is power under the control of informed genius." That's how Tilden puts it.

"I'll go with you," I tell her. "You'll need some technical help."

"No. I'm going without you. What I want you to do is take a hundred dollars and fix the room up any way you need." And she digs into her purse for the money. The surprise is how much cash she's got. At least a thousand bucks, maybe more. All I can see is hundred-dollar bills, lots of them.

□ □ □

After two or three hours of work I manage to turn the storage room, *the lab,* into a wizard's den. First I black out the window with cardboard and a layer of insulation and plywood, so nobody can see or hear a thing. Then along the wall I fit a long table and cut some shelving and strap it to the joists. Behind that, there's a sheet of pegboard set up to hold all the light electronic gear I need. There's a chair and two or three spot lamps. Next to the door I put an old army cot that I picked up at the surplus store. That way I can lie down whenever I need a rest. And on the door I install a deadbolt lock so nobody can get in without asking me first.

With the leftover cash I buy a good stock of tools and some of the raw demolition supplies. A lot of it you can buy in the hardware stores or electronics shops. Most people would be surprised by the kind of stuff you can pick up just a few blocks from their own home. They're the ones who believe that the A-bomb is a huge bulky monster that's pretty tough to hide. Not a bit. It's the size of a kitchen stove. And you can bet that somewhere there's a guy making one the size of a toaster.

By six o'clock Renee makes it back to the apartment with her load of munitions. She's got it packed in cardboard boxes that are sitting in the trunk of a taxi. The driver helps shift everything into the livingroom, and the whole time he's talking about getting all these gifts from relatives and wasn't it incredible that her mom and dad would save all the souvenirs from her childhood so she could appreciate them now.

"Yeah," she says, laughing like she can't believe it either. "They were just great."

Once the door's locked tight she dances into my arms and swings around the room a couple of times. "We did it!" she says, fixing a wet kiss onto my mouth. "We *did* it! You should have seen the deal go down. You should've *seen* it!"

She's talking up a storm, wild with the boxes of equipment sitting in the livingroom, staring back at the two of us. While she's feeling so high I start unloading the supplies and move them into the lab. That's another thing she can't believe. The way I've transformed the place in one day.

"God. It's amazing."

"Look," I tell her. "I've got some delicate work ahead of me. Just setting this stuff in storage takes a clear head. Why don't you fix some sandwiches. Then in another hour I'll really have something for you to look at."

She does it just the way I tell her and I start sorting through the equipment, making sure none's defective, or even worse—faulty. If a fuse or detonator is defective, that's fine. The charge just won't pop on schedule and you can reset it with a little work and spare parts. But *faulty* materials mean you've got gear that's going to get you in trouble. Something cutting in too soon or a short-circuit that fries you just when you're adjusting the timing. Any fault like that hits in, and you can pay with your life.

So I sort through it all and set everything in place and start to test each line one at a time. And after an hour it looks like the whole shop checks out perfect. Every piece first-class. Even the remote detonator's in pretty good shape. It's been through the ropes, you can tell by the scars on the firing panel, but all the electronics shake down just the way they should. Just the way they'd fire in the squad. It's the one piece of equipment I figured she *couldn't* get ahold of. But there it is, sitting in my hands just waiting. That's the beauty of a detonator. *Its patience.*

And when I call Renee into the room she can feel the beauty, too. Ripples right off her face. The way she looks at everything laid out in perfect order, clean and ready to go. She just stops at the hall, not knowing what to say. But I pull her hand from the doorknob and lead her to the table. Then I roll the wire I've been testing onto a wooden spool and lay it next to the other parts that have been set onto the shelves. It's quite a storehouse. Just about two of every special kind of demolition equipment you'd need.

"Sure you know how to put all this together?" She runs her fingers along the pegboard.

"It's the *one* thing I know."

"The army taught you all that in eight months?"

"The army isn't part of it," I tell her. "I just know."

"God." A shudder runs through her shoulders. "It's frightening."

"You were the one who asked for a bomb. You should remember that."

"I know. But it's . . . the power of it."

"The Power's all in how you control it. I'll show you—"

"Yeah. We'll need a show. We can drive into the country." Her eyes flick past me. "Somewhere in the woods."

"When?"

"When Steven's ready to see it." She clicks her tongue against the roof of her mouth and her brain runs through all the details one at a time. "Maybe tomorrow."

CHAPTER 19

On Sunday morning all the equipment is ready to go. Renee has an old-fashioned wicker picnic basket that I use as a loading crate. The dynamite's wrapped in a bag like celery sticks, the fuses are bunched in silver foil, and the remote detonator's folded in wax paper to look like a dozen extra sandwiches. The wicker basket is lined with a checkered tablecloth and the demolition works are surrounded by bags of egg sandwiches that Renee has made, a thermos of coffee, napkins, paper cups and a clump of oranges and pears. The whole thing looks so good that I take a polaroid of it and hang the colour picture on the lab door. Then Renee comes along, laughing to herself, and writes in red ink at the bottom of the picture: OUT TO LUNCH.

But the joke stops when Steven arrives. He's wearing yellow pants and a checkered shirt, and with his blond hair and those wire glasses that glint in the sun, it's too much to believe.

"People can see you from a thousand yards," I tell him, "you might as well advertise the goddamn fact."

A hazy look creeps over his face when he realizes what I'm saying. Renee and I are wearing browns and greens that'll blend in anywhere. "I'll change," he says. "It'll just take five minutes."

We hop into the Camaro and he directs the way to his apartment. Then he scuttles into the building and Renee and I sit with the car idling.

"I'd like to know what you see in him," I tell her.

"I don't see anything, Billy." She cuddles next to my shoulder and drops her hand onto my leg.

"Yes, you goddam do. It's his ideas you're after."

"Dammit," she sighs, and lights a cigarette. "His *ideas* aren't so different. *It's that he knows how to make people do things.* Things they'd never do otherwise."

When he's dressed for the woods, Steven climbs into the back seat of the car and we pull onto the freeway. After a few miles he starts talking about his politics, so I turn the radio up good and loud. That way you can't hear his dry, empty voice and Renee can sing along with all the songs. The more we pretend we're on a picnic the better.

But it doesn't work long. He grabs Renee's shoulder and signals her to turn the music down. When that's done he kicks in with a lot of directions.

"Turn north on Highway 38. It's about six miles up."

"What for? I thought we were going into the woods."

"We are," he says. "I've got a special site planned."

"Where?"

"You'll see," he says, and slinks back into the seat like he owns the car and I'm a hired chauffeur.

The way he sits is like a prince, his nose up in the air and his eyes gawking out the window. It makes me sick and I turn the radio up again to try and block him out. But every minute or two my eyes glance into the rearview mirror and there he is in his glory.

A mile from the turnoff, he pokes his head forward and touches Renee's shoulder again. She turns the radio off this time. "This is it," he says. "Next turn."

I'm planning to race past the turnout, but something in my brain takes control and the car pulls right onto Highway 38. It's like a magnet, the way the car turns, and I realize no one's driving except Steven. He's turned me into a robot that points the Camaro and pedals the gas. Don't know how in hell he's done it. Maybe with some special technique like they used in the hospital. It's crazy. From that point on, I decide to go his way until we hit his special site.

"Take a left turn past that big white barn ahead."

The Camaro runs onto a country road and starts climbing a hill. After a few miles the fields peter out and the woods come into view.

"This is it," he says. "You'll see a dirt road on the right. Pull off there and open the gate."

At the turnoff there's a wooden fence with a sign reading TRESPASSERS WILL BE PROSECUTED. We park in front of the gate and Renee breaks open the latch, waves the car through and clamps the fence shut behind us. When she climbs back into the car Steven starts a fresh batch of orders.

"Drive along about five miles. I'll tell you where to pull off. We can screen the car in some bush, then walk in about two miles. It's not bad. Mostly level ground."

The car wheels down the road, an old road with two ruts and long grass growing in the middle. Above us the maple and fir trees are swaying in the wind and their branches cover the road. It's like driving through a tunnel with the cool green trees waving back and forth. I keep thinking that the branches are big hands waving good-bye. Then I hear the whispering: *bye-bye, bye-bye*.

After the car is hidden I'm back in control. Steven reaches into the trunk for the picnic supplies and that gives me a chance to step on him.

"What in hell do you think you're doing!"

A fluff of hair catches the breeze and his face twists in surprise.

"One bad move and you've got us *all* dead." I inch up to his head and look straight into his eyes.

"*All* of us?" He raises a blond eyebrow like he's caught wind of something.

"Yeah." I pull the basket from his hand and open it up to check the goods. "Instead of *none* of us."

Telling him that works like a charm and his worried eyebrow sinks back under his glasses.

When everything is set he leads us down a path. Renee is behind him and then me. The trail's pretty rough and overgrown in places, but it's brown, hard earth and easy to follow. Every time there's a fork I memorize which side to take so we won't get lost coming back. Especially if there's some panic. It's easy to start running in the bush and get lost before you know it. Then you have to *think* your way out and that can be tough. If you're in a hurry, thinking's the worst thing to try. So every step we take is like a photograph and I run a little movie through my mind, planning what to do and how to do it. When we reach a clearing he waves us to a halt.

"See that transmission tower?" His finger points to the distance and you can see a steel tower on the crest of a hill. The electricity line runs down the ridge into the valley behind us. "That's what I want to try."

"You want to blow the tower?" Renee's been quiet so long it seems strange to hear her voice.

"It's one of the lines from the new generating station. It's got to go." Without another thought he pushes forward until we get to a second clearing. This time the tower is dead ahead, a big steel monster with its feet spread like a bull dog and its arms stuck into the air. With the wires coming through its fingers, you'd think it was a puppet on a string.

"What do you think?" He looks at me for the first time like I'm a human being. For the first time my ideas count.

"I think you should've goddam told me you wanted to blow *this* up."

"What's wrong?"

"I thought you wanted a demonstration. *One* demonstration."

"I do."

"Well this's got four legs, Steven. I got *one* charge. You have to knock out at least three legs before that tower even starts to bend."

For the next five minutes we stare at the tower and the way it shines in the sun. With the birds singing and butterflies flitting past, it turns ugly and dangerous. I can see why Steven wants rid of it.

"Let's have a sandwich." Renee takes the basket from me and spreads the tablecloth on the ground. She opens the sandwich wrapper and passes the fruit around.

But my stomach starts to shrink and fill up with bad juices. There's no way I can eat. I take some coffee instead and let my eyes run over the tower, back and forth as though I was the one who made it. Then the answer falls into place like a dream.

"There's one way you can do it."

"What's that?"

I point my finger three-quarters to the top, where the arms shoot into the air. "Put a charge up top. Then—WHAM—blow the bloody head off."

This idea keeps him quiet for another minute or two. Then he turns and gives me a smile. "How do you plan to get it up there?"

"*I* don't," I tell him. "Climbing towers is my short suit."

He waits another minute. "Then how do *I* do it?" he says.

Suddenly I realize that up to now he's got *me* doing everything. Now it's his turn to learn a few puppy-dog tricks.

"I'll show you." And I open the dynamite wrapper and pull out some electrical tape and binding wire and all the other stuff. After a while the whole kit is ready to go. All the fine points are talked about, the best way to mount the charge, the best place to plant it, how to carry it, what to do if trouble comes.

"And it won't go off without that remote?" he asks.

"You never know. Could go off right now." The dynamite is sitting in the middle of the blanket and everyone gives it the cool eye. "But chances are good it won't."

"Okay," and he grabs the things I've laid out. "Don't move until I come back." There's a little bird in his throat. "All right?"

"Sure." Renee touches a hand to his knee. "We'll be right here."

When he's at the base of the tower my brain starts to dizzy. I can't believe I've got him going up there. He puts a foot onto the steel girders and takes his first step. Then another and another. After about ten feet, he stops and looks back to us.

"Keep going," Renee yells and waves her hand.

"Yeah. Keep going," I say, but it's just a whisper that only the two of us can hear.

He looks like a bug crawling up the leg of a monster and the further he goes the dizzier it gets. The fact that he controls Renee so easy, and that she does the same to me—it all boils up into a wild storm that makes my skin start to crawl. I reach for the wax paper and unwrap the remote detonator with no real care for the delicate settings or switches.

"What are you doing?" Suddenly Renee jumps up and tries to grab the remote from me. "What the hell are you *doing?*"

"I'm not doing anything."

"Look, it's one thing to think what you're thinking, but it's another to do it."

"I said I'm not doing anything. I'm just getting set up."

"The hell you are! Christ! You're trying to blow him off the damn tower!" And she runs to the tower and starts yelling at Steven. He looks down and right away figures something's soured.

"Get down quick!" she yells, and he just about drops, he's so fast coming off the girders. Then she grabs the dynamite from him before he knows a thing. It's all in one second: he hits the ground, she grabs the charges and tape and wires. Then she's ten feet up the tower before he knows the difference.

"I'll do it," he hollers, but she keeps scrambling higher and higher without a word.

"What's going on?" he ambles over to me like a kid who just had his favourite baseball stolen.

But I'm not giving an inch. I stick the remote back in the wax paper before he has time to sit down. The rest is all poison. My body's gone frozen and my eyelids can hardly blink. Watching her go up the tower is plain hell. She read straight into my brain and instead of letting things go as they should she slaps my face by taking Steven's turn. I start thinking I should blast the remote anyway. Then somebody starts yelling: *Get her. Get the damn bitch*, but I'm too frozen to do what anybody says. Only my teeth are free, grinding back and forth, grinding so bad you can hear them.

"What's going on?" He gives me a dark look, but it doesn't slack me up at all.

Near the top of the tower she straps the charge to the main girder with the tape, and after a minute she hikes down. When she hits ground it's like a snap of the fingers that breaks through my trance. Everything inside me turns to water and at last I can think clear. Steven looks at me again and I give him a smile.

"Thank God she made it," I say.

"Yeah."

After she reaches us she doesn't let on a word. She pulls the remote out of the wax paper and hands it to me. "Now," she says, panting, exhausted from the climb on the tower. "*Now* you can do it."

"Wait a minute." Steven squats to the ground and begins rolling the food into the wrappers. "We've gotta get everything cleared up and set to go."

But I don't give a fat damn about evidence or the rest of it. From now on, I'm ready to let things roll any way at all. If we get caught, we're caught. If we get killed, we're dead.

"I said *wait a minute!*" He grabs the detonator box and sits it on the grass. "We're gonna do this the right way." He's just about finished with the picnic supplies. After everything's stuck back in the wicker basket, he searches through the grass. There's the crust from an egg sandwich he'd thrown away. He picks it up and stuffs it into his mouth.

"Let's go!" He pushes the basket into Renee's hands and grips the detonator tight and leads off into the bush.

At first my legs don't budge. Then Renee touches my arm and squeezes. "Come on," she says. "Let's just blow it and go home." She looks deep into my eyes and there's no blame or anger there, just that cool deep green lake of her eyes.

When we reach Steven he's crouched next to a fallen fir tree. "What's the range on this thing?" His face is white as milk and boiling with impatience.

"A hundred yards."

"And what'll happen when that tower blows?"

The big tower looks straight down on us, its hands reaching into the bright sky, screaming to have someone untie it from those wires.

"It'll crack in a million pieces," I tell him. "Or maybe just one. You never know."

"Christ. You're *supposed* to know."

"Well he *doesn't,*" Renee says, "and *neither do you.* So let's do it and go." This time she's mad at Steven. To her the whole thing is his fault. What a bastard he is.

"Give it to me." I take the box from him with a mean look. He's been holding it like a new deck of cards, unsure what to deal. "This is what it does!" I yell at him.

His face boils up again. "What?"

I click the toggle switches so the remote is armed and loaded. "I said, stick your head up and watch." But I duck down tight under the dead fir tree. "That way you can count how many pieces there are."

They duck, too, and I hit the trigger. At the same moment the blast cracks through the air with a terrible shock. It's like magic. Like everything in life shows clear with one flash of light. And in that one magic instant it all comes home to me. What the Power *really* is. It's the Power to stand up and say, "I *count,* godammit. It's *me* you should've listened to!"

After a few seconds the echo rolls down the bush and over us like a wave. Because the charge is mounted so high, the noise is going to travel for miles. A shower of steel whips through the tree branches. You can hear it: *wiff, wiff, wiff.* A hundred rivets and bolts strip the leaves and limbs free. Then there's a huge crash that rumbles through the earth. The sound of the tower breaking loose and hitting just fifty feet away. Finally the power lines start rippling and singing in the wind. It's like a tight-strung harp that has every string pop at once. Except the strings are inch-thick power lines droning a sick and deadly sound.

"Magnificent!" Steven jumps up and stamps his feet to the ground. "Magnificent! Absolutely magnificent!"

Everybody's smiling and laughing and both Renee and Steven start slapping me on the back, saying what a beautiful thing it is. In fact the tower is more ugly now than before. It's broken right through the middle. What's left standing is jagged and crippled. The top has crashed down helpless and the great arms that held the wires high are a misery of twisted, blackened metal. The power lines have all snapped in different places, some of them falling straight to the ground and others drooling over the bottom of the broken tower. You can hear the electricity still trying to get through. It flashes at the ends of the wires, hissing like snakes. The death whimpers of a monster.

After a minute Steven turns on the tension. "Okay. *Let's go.* They'll probably have people out in less than half an hour." He leads us back through the forest at a good clip and a quarter mile down the path everyone breaks into a fast jog. The woods become deep and mysterious and we're invaders full of wild fury, unsure where we are or where we're going. Renee begins laughing and so do I. It's crazy because there's nothing funny, but we can't stop, we're so full of laughter for what we've done.

When we're in the Camaro it's just as bad. Renee is talking up a storm about how it sounded and what it looked like. Steven keeps saying to shut up and drive careful and take this turn and that. But on the skinny dirt road there's only one way to go and all his directions are wasted.

"*You* shut up!" I tell him and turn onto the blacktop and roar down the road. The Camaro's built for fast stuff like this, so I beef it for everything she's got. When we reach the big white barn I slow down. If anyone sees us here they'd remember a speeder, but never anything rolling past at a crawl. Once that's out of sight I crank up the engine again and we head out of the country onto the freeway.

The radio news announcer breaks a flash bulletin about a blackout that's shut down three districts west of town.

"That's us!" Steven crows, and he slaps his hands together and pushes the wire glasses to the top of his nose. He looks like a madman in the rearview mirror and I can hardly wait to drop him. Now the tower's destroyed, I just want him to disappear. Evaporate like a pool of black gutter water.

"Slow down," he says, "slow down! The last thing we need is a speeding ticket. Christ, everyone's under suspicion."

The hell with him. There's a demon in me now that tramps my foot to the floor and we barrel past a line of six cars and do a triple weave across three lanes of traffic. Renee sets her hand on my thigh and massages back and forth. One, two, three, four, her fingers work up and down, side to side, gentle, smoothing, easing. In a few minutes she settles all the nerves in my leg, easing everything down until my foot takes the pressure off and we slow to about sixty-five.

"That's right," she says, and she lights a cigarette and passes it to me. "*Perfect.*"

CHAPTER 20

The university district is extra slow, plugged with cars and bicycles, and when we turn onto Third Avenue the traffic's worse. Somebody has double-parked and only one lane is open to cars coming and going. The front of Steven's apartment building has the worst of it.

"Hey, look at that." He points past Renee's head to the building entrance. Two or three men are standing in dark suits. They look like football players. "And that." He points to one of the double-parked cars. "It's a squad car. See the gun rack and radio?" He ducks onto the floor and whispers up in his dry voice. "Just drive slowly. For godsakes don't stop or speed too fast."

Driving past, I take a closer look. It's the police all right, dressed in plain clothes. Their hair's cut short and straight and their faces are square and empty-looking, like nobody who lives around here.

"What'll we do?" Renee asks when we've turned the corner.

"Go to your place. I'll make some calls and find out what's wrong."

After the car's parked we breeze into the building like ghosts.

Then I remember the picnic basket and the detonator. The last thing you want is a carload of evidence left outside. I go back and open the trunk and for a minute I just gaze into the emptiness, trying to sense what's going on. A few blocks away you can hear sirens. Maybe police, maybe ambulance. You never know.

Inside, Steven's on the phone. Renee and I sit at the table smoking, listening.

"Karen, something's come up . . . Yes that went fine. Don't ask any more about it. Something new has happened and you have to do something . . . No, it will have to be now. Call her back and tell her you'll be at least another hour . . . Yes. Extremely important."

There's a long pause and he twists the telephone line in his fingers and stares at the wall. You can see his brain shuffling facts around like a computer.

"Good. Now this is what you must do . . . No, this is first. Don't call anyone else. First, go to my apartment building. There'll be plainclothes police there. At least two of them, and probably five altogether. Explore the place as much as possible. Enter the building and see what you can find out. Walk past my door and see if anyone's there. If no one's in my place, then get chatty with my neighbour and see what's going on, okay? He's an old guy in number ten . . . No, you won't have to do that. And don't call or see anyone else from the group until you hear from me . . . And *very important:* once you're out of the building call me back from a pay phone. I'm at Renee's. You know the number?"

When he hangs up he slumps into a chair with a dismal look on his face.

"What's happening?" Renee asks. She gets up and fills the kettle and sets it on the stove.

"Nothing is confirmed. Could be a police bust. You can bet they've been watching. And if they get one of us, they'll squeeze for the whole group."

And you can see his worst fear settling into his thin white face. He almost looks like a china doll, brittle and cool, ready to crack in a minute. But his wire glasses manage to hold the face together somehow. The glasses are the smartest part of him and he pushes them up to the top of his nose.

We drink coffee and smoke cigarettes and talk about little things that don't matter. The excitement of the tower explosion has shrunk to a knot in our stomachs. He turns on the radio and listens for more news, but there's no real truth to the news. Just the fact that three western districts are blacked out. The rest is about a freak lightning storm that hit the lines.

The telephone rings and he snaps his fingers at Renee and points to the phone. "Answer it. I'm here only if it's Karen."

It must be Karen because she passes the phone over. He stares into the wall and twists the line in his fingers again. Mostly he listens, and towards the end he throws in some questions: "So how many were there? . . . And only on the second floor? . . . But *not* my apartment . . . But no one saw that for certain . . . And nobody's saying . . . Yes . . . Naturally . . . All right . . . No, I can't answer that yet . . . I'll call you . . . Right. Thanks."

This time he sits down and his face is softer but full of the unknown. "The police were there, all right. When Karen arrived they'd already gone. But she asked my neighbour on the second floor. That was the only place they'd searched. Apparently there were three of them combing around."

"Sounds dangerous," Renee says.

"I don't know." He leaves his lips in an O shape and blows gently. "I don't know," he says again.

"There's only one way to find out," I tell him.

"Oh?" He still has his lips rounded. "Find out what?"

"What they got from your place."

"Really? And what exactly do you think I should do?" he says.

"Go in and see."

He makes the hint of a smile. "Jump into the fire, huh, Billy? I think you'd like that."

"It's just what I'd do."

"Thank you," he says with a sneer. "I'll keep your advice in mind."

But before I give him any more advice, a loud knocking cracks through the door. It bangs on the wood panel and echoes down the hallway into the kitchen. It hits so hard the beat of my heart jumps and pounds with the knocking rhythm. *Bang, bang, bang.* Like the ghost of death itself.

"Christ," Renee whispers and squeezes her cigarette into the ashtray. "Did you lock everything in the lab?"

"No." I grab the wicker basket and slip down the hall. I twist the key in the lock, open the door, throw the basket into one corner without thinking, close the door tight and lock it.

Back in the livingroom, Renee is reading a book and Steven's got his nose stuck in the record collection. "Pretend everything's normal," she says. "Take a deep breath and open the door."

The knocking starts again, but this time it's harder and more sure of itself.

"Who is it?" I yell.

There's no answer. Just knocking that won't let go.

I crack the door open a couple of inches.

"You car outside?"

There's a Chinese man, short with black straight hair. There's no way he can be a cop. "You mean the Camaro?"

"White car?" He pauses a few seconds and looks down the hall to the front doorway. "You leff the trunk open. People steal you everything."

"What?" I open the door wider, trying to understand his Chinese talking.

"I check already. Nothing there already. Is all gone." He lifts his hands in the air and shrugs. Then he turns away and walks up the stairs that wind above the lab in the apartment.

I step into the hall and pull the door shut. Then I slip out to the car. The trunk *is* open. I walk over to it, tuning my ears for the sound of sirens. This time there's nothing. Except for the spare tire and the jack the trunk is empty. I close the hood quiet as possible, trying to think everything through. Didn't I lock the trunk before? I check my pocket for the keys. There they are. Silver metal shining in my hand. *Play it cool, Billy.* Yes. Don't lose it now.

"It's just your neighbour." I stick my head into the livingroom. Steven and Renee are sitting together on the sofa watching some T.V. news report.

"Thank God." Steven pulls himself out of the sofa and turns the T.V. set off. The look on his face is supposed to tell me to leave so they can have another of their secret talks, but I lock my feet to the ground and squeeze all the spite into my fists so he knows there's no more pushing me around.

"Okay. That gives us some time. Obviously the police know nothing about you or they'd be here by now." He gives a little smile to Renee and scratches his nose. "But we have no way of knowing how long you'll be safe."

Renee nods once. "But I wonder how they got on to *you*."

"The only real question is when they came. If it was after eleven-thirty or not. After the power went down. If it was before, who knows, they could've been there for anything. Break and enter, petty theft, obscene phone calls even. But afterwards—it'd be ninety-nine per cent sure they had us nailed on the tower job."

"Yes." She nods again and settles into the chair. "There's no question about it."

"The main fact is we need a safe house. We should get on it immediately. Chances are if they've got me cased, they also have two or three others staked out, too."

"And then they'd pull us all in at once."

"That's what Karen says, too." Steven clenches his fingers together so they make a little bridge. "This's no time to begin taking chances. In fact we should be doubly cautious about everything."

"What do you mean?"

"First thing, we should find a safe house somewhere on the other side of town. Maybe on the north side. When that's secure, we establish a new contact point for everybody."

"How do we do that?"

"Don't worry." He grabs his jacket in one hand and pushes the glasses up his nose. "I think I've got the perfect place."

Everybody stands up and Steven whispers something secret into Renee's ear. The way he does it is just like a fox. He bends down to zip up his jacket and slouches close enough to her to make the whole thing look natural. Then he spills his damned ideas straight into her head and she nods to show she's got it. That's when my feet unlock from the floor and push me ahead with a fast shove that I can hardly hold back. One glance shows he can see the fury rising up inside me and his eyes thin down to two slits.

"I'll let you know when I know," he says. "Don't try to contact me."

Then he gives Renee a hug and tells her how *brilliant* she was at the tower and how the whole thing was heroic. After a final slant-eyed look at me, the door slams and he's gone.

"That bastard's lucky to be alive and he doesn't even know it!" I kick my foot into the wall once and then again, so the plaster cracks open like a split skull.

"You couldn't do it, Billy. Don't kid yourself into thinking you can kill so easy."

"Yeah? You don't think so, huh?" All of a sudden a sheen of pain digs into my face.

"Maybe. But it wouldn't be easy on you." She lights up a cigarette and boils some water for two coffees. She's gotten good at pulling all the hell out of me without too much work. You can figure she's building up to smooth everything over. And even though I hate it, I want her to do it so bad all I can do is hang onto every word she says.

"Up at that tower you had all the time you wanted to pull the switch on Steven. But you waited. What'd you wait for, Billy?" She stirs some Coffeemate into the cups and passes one over to me. The way she stirs the spoon around and around in her mug shows that she's got forever.

"Nothing." It comes so easy for her. I was expecting another block in my throat, but now Renee can pull whatever she wants out of me with no blocks or lies. Specially when she's got the coffees and cigarettes and everything's slowed to her pace.

"Yes, you were. You were waiting for me. You were waiting just long enough *to show me* you could kill him." She takes a long drag on her smoke and digs into me with her eyes. It could last forever. She holds on with those green smooth eyes and it's like being on a safety line the sergeants hold when you're jumping down the face of a cliff. "Weren't you?"

"Maybe." Maybe I *was* waiting to show her. The sorry part is I don't even know myself. It's as though she's the only one who knows and everyone's on the edge of their chair to see what she says about it.

"Yes, you were."

"Maybe."

"You *were*."

Now the rope that I've been hanging onto turns into something different. It's a tightrope strung across a canyon, and miles below is a black river ready to swallow whoever falls first. Instead of letting me dangle from one end, she's spinning out the rope, pulling it tighter and tighter so there's less room for play and every step you take has to be sure.

"Stop trying to rope me," I tell her.

"Rope you?" She flicks a bit of ash from her cigarette and pulls closer to the table. "I'm just trying to show you that there's no damned control to anything any more. You're not going to be able to change things, Billy. It's all set out. Nobody's big enough to change it. Maybe if you'd give in a little and let Steven do what he has to without trying to blow it all up, then *maybe* you'd settle in to something more enjoyable for a while."

"It's not just Steven." I can't even look at her. This time there's a long silence so deep each breath is like the last one before you plunge over the cliff edge and into the boiling waters below.

"I know," she says finally and reaches out to hold my hand. "I know." The skin around her mouth is smooth, almost glowing. "It's *me,* isn't it?"

But there's no confession or nothing. All there is, is me falling into the canyon slow as possible. The air sucks right out of my lungs and the muscles disappear from my arms and legs so there's no strength to hold on to anything. The funny thing is that I can see myself going down, like I'm back on the ledge watching myself tumbling into the river. And all the time I'm dropping, one low whisper echoes back and forth in my head: *She's using you, she's using you, she's using you.*

"You know what I think?" I stand up and start walking around the kitchen, pushing from one end back to the other. "Huh? You want to know what I goddam think?"

"Sure." Her eyes are thinned down and she's slouched in her chair, looking at me, with a cigarette smouldering in her fingers. "Of course I do."

"Sure you do," I tell her. It's all coming out. I can't believe it, but it's all coming out, for once. "I think you've got me on a string for so long you don't even know you're pulling it any more."

"What?"

"You heard me!" The sound of my own voice yelling sticks in my throat. I take a second to look into the sink. It's full of dishes and coffee cups. "I'm saying that you don't give a shit for me. That everything you ever done for me is for one thing only."

"What's that?"

"For your damned crazy bomb-making!" I point down the hall to her bedroom so she knows the truth. The hundred newspaper clippings she's got glued to the wall. Every one a story about blowing up airports and factories and everything else in the world.

"And for Steven and all his damned ideas!"

"Steven doesn't have anything to do with us," she says, taking a long drag on her smoke.

"Yeah? Well I'll tell you something. He's got you on a bigger string than you've tied to me. Except in your case, your eyes are shut to it."

She stubs out the cigarette and for a minute it looks like she's going to stand up and walk out on me, but instead she comes over and kisses me full on the mouth until neither of us can breathe. "You're so beautiful," she says, and then, "I don't know. God, Billy, I don't know," and she keeps kissing and kissing until the sex in me takes over and I start peeling her clothes off and start kissing *her* wherever she tells me. Then we're both falling into the canyon, or maybe she's still holding onto the rope and somehow she'll pull us back to the cliff edge. But in the end it doesn't matter, and she starts to love me in a way I didn't think possible, her on top and pulling me deep into her hips, tossing her head back and moving so perfect until we splash into the river at the bottom and start laughing like crazy kids because we just dived off the highest cliff, a cliff so high and jagged that nobody else would try to jump it, let alone dive straight for the bottom. It's like a dream, and when I start throwing my arms into the air, splashing waves every which way, she starts giggling and poking her fingers into my ribs until I have to roll away, away onto the floor where there's no waves or ropes or canyon walls.

Then she leads me by the arm to the bed and we pull the blankets tight around us and hold together like there's no tomorrow.

"Hey, you want to know something?" She wraps an arm across my chest and rests her head on my shoulder. "Huh?"

"Sure." Letting her do all the talking's the best way.

"You really sure?" She's playing like a kid again, trying to coax the fun out of me.

"I told you, *sure.*"

"Well . . ." Her voice drags out to keep me dangling. "See . . . I think we're going to have a baby."

A baby. She whispers it so lightly I can barely hear, then sucks in her breath and shakes my arm just once.

"Did you hear?" She says a little louder, "A baby."

"Yeah." But right away I start wondering if it could ever happen. Wondering, what would it be like? Wondering a thousand questions I don't even know how to ask. But out of all the unknowns, one question keeps tumbling through the back of my head: *Are you sure it's mine? Are you sure?*

"Haven't seen the doctor yet, but I took a urine test." Now she's propped on one elbow, smoothing her hand back and forth across the Fire Eyes tattoo.

"But you're not sure?"

"Not yet. For the next couple of weeks you'll just have to sweat it out."

The thought makes her laugh a little, and then she drifts into sleep, restless and rolling her fist against my chest. The question keeps roping through my brain and every once in a while it ties together with her not being sure. When you think of it, she's never been unsure of anything before.

After a while I drift off, too, into a sleep wild and mean that rolls the storms of the last week back and forth so bad that I start tossing and flipping all over the mattress. I got no way to control it. Everything gets shaken around inside me. Michaels and the way the two of us got cut down by Tilden. Jamison and the power he carries around. The look of Tooler's head turned blue under the gas mask and the smell of death steaming out of Jackson and Sinclair's bellies on the way down the mountain. And now Renee. And how I *need* her so much. Specially how she keeps everything inside me together without it all flying into a million broken pieces.

Then I start playing back the picture of the two of us making love. Do it all in my mind, like a movie, showing all the special ways she has of bringing herself off, the way she likes to take the lead and set things right while I watch, just the way it works on demolition details, with Michaels setting all the fine points and then the two of us waiting for the explosion to burst straight into your heart with all its Power. God, it's a beautiful thing. Then I let the movie play out a little, watching her twist and turn, the look of a soldier in her face while she rides harder and harder. But then the crazy thing is how her mouth suddenly shifts on her face, her eyes suddenly stopped with some terrible pain coursing up her legs into her belly. Then she lifts herself free and collapses beside me bleeding onto the mattress, pointing with one weak finger at my crotch. And when I look down I can't believe it either. It's crazy. But there it is—my pecker turned into a steel bayonet, cold and glinting from the light off the Chinese street outside.

I get up and walk round the apartment slow as I can and look through a few windows to the street and start to figure it all out. There's really no way to set anything straight, is there? Nothing you ever told me about, anyway. The best I can do is pull through with Renee until she can see her way clear of everything. This revolution business. Otherwise, I got nothing. Later I'll still have a chance of breaking free of her and maybe even the army, too. Breaking free of all the lines that have me pinned down, squirming, hopeless and alone like a caged animal. Somehow I know that's what she can do for me. That's what I mean by being *transformed*.

CHAPTER 21

A *baby!*" Michaels's eyes roll like he can't believe it. "Jeezus, buddy, you got in with this broad faster than I figured."

"Yeah. I guess I did."

"Now you got one hell of a consideration to make yourself."

Considerations are what Michaels has been up to all weekend. And he had lots of time to sort them out, especially with the rest of the squad on leave. He was going to go off base, too, except news got up to him that Charlene's mother had a cancer. And now Charlene's decided to stay home with her father to look after the other three kids. Michaels doesn't blame her for that, it's just that Marysville is a good nine hundred miles away. "Chances of seeing her again before discharge are nil to zero," he figures. "That's why I'm seriously considering early retirement. That and this other damn mess."

The other damn mess goes back to the demolition manoeuvres. Nobody's had a chance to set up the Board of Inquiry, but MacEwen says in a week or two they'll be grilling the whole squad. Specially about what happened to Tooler. With Michaels calling Jamison a murderer and everybody else calling it accidental, it'll probably turn into a showdown. Trouble is, there were no witnesses to either story.

"You sure now that you didn't see it?"

"All I saw was you running into that crater and dropping Jamison in one punch," I tell him. But I figure Michaels's version is pretty close to the truth. And with him looking so sheepish I tell the story just the way he told it to me. A lot of times I try to picture it in my head, give it all the colours and smells so it turns to truth right in front of my eyes. There's Jamison holding that rock over his shoulders and Tooler lying on the ground, begging for mercy. But any kind of begging just makes his death more certain. Jamison can smell the fear running out of Tooler's pores and oozing through the skin of the rubber gasmask. It's like a drug to him and he raises the boulder an inch higher, then smashes it onto Tooler's chest, lifts it once more and dumps it down again, so the rib cage snaps into a dozen pieces that knife through his heart and lungs.

"That's what you *think* you saw down there, huh?"

"Something like that." Whenever I look back into that smoking crater of hell it makes me want to puke just remembering all that I *did* see.

He looks at me and rubs his fingers over his jawbone. "Well, I think you better stick to what you're *sure* you saw. Not any guessing about what you *think* you saw."

"Yeah, but what I did see isn't going to help you much when the investigations start pressing for an answer."

"Yeah, well, that's the way it goes, I guess." He shakes his head and fluffs up his pillow. Then he kicks off his boots and stretches onto the bunk. Everything he does looks tired and worn down. Even his smile is exhausted. Where he used to have ivory teeth glittering in the sun, things have changed for the worse. In the dull light of the barracks you can see how those teeth have turned to a flat grey paste.

"What if I was to memorize the details to match the way you saw it?" I keep thinking how bad he needs someone to crawl onto his side. "You know, just fill in the story with the facts."

He thinks this over a minute while one hand rubs over his eyes. "Forget it. You got troubles of your own already."

"Yeah." I slip onto my bunk, too. There's nobody else around right now. One of those moments of privacy you get maybe once a month in the army. "There's even more going on than I told you about."

He looks over with an intent look to his face. "Oh? Like what?"

"Some pretty big stuff. On the outside." But I don't say anything more. If I told Michaels about bringing down that tower, it'd just be another fact he'd have to seal off in his memory. It'd do nothing but pull him down even lower.

"Yeah?" He turns his head back to staring at the ceiling and lets my talking drift. He doesn't want any of it either. He just makes one point and never brings it up again. "That Renee's taken you deeper than you'd ever go alone, Billy. You be careful or all that radical business will wash you down the creek and over the dam. I heard about some power station being knocked out over the weekend. Hell, everybody heard about it." And he looks at me again, looks straight into my brain. "Lot of the brass here seem to have the opinion that it was done pretty professional."

I don't say a word. Just let myself float up to the rafters so I can think things through. But Michaels is still looking over at me. I can feel his eyes digging into my skin. "Think I heard about that, too," I tell him. "On the car radio. Wonder if whoever did it was a Fire Eyes at one time?"

"I wonder," he says with a laugh that snorts through his nose. "Probably Wiggins or Turner, huh? Hey. Maybe it was even Jamison!"

"Yeah. I bet it could've been him."

"Why, it might even have been Sergeant Tilden in on the job."

With all his joking done, Michaels drifts into a sleep full of tossing and turning and teeth grinding that lasts through the night. Watching him there on the bunk, I can tell that something has grabbed him so tight in the middle of his guts that it'll never let go. It's the first time I ever think of worrying over him. And I guess it's the last time, too.

□   □   □

On Friday nights they show movies in the messhall. The special feature tonight is *Vertigo,* which I've already seen, but I sit through it again because I know somebody's got a sex film to put on after the main show. Usually the sex movies are pretty gross, with women screwing animals or playing with candles and bananas, but it joins all the guys together laughing and telling stories like they're all brothers and family. Once in a while somebody gets sick to their stomach, but it's from the raw booze as much as the show.

Halfway through the sex show I have to pee so bad that I can't sit through any more sex parts. I slip through the emergency doors and head over to the fence on the far side of the kitchen and food store. It's a clear night with no moon, and the stars are sharp and glittering.

I find a place that's tucked away and have a pee and just gaze into those stars like they know something important. Then I decide not to go back to the movie. Just go to bed and forget the sex and booze that makes you sick and dream up the perfect woman. A woman who's soft and does what you want without having to tell her a word. One who doesn't kiss you too much and who has small breasts that last without sagging. That very woman's stuck in my dreams more every day and sometimes she's outside my dreams, too. Out in the open, walking beside me for company. Maybe it's you all along and I just don't know it. Anyway, I head over to the barracks, looking into the stars, wondering how they got there and what kind of woman God would love.

And when I'm thinking into the heart of it I hear this moan, like someone talking to themselves, a little grunt like they forgot something. I stop dead in my shoes and listen again.

"Uh-h-h."

"Who's that?" There's only a whisper to my voice—a ghost sheer as the night.

"Uh-h-h. Uh."

This time I know something bad has happened. At first I figure it's a trap, but the moaning gets stronger and I burrow through the scrub next to the fence until my boot hits something soft and the groaning comes up into my ears. "Oh-h-h, uh-h-h."

Then I bend down and see him. It's Michaels—Michaels beat so bad that his eyes are swollen shut. I lift his head and brace it on my knee, but this starts so much blubbering from his mouth that I have to lean him back down and hold both my hands under his neck.

"Oh, Michaels. Christ, what the hell happened?"

But he doesn't come back with a thing. Then I realize that he's never going to. The back of his head's oozing with something clear that's not blood and his arms and legs are smashed up so I can feel his broken bones under my fingers.

Seeing him like this makes me feel so miserable that a wave of exhaustion rolls through my arms. Then I straighten his body out to look comfortable, the way they do in funeral parlours. Once he's settled I put my hand near his nose to test his breathing. After a while it gets weaker and weaker and then I can't trace it any more. There's nothing but the weight of my fingers dragging under his empty broken head, nothing but the sound of my own breathing turning rougher and deeper until finally I'm left there in the cold, crying so bad I don't know how it'll ever stop. Then I notice how all the tears are falling onto his face and what a shame that is, something you'd never see Michaels with if he was alive. So my hand starts flicking the tears away, smudging most of them into the creases around his eyes and mouth, tiny lines on his face I never noticed before.

I guess it goes on like that for an hour or two. I don't know, really. I start thinking about how Michaels had changed in the last few days. He didn't even do that much talking any more. He just kept walking a long, thin line on his own, waiting for the Board of Inquiry to call him up. Then he planned to set the truth out in front of them all and ask for his discharge the same day. Guess his idea was to head up to the north country and team with Charlene. That way at least the two of them could be happy.

But after a while I start humming, or maybe it's you that starts humming, some golden voice singing lullabies that fold a warm blanket over the cold of night. Then a vision starts to rise in the mists, pictures coming like shadows in the fog. And watching them I start to see how the whole thing has to fall onto Jamison and how somebody has to stand up to him before he cuts us all down one at a time. And that's what the shadows show me. How it all works. How I have to draw him into fighting me the only way I know how to win — with my hands. Those same granite fists Michaels showed me so long ago. And the only way to draw him out is to make him crazy for it. Make him grow so damn crazy for killing me that he tumbles right into my hands. But it's not just the fight that's important, *it's showing him up in front of everyone*. Working it so he breaks down in front of the whole squad, so everyone can hear the confession dribbling from his lips like so many pieces of broken teeth.

That's when I twist all the buttons off Michaels's jacket, all six of them, and pull the dog tags from his neck and stick the works in my pocket. Funny how he's still wearing those dog tags. Usually they only hand them out during field operations. But Michaels always wore his, no matter what. They were the only thing about the army he really loved—like they were jewellery. Then I sit with him for another hour, maybe more. You never know how long it takes to say a last good-bye. Then the air blows so cold I start shaking and decide to leave him.

Walking back to the barracks makes me dizzy all through my legs and back. And it feels like someone switched on the compound lights, because I can see everything so clear and straight. But the yard lamps are all snuffed out and the only light is coming down from the stars. When I get to the work shed I have to hold onto the wall to keep from dropping. Everything is clear, but at the same time swimming around like a whirlpool so I can hardly set one foot ahead of the other. After a while the spinning settles down and I make it to the barracks and then over to my bunk. At the end of the row of beds, Jamison is sleeping like nothing's ever happened and the world is just a pure white baby lamb.

Once I'm settled into my bunk my eyes catch a moth flicking around the rafters. Funny how they do it so stupid. Never an idea to their lives. Finally I drift up to the stars, clutching the buttons and tags in my fists, and I let the plan roll through me like a dream. It's a damn good plan and Michaels would love it. Even though he's lying out there dead, waiting for someone else to find him—he would've loved it.

CHAPTER 22

Since they found Michaels's body, there's been a big hullaballoo about who killed him and where his I.D. and buttons went. They grill me pretty hot, but I tell them I was at the movie and even describe all the sex scenes to show I was there. That part is easy, because most of the movies are the same. Nobody noticed I was late, because they were so boozed up and horny. The whole question of murder's hot in the air again and a lot of guys are eyeing one another. But most are eyeing Jamison. Everybody knows he broke Michaels down. Broke every bone in his poor shattered body.

Jamison isn't that big a guy, specially when you see him stripped naked in the shower. But he's got hair all over him, over his chest and down his back and legs and in his ass. The hair on his head's thinned out so he's got bald spots at the front and a little bald crown. But what hair there is is all black and it makes him look like a shadow. He scrubs himself up with white soap lather so it catches all the curls and then he bounces around like an albino monkey before washing the suds off. He thinks this is a big joke and does it three or four times for the guys. But he never laughs.

Not once does he even think about laughing. He just soaps up and tries to wash off that dark midnight fuzz.

Looking at him sucks the bad nerves right out of me until there's not a stick of fear left inside. I know I've got him beat and there's nothing he's going to do to touch me. It's fear that makes mistakes—the shaking at my knees that slows me down just enough to screw something up. And once the fear's destroyed, I can set my mind to do everything perfectly.

When everybody's busy, I crouch down to a hole where I hid the buttons and tags beneath one of the empty footlockers. Right under it there's a tiny space where some rat has made a cave big enough for three fingers to slip into. It's hid so well, I'm surprised I ever found it. And I never would have, except for the first day when we shipped in and Michaels dropped a dime and we both crawled around looking for it. I poked my hand down under the locker and found the money rolled right into the cave. I grab the dog tags and then I take a towel and soap and my shaving kit and stroll towards the showers. When I hit Jamison's bunk my eyes take a fast look around. There's nobody paying attention to me at all. I slip Michaels's dog tags under the sheet flap and smooth it over. And there they are: secret shiny rectangular bugs, cold and poisonous.

After the I.D.'s tucked away, I head into the showers. Jamison is just rinsing off and wraps a towel round his waist and comes over to me.

"Hey, there's Crazy Billy," he says and turns to one of his buddies, who starts laughing.

"Used to call you Lucky, didn't we? Huh? When Michaels was around. Know why they call you Crazy *now?*" he says. "Huh, know why, Billy?"

I nod my head but never say a word. Never take my eyes off the bastard for a second.

"It's cause of your whole face," he says. "Just like the way you're looking at me now. Like your face is glued down. It's so worried about jumping onto the ceiling that someone took a tube of crazy glue and sealed it right down."

He gives me a big frown and walks past, mumbling about how Michaels's dying has sent me off the deep end. But I just ignore that crap and hit the showers, towel off and have a shave. When I come out he's sitting on his bunk, flicking through a magazine like there's no trouble on his brain at all.

But that night, about midnight, comes the first good sign. To begin with, you can hear a rustling noise near his bed. Then a real shudder and the sound of two feet thunking onto the wood floor. I roll over as though I'm stone asleep and look down the row of cots. And there's old Jamison standing beside his bunk, stiff as a scarecrow. He's standing there like a ghost in the night. Cold and terrified by his own freak existence. Just standing there holding the dogtags in his hand and shaking with the slightest twitch where his fingers touch the chain.

□ □ □

The look on Jamison's face is pretty tight for the next couple of days. All of a sudden, he's looking at everybody else the same as they look at him — like a filthy spy.

Then I wait. There's only one fish in the lake and that's the one to catch. I keep looking for the right signs. With Jamison it's the way his jaw works: he's always chewing as though his mouth's full of gum. When I see there's no gum in his mouth and he's just gobbing down air, that's when I know he's ready for another nibble.

One night about four A.M., when everyone's in the best part of sleep and they're snoring or dreaming of sex, I get up and take two of Michaels's buttons and slip them into his boots. One button for each foot. Once they're tucked away I pretend I'm on my merry way to the pisser. It's easy. There's the boots at the foot of the bed. Then *plip, plop* and the buttons are in and I'm off to have a pee.

Next morning things are busy as soon as they sound reveille. But not so busy that everybody doesn't stop to notice Jamison scrambling around after he shoves on his boots.

"Goddammit! What's going on?" He hops around like he's dancing on hot coals. Then he dumps the boots upside down and the two metal buttons tumble onto the floor. Everybody sees right away that they've got to be Michaels's buttons.

MacEwen picks them up and looks square into his eyes. *"What the hell are these, Jamison?"*

"How the hell do I know?" he says, and loosens his jaw down like a heavy bucket. "Some Cock Nose playing tricks on me.

That's what it is." Then he starts marching up the row of beds where everyone's staring at him.

"One of you A-holes plays a pretty shit game of poker." He stops in front of Wiggins. "And I want to tell you the stakes are high. Very high," he says, and Wiggins looks off to the wall, ashamed of being put down so hard.

That day the Military Police haul Jamison off for about ten hours. Everybody's quiet about the whole thing until he comes back. He doesn't say a word, either, and that makes everybody even quieter. After a week the idea gets around that the M.P.s can't prove a thing about him.

The second step of the plan calls for more of the same, except to stick him even worse. A new twist dreams into my mind where Jamison starts eating the dog tags and all the buttons one by one. He sets the buttons onto his tongue, then swallows real slow and you can see the hard disks slip down his throat and into his guts where they turn gangrene.

But instead of putting them straight into his mouth I buy a deck of Winston cigarettes, the same brand Jamison smokes, throw out half and wrinkle the package until it looks used. Then I drop another button into the pack and flick it a couple of times, to make sure the button flies free.

Next day in demolition class I spot a chance to load the pack into his pocket. Halfway through the class Jamison gets up for a pee and leaves his coat on the chair ahead of me. Everyone's in a dozy mood, because Sergeant Tilden doesn't have the way for words that he has for marching and the best he can do is drone the facts into everybody. It's always been that way with him—he's never much more than another voice barking in the back of my head. So when the time's right I take a deep breath, slide the new cigarette pack into one of his pockets and start to fish out the old pack. But just when I get the feel of it, Maxwell, Jamison's old buddy from the whitewash fight, starts to eye me like a cop. You never know about a guy like Maxwell—he's never exactly with Jamison—but he has the *look* of a spy. I pull my hand out quick, like it was never there, but he keeps his eyes tight to my face until a fear starts to perk into my spine. By the time Jamison sits back in his chair, my guts have turned into grease. Now Jamison has two decks of Winstons instead of one. And the one's loaded with all the proof he needs.

The rest of that afternoon is one long storm of mental hell. I can't quit thinking Jamison will find the phoney smokes and pin it straight onto me. Specially with Maxwell as a spy. The fear crawls out of my stomach like a snake. Right up the spine and into my brain, where it curls around all the nerves and starts to squeeze. And when it pulls tight you're finished, because there's nobody home up there to settle you down so you can think straight. Everything inside goes on alert and it shows all over your body. Your fingers shake and your knees shake and finally your boots shake so bad you can't walk. The worst of it is grinding in my teeth, the slow, steady twist of the jaws digging against each other.

After dinner I head direct to the barracks and rack out like I'm sick. Nobody pays attention and I lie there with my eyes half-closed, looking through the eyelashes at the guys starting up a game of blackjack.

Half an hour later, Jamison strolls in and sets a place for himself at the card table. Everybody's pretty cocky when it comes to poker, so they're making bets and writing I.O.U.s and betting their girlfriends' right tits. And when Pollock starts talking about sex parts, Jamison jumps straight onto him.

"Pollock, how in hell can you bet Marianne's right tit when she don't have no boobs at all?"

Pollock raises his eyebrows and stares down over his cards. "Bigger tits 'n yours," he says, and makes a smile like it's all a joke anyways, so why question it.

But Jamison keeps on for a least twenty minutes talking about Marianne's invisible tit that he says is covered with pimple scars and how you'd get V.D. from sucking on it, which you couldn't do anyhow.

"Why, you'd be better off bettin' your balls than Marianne's tits," he says, and slacks down his jaw.

" 'Cept you'd have no balls to match me," Pollock tells him quick as a cat.

"Don't go beggin' for it," Jamison warns, "or else you'll end up with a high voice and no round dice."

"Yeah?"

MacEwen looks the two of them over and slaps his cards onto the table. "Just play your bets," he says. "You guys are getting goddam boring."

"Boring, huh?" Jamison looks at him and leans back in his

chair. He pulls out the pack of Winstons and holds it in his fist. Then he taps the soft pack against his fist, the way they do in movies. One cigarette's supposed to pop out a few inches and you fit it into your lips. But Jamison knocks it twice against his fist and Michaels's button flips onto the table and rolls into the poker pot.

"Jeezus, will you look at that!" Pollock stands up and points down to the button.

MacEwen folds his cards into his hands and looks careful at the poker pot and blows through his lips like he's whistling. But no whistle comes out, just warm, steady air.

"Jeezus," Pollock says again, "you got a whole fucking *collection* of those damn things, don't you, Jamison?" He throws his cards onto the table and stares him into the floor.

But Jamison isn't saying a word. He glues his eyes to that shiny button like it's a curse with his name etched into the surface. Then all the blood drains from his face until he's pale and pasty-looking, and his hair looks even blacker than before because he's turned bleach-white, so even his lips are dead and grey.

Everybody jumps up to look at the button on the table. They start calling him "bastard" and "cutthroat" and "dead man," and he can't say nothing back, because his brain's seized up and no one's working his lips or his throat or slacking down his jaw.

□   □   □

"Hey, Crazy Billy, pull off a second." It's Jamison talking. I can tell even before I see him. He's the only one who calls me Crazy Billy. Figures he's got me keyed with the idea that I'm falling straight to slush without Michaels around to hold me up. It's his way of trying to step on me so it'll make him an inch higher. There's always some piece of human misery who thinks they're born in God's hip pocket and they're going to step on you and climb up on your back and tell you you're nothing but worm-brain.

I ignore him and keep stacking the rope and wilderness gear into the storage shed. It's dangerous having to take Jamison on with nobody else around. That's how he got away with killing Michaels. No witnesses.

"I said pull off a second." He puts a hand on a set of dusty old packs that I'm shaking out.

"What for?"

"Cause I need to talk. And when I'm talking I can't have your mind drifting off somewheres." He moves in front of me and eyes me straight as he can without blinking.

I look into his face and notice that he's even got short, black hairs growing on the ball of his nose. Little digging hairs like a mole's. Then I decide I'm not having a word with him. I can look at him forever, but it's a mistake to get talking.

"Listen. Maxwell told me something kind of interesting last night."

I keep my eye fixed on his nose, without a hint that I even heard him.

"You know what that something is? Hey? . . . I'll tell you. Three days ago he saw your fingers taking a walk through my fatigue jacket."

That's when I feel a river of trembling running down my back. And then my teeth starting to grind together like a dog gnawing on some old bone.

"And you know what else? That was just before I found that extra pack of cigarettes in my pocket. Funny thing, that was. You know, I was planning on quitting when I finished the first pack. And then I find the extra one. And you know what?"

I give a little blink, but my eyes are locked onto his face so I look like a rock. A piece of raw granite.

"You know what?" He pushes my arm so I drop the equipment pack I'm holding.

"What?"

"I'll tell you what, you crazy fucking jerk! That extra pack had Michaels's goddam button in it."

"Oh, yeah?" The teeth are gnawing so bad that spit's beginning to wet along my tongue and lips.

"You're goddam right!" His eyes puff up like two snakes. "And don't play crazy with me when I'm telling you. Cause there's one thing you gotta get straight the first time. So listen up," he grabs my arm and just holds onto it like it's a telephone and he's talking right into my ear. "If any more of those buttons you're hiding show up anywheres near me, then I'm gonna drive you so bloody crazy you'll wish you was dead. You got that, Cock Nose?"

His hand starts to squeeze on my arm and I can feel some big animal in me starting to wake up.

"You hear that? Don't push me or you'll end up *killing yourself.*"

The animal's got big jaws and I'm doing my best to clamp them shut before I tear into him so bad that I can't stop it. My teeth start grinding back and forth and my tongue drops deep into my throat so it won't get trapped in the way. Then this low moaning noise starts purring in my chest and I know it's the animal getting set. It sounds like a machine and the noise comes out of my mouth sure and terrible: *Gggraww*.

But before I rip into him, Jamison's face turns a shade lighter. He's starting to figure how dangerous things really are. He must've seen the animal and the big teeth and the picture of his throat ripped out of his neck. His hand lets go of my arm and he steps back two paces.

"You're crazier than hell already, aren't you?"

I keep grinding my teeth, sharpening them together and looking at the way he moves to the door.

"You just remember what I told you. That's all you gotta remember." And he backs from the shed with his eyes fixed on me, terrified like some broken rat.

Once he's gone I'm stuck with my jaws locked together and the animal still ready to kill. It's all through my insides. In my legs and arms and in my mouth. It's grinding away like a Doberman pulling on his chain, trying to snap the face off some thief. And on the other end of the chain is somebody straining to the limit, holding the wild animal down as best they can, whispering: *Don't say a word. Don't say a damned thing.* Maybe it was you even then. Coming out of nowhere, trying to settle things down, trying to hold me together and keeping that mad dog under control. It was a hell of a job.

□   □   □

Through the next few days, I watch the battle between that crazy, mad Doberman and the leash holding him down. It's a battle going on all the time, so even when I'm eating or sitting in on demolition class he's straining on that chain. And, strange as it is, I never really worry about what's going to happen. I just watch the chain cinch up tighter and tighter.

If Michaels were still around, maybe it wouldn't be so bad. He always had a good idea to set things right. Always knew how to move his way through a crowd of noise and push past all the voices and dogs of hell they let loose in the world. He'd be saying, *Bill, now you just stick to your guns. And remember to squeeze*

those fists tight when the time comes. Squeeze them down to rock.
And he'd look at the dog fighting the chain and say I was having a
vision and the best thing to do is just watch. *And make sure you
don't go believing it too much. Maybe just take a warning.* But
that dog is getting worse. Sometimes he gets straining so bad that I
have to lie down more often. Whenever there's a little free time,
which is just about never, I rack out and stare into the barracks
ceiling. My eyes are like movie screens, just running the battle
scene over and over. First, the dog creeps away so the chain's not
too tight, but just as he's about to make a break, this guy—he
helps me out sometimes—wakes up and grabs onto the leash so he
can't bite into somebody. Then he says something like: *Lay down,
Kane. Lay down and hush.* And the dog never tries to bite into the
chain itself or pull any tricks that'd break him free. He just uses
brute force and an idea that one day he's gonna make hell pay. I
can see the dog clear as day—wild and furious and raw.

One night, just before lights-out, something starts shaking my
heart so hard it pounds like I'm running the obstacle course. I
don't know what it is, but it shakes me off the mattress and pulls
me out into the front of the bunk hall, where the lockers are
stacked against the wall. MacEwen and Pollock are leaning against
their locker and see me staring past them.

"What's up, Billy?" one of them says, and gives a wink to the
other.

"Nothing." I stand there, realizing I've gone brittle in my legs,
so I bend them a little and start flopping my feet around.

"You practising for dancing?"

"Yeah."

"Well, get a little more swing in your butt then. It takes a bit of
ass to make the women take any notice."

They start laughing it up, but I don't say a thing. And when
we're all staring at one another for two or three minutes I can see
them gulping down air and looking red-faced. Then they make another joke and push past me into the bunk hall.

I check around to be sure nobody's spying. When everthing's
clear, I bend over and slip my fingers in to the cave under the
bootlocker and haul out the last three buttons and tuck them into
my fist.

I stand up and open my hand to look at them. Suddenly they
seem hot enough to burn holes straight through my fingers. But

the feeling drifts off when I tell myself they're just buttons. Cold and dead and fresh buried in the little cave.

Then my heart beats up a frenzy again and I start wondering what the hell I'm doing with the buttons in my hand and no real plan. The only thing that seems right—seems perfect—is the *timing*. And somewhere inside me there's an idea, and a damn tough one, even if I'm not filled in on the details. I squeeze my fingers shut and walk into the bunk hall and take a look around. Nobody's up to anything special. A few guys are sleeping and some are reading comics or skin magazines. I take a deep breath and look down the row to Jamison. He's at the end near the showers, lying on his bunk with an army cap pulled over his eyes. He likes to wear the cap pulled low, so it covers his bald spots and you can't see him eyeing you. When he's resting he pulls it even lower. I take a few steps and listen to my feet hitting the floor quiet as a leopard. There's just my breathing and my heart, which has stopped flooding and shifted to a slow, steady idle.

When I'm about ten feet away, I slip one of the buttons from my palm into my fingers. Then I fire it straight at him. It's like a stone fired from a slingshot. It arcs through the air, but keeps a steady line on target and bites into the corner of his chin. It wakes him up pretty fast and he flips his hat off, so he can see what's going on. But before he can think, I shoot off another that picks into his eye.

"What the fuck!?" he says, and jumps up next to the wall.

"Tell them!" I yell at him, the last button burning in my fist. *"Tell them you fucking did it, Jamison!"* A sudden look comes into him that's full of hate and poison. *"Confess!"*

"Okay, Billy. Okay, you've goddam gone too far this time!"

But I've got one more button ready to go and he holds up his hands to cover his face and chest.

"MacEwen, Pollock," he yells. There's a mouse in his voice that jumps so high he can't tell them anything. "MacEwen! For Christsakes, can't you see he's gone crazy!"

When he starts blabbing this out I fire the last one pointblank, square into his mouth. The way it hits is like a hard punch that snaps him awake to what's really happening. The button lies flat on his tongue and he brings it onto his lips and spits it back at me. Then his hands turn into fists and I can tell he's ready.

CHAPTER 23

One thing a sergeant's got to have is a big voice. And Tilden has a voice bigger than most. When he barks out an order it comes straight from his chest—a huge cage of a chest that he carries around like it's the heaviest load in camp. When he walks into the room he packs more hell than a general and just by looking at you he can tell you to scram or shut up. And he's got as much bite as bark, so when he orders something you have it done yesterday.

The very second Tilden blasts, Jamison's fist is stripped in midair. Everybody's standing around us in a half-circle, with Jamison next to the wall and the bunk beside him. "What in hell is going on here, Jamison? I want to know *now!*"

Everybody snaps to attention. Two or three guys shuffle their feet so the buttons are covered and Tilden won't see any evidence.

"I said *I want to know now!*" He strides back and forth, trooping his chest in front of us. Nobody says a word, and Jamison slacks his jaw like he's about to say something.

"Nothing, sir." MacEwen pipes in from behind me. He's trying to cut things off before Jamison starts squawking.

"Nothing?" Tilden moves so his face is just inches from

MacEwen's. He can smell a liar and he puts his nose next to MacEwen's mouth. "Then what the hell is Jamison's fist doing two inches off Deerborn's face?"

"Practising, sir." This is from Pollock, who's standing on the far side of the bunk. "We're all just testing our reach and reaction time. Bill there, he's got the fastest reaction of all. Moves his face out of a punch just like Ali."

Tilden doesn't go over to smell what Pollock's saying, because now he knows everyone's in on the cover-up. The look from his eyes tells everything: bull roar. Soon as you mention Mohammed Ali, then it's one hundred per cent bull roar. He stands there a minute or two, then comes over to me.

"What do you have to say?"

I don't have no plan at all, so I let my mouth say whatever comes out: "It's just a slice of life, Sergeant Tilden."

He scrinches his face up so you can't see his eyes. "Now what the hell does that mean?"

I look off in a blank. I've got no idea what it means. It just came out like anyone could've said it.

"What he means is that he'll take it any way I cut it." Jamison says this like he's got battery acid in his mouth.

Tilden swings back to Jamison. "Tell me more, Jamison."

But he takes a quick look around and sees that everyone's playing for the cover-up and he better, too. "Nothing, sir. It's just a way of saying my punches are better than his reactions. That's all. I was trying to prove it when you caught us out."

This time Tilden says it outright: "Bull shit," and he swings around to eye us all. "Now, I don't want no more barracks fighting of any kind. This squad's already the worst in the last five years here. We've had three fights, six drunk and disorderly and *four dead*. That's all in eight months. If you boys think the brass aren't looking hard at this Fire Eyes unit, then think again. The knot's pulling tight on our necks and it's not going any further. Understand?"

"Yes, sir!" we all bark out at once. When he starts talking at length, you know the worst is over. After he ties the speech up, we snap to attention and head back to our bunks.

A little later, Wiggins comes to my bed and whispers to me. "You better stay with somebody from now on. Jamison will see to it, if you don't."

I look into his eyes a minute. "How long do you mean?"

He scratches his nose and raises his eyebrows. "Forever, I guess. Or until Jamison is through."

"Through with what?"

"Through with everything," he says, and shoves off to his own bunk.

So for the first time in his life Wiggins has some pretty good advice to hand out. And for the next three days I'm sure to fix myself in with at least two other guys, no matter what we're doing. Off in the distance you can see Jamison on the edge of things like a hungry buzzard. You can tell everyone's grown to hate him, but somehow it doesn't matter. Even though there's seven of us and only one of him, he's still got the power. He's the only one with a plan. He's got a system that's going to step on us, one by one. I had a plan but used it up. And it worked good, but now I know it didn't go all the way. Not like his plan. His plan is staked out so he's got your gravestone set, with a little epitaph carved into the rock. He's going to finish you and he knows where, when and how.

And three nights later I'm on my own for at least half an hour before I even think about it. The boys are playing poker and Maxwell's run out of smokes and I'm walking by when he pegs me for a favour.

"Just a pack of filters," he says, "any kind."

I look at him like I don't want to do it but he starts in on a memory.

"Remember how I subbed for you on K.P. last week?" Kitchen Patrol is when you get assigned to peeling patatoes and carrots and whatever else is brewing that night in the mess. Usually K.P. is a punishment, but lately everybody's been living by the books, so K.P.'s become a routine detail.

"Yeah?"

"So now I need a break, Billy." He frowns like he can't believe I'd hold back on him. "Look, I've got two aces showing and two cards coming. I'm out of smokes and three hands down in the game." His lips curl up as though there's slices of lemon stuck in his mouth. "I can't pass now. Just get me a pack of filters."

"Okay."

"Me too," says Turner.

"And me," says MacEwen. "Make mine Luckies."

I collect the money and swing outside to the shop. The night air hits me like a dream and I look into the stars and the moon and see the magic. It's so wide and beautiful that I take a detour to the edge of camp, where there's no lights around and the sky can pour straight into my soul. When the stars speak to me they don't use any words at all, they talk direct to my mind, and it's as though that's where my brain comes from and words are stupid, useless things that get in the way. I open myself and let the moonlight in and never ask it any questions. Without questions it'll tell me everything. It makes me feel breezy, as though I've got no body, and I start thinking about the story of me being found in a paper bag and how I must've spent that one night on the road just staring into the face of the moon. It's like a father to me. Big and silent and knowing everything because it's seen everything. If I didn't know better I'd start praying to it, because it's the kind of mystery I can touch.

Then I turn a little to one side. The wind plays onto my shoulder and I know that someone's come up on me by the way a shiver runs down my arm. That's when I realize I'm alone. I take a deep breath and tighten my fists. For a minute I think I should run. But that'd be the worst thing.

"Hey, Crazy Billy."

I whirl around to show him I'm ready no matter where he is. My fists are tight and I can feel my fingernails biting into the palms.

"Hey, don't act so spinny, Billy." Then I see him coming from the fences where it's darkest. He's got his jaw fixed so it's almost a smile. And his arms are wrapped behind him like a picture of Napoleon.

"You look a little scared," he says. "You're not scared, are you?"

Get in first. Tighten those fists and lock in with a reverse punch. Wait for him and you've had it.

"Just a little scared? Or is it crazy? Yeah. That's it . . . I said I was going to drive you crazy."

Wait for him to get two or three feet away and then slam it. The voice that's holding the Doberman's leash is going to let hell loose. But I can't find the Doberman and there's nothing inside me to kill him with. There's only me and my tight fists.

"And you know how I'm going to do it?" He's inching closer

but not close enough. "I'm gonna put you on your own. In solitary." Then for one second his face cracks a hint of a smile. Like he's got a joke on his lips that only he knows.

That's when I move. With that thin joke there's something wrong in him. I jump for his face and just when I'm closing in, I can see what he's hiding behind his back. A thick shaft of hardwood that he swings over his shoulders. It's a baseball bat, and it comes down on me, down like a long black nightmare.

□   □   □

"Hey, Billy. You come to yet?" Jamison is using a whisper the first time I hear him. "I said, you come to yet?"

When he's talking I realize that only one ear is really working. My left ear is covered with dried blood and dust. Even cleaning it off does nothing to help me hear any better.

"You've ruined my goddam ear, Jamison!" Yelling this out is like being smashed in the head again. Just opening my mouth shoots a dull pain through my neck and into my chest. It's like an ocean current throbbing every time my heart beats.

"Gee, Billy . . . that's tough." He laughs, and I hear a tapping sound. "Can you hear that noise, Billy? I want you to know what that noise is."

I don't say a word. Instead I start feeling around. Somehow he's got me pinned down so I can't move. I'm curled up like a snail with my head pressed onto my knees and my feet pulled in tight against my ass. Only my arms are free but even they can only move about three inches before they hit a metal wall.

"That noise you hear is a baseball bat hitting on a steel drum, Billy. It's the same steel drum that you're squatting inside right now. Sounds just like a church bell, don't it?" He hits the bat onto the drum and it sends a shudder through me. "I'd say it's a forty-gallon drum. Frankly, I thought I could squeeze you into a thirty-gallon size. But you're pretty pudgy in places and you don't bend too good. Specially when you're unconscious!" He laughs, and I realize it's the first time I ever heard him give out a good laugh. It rolls on the back of his throat, heavy like a dog's barking.

I pass out again, into that blank space of mind that's empty of dream or memory. Then I'm pulled back with more of his whispering.

"Now, don't you go falling asleep, Billy. You've got a desperate situation on your hands. A real desperado. See, I'm gonna be leaving soon and you're gonna be on your own. Just you and your Crazy Billy mind."

I put my hands on the face of the drum and let them explore. He's got me fit so tight that I can only move so much. One thing's certain: I'm trapped good, with the barrel pulled right over my head.

"Now you're stashed away where nobody's gonna find you. I mean nobody. And the sun'll be up in a few hours. By noon that drum you're in is gonna be like an oven, Billy. And by three in the afternoon you should be done about medium rare."

He starts laughing his dog laugh, and I try to rock back and forth to tip the drum onto its side. I push back and forth like I'm in a baby buggy, but nothing happens. It doesn't budge an inch.

"And by chow time you should be smelling like a pig on a hot spit. Maybe then somebody'll *smell* you out."

He taps the top of the drum a few more times and goes on about how everyone's going to miss me, specially him, and how he enjoyed me throwing all Michaels's buttons at him. Then he hits the drum once more and is gone. I listen for a while and pass out a few more times. But I never hear a word from him again and the darkness grows hard and cold.

And within an hour the nightmare starts to crawl onto me. It comes in pieces at first and then it comes in lumps and starts to feed on me the way you see insects swarming on a dead mouse after it's been lying still a few days. After a certain point the nightmare gets so big that you can't even tell it's a nightmare any more. The nightmare *is* you. Then the part of you that says everything's just a horrible dream disappears. Finally what's left is the horrible dream all on its own. That's when there's just the insects scuttling around and no more mouse.

At first I start tapping on the drum so somebody can hear me. My teeth start grinding together again and my mind begins rolling and soon I'm counting the number of knocks, just like I did as a kid when I counted into the millions. When one knuckle starts to bleed then I switch to another and then another until I use them all up and have to start banging with the bleeding ones.

Then this voice comes into me. It doesn't say anything but it hums a tune, a lullaby or some baby's cradle song. You can barely hear it just under the ear, a whisper of a song that tries to rock me asleep. It's a lady's voice and I let her carry me off. Who knows where it takes me? Just away. Anywhere away from my body, anywhere I can stand up free and stare into the sky. If anyone could listen they'd be carried away and never open their eyes again.

I start crying because my knuckles are bleeding and my ear is ruined and my back is so broken down from being squeezed into the drum. The beauty of the woman's voice can't hold back the tears, but its singing rolls on while I'm crying and grinding my teeth and hitting my hand on the drum.

Then I see the Doberman. Just when my eyes are teared out, the Doberman flashes his teeth and breaks from the chain that's been holding him tight so long. His mouth's white with foam dripping from the points of his teeth and he starts lashing out. First he rips into the steel drum, banging into it like fury. He grinds his mouth against the metal wall and pushes his snout onto the floor. When he sees he can't get free he turns on me. He starts biting on my arms and knees and into my legs where he can reach them.

And when the heat comes into the drum, it's just like Jamison said. To start, it's a slow cook. Then the juice pours in and the dog and the woman and the counting are all pulled into one swarming animal that smothers onto my face. It's a big white mask that fits like a skin with no holes to breathe or see or hear. It's a death mask, and when they pull it onto my face, everybody snugs it tight so there's no tomorrow. That's when I disappear. That's when the nightmare is bigger than me and the insects have left nothing but broken bones behind.

CHAPTER 24

Death has a beauty untouched by sleep or dreams. There is no hint of disturbance and no wish to return to living. When I was dead it was the great emptiness that wrapped me up and held me in its cold white arms. And after they brought me back I was never afraid of dying again. The plain truth is that there is nothing to be afraid of. Death *is* nothing.

From what they tell me I'd been dead at least an hour before they got me to the hospital. Then they plugged me into the machines and pumped me up with chemicals and threw the switch. When my heart kicked in they probably shook hands and said what a miracle they've performed. But having a heart roll over sixty times a minute or having a pair of lungs breathing in and out doesn't mean you're *alive*. In my case, I might as well have been locked in a coffin for another week before anyone cracked the lid and let me see a shaft of light. For seven days I lay in that black box without one of my six senses telling me I was a living human being. They had machines feeding me and the shit nurses cleaning and washing me down. But I never had a clue to any of it.

Then one day comes that crack of light. It's like finding a door in a wall you think is totally sealed off. And the fact that it opens at all is more a surprise than seeing someone standing there looking down on you. It surprises me so much that all I can do is move my hand up to my lip and stick a finger in my mouth and just think about it. Then I realize I'm sucking on my hand and that I'm alive again. It's the first thing I remember doing: sucking away like a newborn child. A little smile comes on my face and whoever it is staring at me smiles, too.

It takes three or four tries at opening that door before I get used to the idea. Every time I can feel myself warming up more and more until one day I *see* somebody standing next to me, asking how I'm doing.

"Christ, Billy, it's good to see you looking better," he says, and gives a big grin.

I look into his face. It's a face full of old pimple marks that have made dozens of tiny scars over the cheeks and chin. But those pock marks don't prevent any smiling or holding my hand.

"How are you, Billy? Come on, give me a little smile, huh?" He's pushing for an answer, but all I can do is look into his face and wonder how it looks so sore and happy at the same time.

"That's enough for today," says another voice. "Try again tomorrow."

When he's gone I slip back into the coffin and the door slams shut. But he keeps coming back and finally I get to smiling and squeezing his hand when he talks to me. After that's happened a few times I manage to keep the coffin lid open even when he's gone. That gives me a chance to do a little thinking on my own. I decide that the next time he comes in I'm going to break over the edge. No more squeezing and grinning. I've even got something all planned to tell him.

"How's it hanging?" he says right off the top of his next visit. He comes and sits on the bed and winks at me.

I look at his lips and put the words on the point of my tongue, but nothing comes out. All the thinking's in place but it just won't talk.

"The guys send over their good wishes," he tells me, and takes hold of my hand.

With my hand locked into his, I give a tight squeeze that jumps him off the bed. I dig right in with my fingernails leading the way.

"Hey!" He pulls the hand free and rubs it as though someone's bit into him. "What the hell's the matter with you?"

Then I say it in a voice that startles me because it's so weak and tired: "Keep it open."

He looks at my face as though a spider's crawled onto my forehead. "What's that, Billy?" It's almost a whisper. "What'd you say?"

"Keep the coffin lid open, willya?" I try to put on a smile to show that hurting him with the handshake was a joke.

"By Christ, you're back to normal, aren't you?" He runs his fingers through his hair and rubs his hand again. "Aren't you?" he says.

□　　　□　　　□

Once I start talking, the doctors are beside themselves with the miracle they've made. Their next move is to increase my visiting hours and get Wiggins to come in every day. It's Wiggins that opened the grave to begin with, so they stick by him to the end. My problem is to figure why he ever comes at all. But he's stuck on being my best friend and puts on that he's the one who saved me. And in truth he *is* the one. Without him I'd be dead long ago. Dead for good.

"I tell you, Billy, you were a terrible mess when I found you." He's sitting on the bed with one knee hoisted onto the mattress and the other leg propped on a chair. "Jamison came close to killing you before he even stuck you in that drum."

"Jamison? How'd you know it was Jamison?"

"Easy—but I'll tell you about all that later." He rubs a hand over his poor face and thinks back. "When I found you, you *were dead!* No pulse or nothing." He raises his blond eyebrows like he still can't believe it. "And you were cut up something fierce. Your head was cracked open next to your ear. Every one of your fingers was bleeding. And there was those marks where he'd bit into your arms and around your legs. Right through the goddam fatigues. Now, what kind of man could bite into another like that?" He lets this idea sit like a dark cloud in the sky.

"A mean one," I tell him. But I don't mention the Doberman.

He shakes his head miserably. "Worse than mean. There's no

word bad enough." He rubs his face again and keeps a hand to his cheek while he's talking. "And after taking your pulse, I don't know what I did for a good ten minutes. But then something came into me and I started hauling you next to the fuel depot and propped you onto the shed wall out of the sun. All that time I'm talking to you like you were alive. 'Come on Billy,' I'd say, 'let's move out of the fuel dump to the depot.' "

"That's where you found me? In the gas hold?"

"Yeah. In one of the empty drums. And I think it was just talking like that that made you really come alive." He smiles like he's the miracle-worker now. "Think so?"

"I guess."

"Anyways, then I phoned the medics and they got you in here fast. It wasn't five minutes before you were put on maintenance with all the doctors' machines and transfusions."

I look into his eyes and see how blue and clear they are. That's where he hides his beauty—in that clean ocean water of his eyes. I want to tell him *thank you,* but the words just don't come out. Best I can say is, "Those doctors are good."

"Yeah," and then he looks off as though he can't stand to be around any more. "Look, Billy, I've gotta go. Sergeant Tilden is real push-push these days." He lifts his knee from the bed and steps down to the floor. "I'll be in tomorrow, maybe."

But just as he's leaving a question comes to me: "Wiggins, how'd you find me to begin with?"

He looks like that's the sixty-four-thousand-dollar question. "I don't know. It was like a magnet. I was just walking around the drum dump. One of the drums was wedged up with concrete blocks and there was something funny to it. Just the way it looked. All pinned down like none of the others. Then after I got close I could smell it." He smiles a half-smile that pulls his lips down at the corners. "You messed yourself pretty good, Billy. You had shit all over you." He says this in a whisper, almost like he doesn't want me to hear it. Then he waves his hand in a half-salute and leaves.

Within a few days everybody's real happy about how great I look and how I've started talking. They force me to walk up and down the hallway to build up my muscles. After almost two weeks on your back, there's a lot of slack growing into your arms and legs. But the nurses build me up day after day, get me swimming and lifting weights. Then they explain there's going to be an inquiry as soon as I can face up to it. But two days before I'm supposed to meet the M.P.s and the board, Wiggins hits me with the news.

"Jamison is dead," he says. "Just happened yesterday."

Hearing it so sudden clips me off balance and the best I can do is stare into his face. "Who told you that?"

"Nobody *told* me. I saw it with my own eyes."

"You *saw* it?"

"Yesterday," he says. "We were all taking turns in the demolition lab. You know how they work it. Everyone is practising on a banger one at a time and the instructor is watching it all through a T.V. camera. But the first time Jamison is on a live detonator he accidentally triggers it. Christ, it was just a flash. There was nothing to see, really. There's a blip of hot light and he pushes onto the floor. He was dead before he hit bottom. That's what Benson says. He should know. But Tilden's madder than hell. He keeps telling us we're washouts and the worst he's ever had in the Fire Eyes. *Ever.* Says he hopes none of us re-enlist when our time comes up."

I think this through a couple of times to see what it all means. If he's really dead, then it's perfect. Everything goes onto his shoulders. Michaels's murder *and* putting me in the drum. "You're sure he's dead? Not just hurt?"

"No question. He's heading six feet under come Saturday. The guy's got no living kin. And he only lived once," he grins, "not like you. Not like a cat."

Somehow it just can't be. It all seems *too impossible*. "But what happened? There's got to be more to it."

"I told you. He sparked a detonator and went down. Maybe his fingers were wet and there was some static. Who knows?" Then he smiles. "The mean bugger just *ate sky*."

"And what's the proof it was him who tried to kill me? You said you had proof."

He rubs his face a couple of times, as though he's trying to decide whether he should shave. A smile grows bigger on his lips and he sidles up and looks me straight in the eye. "He told me," he says. "Told me *personally*."

"What?"

He gives a little laugh like a kid might do when he's figured a jigsaw puzzle. "It was the best part of all. In the middle of the night just after you were brought back to life. All the guys went crazy in the barracks. That's when I heard him mumbling under the covers. I couldn't sleep because I was still thinking about finding you in the fuel dump. But he's gabbing away to himself under the covers. He was *sleep-talking* for Christsakes! So I get up and go have a listen. It's just like a bloody telephone call: 'You shouldn't of left him. They'll find him. Somebody'll find him. So what—he's crazy. Crazy Billy. You still shouldn't of left him. Billy'd be better dead. Billy'd be better dead.' He said it over and over like that: 'Billy'd be better dead.' "

Just hearing Wiggins repeating what Jamison said is enough to make me sure it's true. Somehow Wiggins has Jamison's voice down perfect, like it was Jamison stuck right inside his throat. "Are you going to tell the brass at the board?"

He looks off a second to think. "If they ask me, yeah. That's what I already told the M.P.s."

"And if they don't ask?"

He scratches his ear and glances back to me. "Yeah. Yeah, I think I will anyways."

I give him a smile to let him know that this is the best thing he could do. For the first time I can see a crack in the door—a way to break out of the army straight and clean. If the courts play it fair, I could be on the outside in a couple of weeks. With a witness like Wiggins, and Jamison being dead, and me a medical miracle, I sort it all through and figure my chances are better than even, specially with a short run of good luck.

CHAPTER 25

Renee turns her T.V. on. It's an old black-and-white that throws a hundred shadows into the room. With my eyes half-closed and the light of the room barely streaking past my eyelashes, they seem like ghosts dancing across the floor, waving and flickering, unsure how they're going to haunt your soul.

I stretch my legs along the sofa and pull the blanket tighter around my shoulders. It's been a week since my discharge from the army. At first I figured on a big celebration, but none of the wild times ever really happened. Even though there was good cause for some partying. First, the army gave me a complete release from all the killing that'd been going on. Nobody could find me guilty of a thing connected to Michaels or Tooler. And in the end there was nothing pressed about stripping the mask off Jamison in the death pit. It was Michaels who did that, and the lawyer made a big point about me being the "unfortunate witness to a tragedy beyond my control." All three judges agreed I was clean on that count. Then Schneider, the lawyer they attached to my case, pushed ahead to get a lump-sum payout against the damage that caused my disability. He called in the two doctors who brought me back to life and had them testify about the damage Jamison had done to my ear. How I'd lost ninety-five per cent of the hearing in the left ear and there was no guarantees that the ear wouldn't be all deaf within a year. That kind of disability he figured was worth ten thousand dollars minimum. In the end I got forty-five hundred.

Two days after the proceedings, Charlene telephoned to see if I could sell Michaels's car and send her the cash. The bills were starting to pile onto her family and she wanted some quick cash if she could get it. She started crying right in the middle of the call, specially whenever she mentioned Michaels's name. I said I'd do the best I could for her and tried to keep everything businesslike so she wouldn't end up with a nervous breakdown outside the phone booth in Marysville. Then I drove the Camaro over to a few secondhand dealers who spewed out a lot of B.S. about the car being worth just under two grand. So I ended up buying it myself and wiring her three thousand dollars. Then I sent up a flower wreath to have set on Michaels's grave, along with a note written out by the flower salesman telling Charlene how sad it was that Michaels passed on and how I knew he loved her. I figure he kind of loved me, too, at least in the way I loved him, but I never mentioned that to her or anybody else.

And maybe that's why—because Michaels is gone—that we never had a discharge celebration. Maybe it also explains why I can't do much more than lie on the sofa here, watching T.V. Either that, or I just watch Renee pasting more and more news clippings onto the bedroom walls. Now she's got the whole room covered with news stories. And all of them about the same thing. The I.R.A., P.L.O. and a hundred others around the world. As though everybody's got their own private army set to launch a first-class undercover strike. And the way she does it is like someone in a trance. Leafing through her stacks of old newspapers, cutting out a story whenever she finds one that catches her eye, then squeezing some Lepage's glue onto the backside and pressing it to the bedroom wall. Then she adjusts the paper three or four times to set it just right. And if the glue starts to dry before it's laid out perfect, then she cuts loose with a hell of a swearing scene. The whole thing's crazy. But I don't say a thing. After what Jamison did to me, there's no telling who's got it worse, Renee or me.

"There it is," she says, adjusting the tuning knob. *The People's*

Forum." She settles into the chair opposite me, then pulls herself up to the edge of the seat. "They're having Frayburg on, the Nuclear Power Commission chairman who okayed the power plant."

I open my eyes a little wider to watch the show. There's two guys sitting in stuffed chairs wearing suits and talking up the details of the power plant. Frayburg sits back and smiles a little whenever Bennett Paulson, the guy who runs the show, tries to grill him with a hot question.

"There was never any *need* to go the referendum route," Frayburg says. "We had a government mandate to proceed with the implementation of the plant—"

"—you mean without asking the people—" Bennett Paulson's really good at interrupting any snot he doesn't like.

"—the government is *elected* by the people," Frayburg interrupts right back so fast it puts a sneer on Bennett Paulson's fat face. "And the government legislated the right to proceed according to their democratic authority."

"All right, we'll go to the phones right after this break." Bennett Paulson points a thick finger at the T.V. camera to show everybody they can grill Frayburg, too, if they've got the guts. Then a Heinz commercial comes on.

"Christ, can you believe this asshole?" Renee stands up and starts pacing around the room. "He doesn't even know what he's talking about."

"You should phone in," I tell her, "and let him know."

She looks at me a minute and then pushes around the room again. "And Paulson's on *his* fucking side, for Christsakes!"

It doesn't seem that way to me, but I don't say anything. Lately I've gone along with everything she says. It's easier that way.

"They're all part of it. That's why. They're all getting paid for saying the same thing. Frayburg, Paulson, everybody. Don't you *see?* It's like even this show's put on to fool everyone into believing that somebody's really *questioning* things. But they're not. It's a *show*, for fucksakes! Just a goddam Hollywood parade of lies!"

"Yeah," I say, puffing on a smoke and flicking the ash over the side of the sofa into an ashtray that's lying on the floor. It's true. When you look at it really close, everyone's lying one time or another. Some people do it all the time. Even Jesus said nobody was completely clean.

The People's Forum comes on again, and Renee moves to the back of her chair and grips the seat back with both hands. Somebody phones in and asks Paulson what they're going to do about all the nuclear wastes. He tells them they'll all be buried in limestone vaults. Then somebody else phones in and congratulates him for going ahead with the plant. It's a lady who figures we need the power and if the government says it's safe, then that's good enough for her.

"Shit!" Renee thumps her fist against the chair. "I'm going to ream that bastard." Then she grabs the phone and phone book and starts dialing a number. A few seconds later she gets a connection.

"Give me Bennett Paulson," she says. And then, "Yes, I'll hold."

"Are you on?" I sit up and look from her to the T.V. and back to her again. I've never known anybody who got on T.V. before.

"I'm next," she says, covering the mouthpiece with a hand. There's a little smile to her face and then a worried look as somebody says something to her over the line. "All right, I'm ready."

"Next caller, go ahead." Bennett Paulson waves his hand to the T.V. camera again, but there's no talking coming through. He clicks some kind of switch and says "next caller" again.

"Yeah . . . I'd like to speak to Frayburg." It's Renee. I can hear her talking here and then on the T.V. a few seconds later.

"You're on the air. Go ahead."

"Frayburg?"

"Yes. Go ahead." Bennett Paulson's starting to sneer again and he shakes his head.

"Look, I'd like to know what you think you're doing?" Renee's voice is a bit shaky but she gets through the first sentence in one run.

"Doing? About what?" Frayburg lifts his eyebrows and sinks back into the chair.

"With this nuclear waste. Who do you think you're kidding? That poison is going to be around over twenty-four thousand years!"

"Well, it's not a question of dumping without management—"

"Yeah? You can guarantee someone'll be around to check it out in two thousand years? Five thousand years?"

"Of course, there will be ongoing—"

"There'll be ongoing bull shit, that's what there'll be! And I'll tell you, Mr. King of Shit—" But she doesn't get to yell out anything more. The T.V. cuts her off before the "bull shit" comes through, and Bennett Paulson pouts his fattest, deepest sneer so far.

"There's always that idiotic fringe out there, soaking their granola bars in goat milk. Please, if you're going to call into the show, keep your comments on the civil side of rational debate." And he shrugs to Frayburg as if to say, "Look, there's a million creeps out there and some of them always call in to bugger the show."

But Renee has turned a kind of white. She's still holding the telephone in one hand and breathing so slow and stiff I can hear the wind sucking in between her teeth. It takes a good two or three minutes before she can ease off and put the telephone back onto its cradle. Then she walks around a little bit, not saying a thing. Finally she pushes herself down the hallway and into the bedroom. When the door slams it means she's been pressed to the limit. Nobody can make her back off now.

□ □ □

Two or three hours later, the sound of rain splashing onto the street wakes me out of a dead sleep. I walk to the window and watch the streams gush from the roof gutters onto the sidewalk to the sewers. Strange how water always knows where to go with itself. Never a question to it. Listening to the steady smacking against the concrete sends a cold shiver along my back, and I pull the curtain tight and decide to put on a record. When I turn around, Renee's at the door.

"Hi." One hand's holding the collar of her blouse together at the throat.

"Hi." I didn't hear her come up on me at all. She's like a cat now.

"I was just wondering where we go from here," she says, moving over to the sofa and sitting down. "I mean, now that you've been out a week."

I sit down in front of the record collection and start flipping through one by one. It could take a year, there's so many records.

"And what's going on between us?" She lets go of her shirt collar and lights up a smoke.

Pressing. I can feel the way she's digging at me. It's coming at me from every pore in her body. She's got something she wants to squeeze out of me one drop at a time. I pull a Billie Holiday record out of the jacket and put it onto the turntable. A few seconds later she's singing "Summertime," the story of this little baby whose life is so perfect and he isn't even old enough to know about it.

"I don't just mean the sex," she says. "Though it is good for me."

How she likes to control it, she means. But there hasn't been any of that this time. In the whole week together she hasn't made a move. In fact, there's a thin sheet of ice been skimmed all around her. Too cool to touch.

Then something about her makes me think of the baby. It's in her face. Like a question sitting on her skin, in the cheeks and along the jaw.

"What about the baby?" I ask her. It's almost too hard to ask about.

"You think you can handle a baby?"

"Well, you're supposed to love a child," I tell her.

"Are you? Did they love you? Huh? Or me?"

"No." The pain's starting to come into my ear again. Just a little ringing at first, a delicate buzz dancing above Billie Holiday's voice. "But just because you can't go back and change the past doesn't mean you can't fix the future."

"Oh." She stands up and walks to the window and looks onto the street. The rain's still coming down hard. "And you think you're capable of that? Do you?"

I don't know what to say. The worst part is seeing her drift so far from me. Talking about things you can never know. Not until they happen, anyhow.

"Well, I'll tell you. You deserve to know." She turns and looks at me. I'm still squatting on the floor next to the records. "They still don't know. I'm two periods late, but there's nothing positive showing on the tests. So now you know: we *don't know*."

"Okay," I start to rub the noise off my ear. Two fingers pressing along the rim. "I guess that's all right."

"Yeah. I suppose." She's walking back and forth in front of the window now. Pacing eight steps at a time. "The doctor said it could just be stress. That maybe I've been under pressure that I'm not conscious of. That's the word she used: my *unconscious*. Jeezus, it was like I was sixteen years old and they're pinning this psych complex on me for trying to replace my damn mother."

She's talking crazy again. When you're a good talker the way she is, sometimes you can drown in the flood of ideas pouring out your throat. But I don't know what to do for her. Maybe just keep the flow running. "When you think about bombing the tower, you know, that could do it. Lot of the guys broke down under the noise alone."

Then she twists around on one foot. Her voice screams at me: "Fuck the noise! I'm talking about *me!* Don't you understand that?"

But the only thing I understand is the ringing coming louder and louder into my head. At first it rolls over Billie Holiday and then it washes out her yelling and then everything sounds like it's coming from under water. And while Renee's twisted around, looking down at me, all I can do is hold my hands over both ears to keep my head from bursting under the pressure of so much screaming at once. Then a huge waterfall roars through me, tossing a million wailing gulls over the edge, all of them breaking free into the air while I slide over the falls into the emptiness. Then I hear a whisper cut through it all, break right through the thunder and say, *Hold on, Billy, hold on.* And I grip tighter onto my head, tighter and tighter until I can feel two hands prying my fingers away from my ears.

"Billy. Billy, stop it."

But it's hard. It's so damn hard to let go.

"Please, Billy. *Please.*"

Then I open my eyes and Renee's kneeling in front of me, holding my hands in hers and running her fingers back and forth over my own. It's like something sacred, kneeling on the floor together, our four hands steepled like we're praying for a miracle.

"Things just aren't right any more," I tell her when my breath comes back. "Jamison said he'd make me crazy. Sometimes I think he might've —in my ears."

She looks into me like her heart has slowed to a stop. Then she curls next to me, sets her cigarette in an ashtray and shifts my head around so she can see the ear. Then without saying a word she touches her tongue along the edge of the ear, licking back and forth, dipping into the pit as slow and gentle as that lazy cigarette smoke trailing along the lamp toward the ceiling. And the whole time it feels like somebody put a conch shell to my head so I can hear the sound of the ocean rolling onto the beach. But instead of the ocean, all I can hear is the sound of whales moaning under the seas, running in front of a hundred steel whalers steaming down on the tide.

□   □   □

That night we drive around town looking for some fun. Renee says we need to lighten up, so she picks out a black-and-white comedy show playing at the Arts Cinema called *The Mouse that Roared*. It's about a little country that figures the only way they can win in life is to lose a war to the U.S.A. But it turns out that the way they win is by winning bigger than anybody could've guessed. It's worth a few laughs, but the best part is watching Renee. She's laughing when nobody else would think of it. And that gets me going, too. After the show we push on to an all-night restaurant and order the ritz specials, right down to desserts. With all that extra cash in my pocket, I figure there's no point skin-flinting my girl. Specially when she needs to be won back so bad.

Once we get back to the apartment it's about three in the morning. Renee sets the kettle up to make coffees. Needs a little late-night snack, she says.

"You giving any thought to what you're going to do next?" She sets two cups down with a pitcher of milk next to mine. "I mean, now that you're finished with the army."

I'd mulled over a few ideas but nothing clicked into place. "Not really." Then I take a chance on a bit of truth. "I was waiting to see how things might work out here," and I tap the table so she knows I mean *right here*.

"Mmmm." She holds the mug to her lips with both hands so most of her face is hidden.

The two of us tie our eyes together and then shift away. Then back again. It's like a little dance. The eye dance.

"Well." She clears her throat and sits up so both arms are propped onto the table. "I've still got some work I'm going to be doing—"

"—with Steven," I cut in. Just the way her hands are folding together shows what she's thinking.

She blinks once. "Yes."

"Well, you can count me out of it."

"Why?"

"Because!" Because he's a goddam rat in my belly. Because he's a punk. Because he deals in stolen army demolition gear. Because he's got no guts for anything more than ideas and a lot of fat talk about changing the way the world runs. But I don't tell her anything about it. None of it would come out right.

She drinks another sip, hiding her face again, then she puts the cup on the table and looks straight at me. We eye-dance a bit and she starts in with a new plan.

"Look. You've done a lot. Just knocking out that one tower did a lot."

"It did?"

"Yes. It put their system down for three weeks. And a whole new security network has been set up. That diverts a lot of employees away from production. Makes everything sluggish at first. But once they get used to it, they'll be tough to break. In another month or so it could be impossible."

"Who cares? Why do you want to knock them out so much, anyway?"

"The plutonium. I told you. It's poisonous. A single atom can lodge in your lungs just from breathing a fresh breeze a hundred miles downwind from the reactor." She points to one end of the room. As though you could catch it in the hall. "Then you get cancer. *You* die, but the poison escapes and kills something else. Maybe a deer this time, who knows. Then *it* dies. The whole chain rolls on for *twenty-four thousand years.*"

She looks at me like this is the most important fact anyone could understand. But who really cares how *long* it is? Most people are lucky to hit fifty.

"And what's worse, the waste plutonium is used to build atomic weapons. More than *fifty thousand* of them."

"Hmmm." Thinking about A-bombs reminds me of those movies they showed in the army. Films of Hiroshima. What a hell that was. Nobody should even have a taste of it. *That's* something worth stopping. "So what do you want me to do about it?" I ask her. I mean, what *can* anyone do?

Her eyes light up and she presses her arms forward to grasp hold of my hands. "Just one more. That's all."

"You mean knock out another tower?"

"No. We're going to hit the computer. Take out the brain behind the whole head office."

I look off to the wall. That's getting pretty big-headed. You
need some real fire-power to mow down a steel-and-concrete
building like that office. Unless you add incendiaries. Wherever
they have a lot of plastics would be perfect. Plastic burns through
anything, once you get it going.

"But we have to do it before the security nets starts working ef-
ficiently." She lights a cigarette and passes the pack to me.

"When?"

"I don't know. When I hear."

When she hears from Steven. That's what she means. He's pulling every single string, right down the line. He lifts a finger and a
whole row of puppets dances some junk ballet. Christ. The worst
part is knowing I'm one of them. Knowing I can't say no. Being
tied to Renee as though my life would slip away to nothing if it
weren't for her. And it would. I know it would. I've got to hang
on with her for a little more.

"Then *just* one more," I tell her. "You've got to promise me it's
the last one."

"All right."

"Promise."

"Okay."

□   □   □

When the phone rings, a little before noon, I'm already in the
kitchen, mixing some orange juice, waiting for Renee to wake up.
The woman on the other end is someone new. Someone in a hurry
and tight in the throat.

"Is Renee there?"

"She's sleeping."

"Oh." The voice has to think this over. "Maybe you could
wake her. It's important."

"Take a message?"

"Mmm." She tightens right down to a whisper. "I'd sooner
speak to her personally. It's a very personal matter."

"You the doctor?"

"No."

"Then who's calling her?"

"A friend."

That sets it. Whoever it is works for Steven. I'm just about to
smack the phone down when Renee slips into the room rubbing

her eyes with one hand and trying to tie her bathrobe belt with the other.

"Who is it?"

I flatten my hand across the mouthpiece and tell her "nobody," but at the same time the voice yells out for Renee.

"Give me the phone." She holds out her palm and shakes her head with shame that I'd lie straight to her face.

"No."

Then her face turns to hard steel and she fixes an edge to her eyes I've never seen before. For the first time I don't mean a thing to her.

"*Give me the phone.*" Everything hangs on whether I hand over the phone. Everything.

She grabs one end of the telephone, not forceful, but with a slight twist she pulls it free, puts it to her ear and turns around like she's locked in a telephone booth.

"Yes?"

There's a long speech and Renee takes out a notepad and begins writing down directions and an address with the phone pinched between her shoulder and ear. The whole time she's trying to keep it secret, hunching her thin back towards me. After she's hung up, she rips the paper from the pad and folds it into the little silk pocket of her robe.

"There's only one thing left," she says. The hard steel is still in her face, but she won't look me straight on. "Everything's ready except the bomb. I'm asking you for it directly because of what we said last night. From now on there's no more games."

"Except Steven. He's the master of them," I tell her.

"Nobody's the master." She clips into the bedroom and pulls her clothes on fast and angry. "Now look," she says, gathering her purse and counting the loose change, "I'm going out for a couple of hours. We need this other bomb for tonight. It's that simple. You either make it or you don't."

"Where're you going?"

"Out."

And when the door slams I realize I'm on my own, with no one left to stand by me at all. The more I listen to the emptiness in the hall and kitchen the more I can hear the whirlpool opening in the back of my head. The dull rushing sound of it, the gentle sucking that pulls so slight at first, then drags you down, under and away.

CHAPTER 26

The lab's set up like a cave. From the hall it looks like any other room except for the deadbolt fixed to the door. That gives it something special. But it's only *inside* that I feel the Power come over me. And like I told you, the Power is everything. It slips over my shoulders like a cool hand and brushes against the hair on my neck. Sometimes I think it could be just a draft of air, but it works across my shoulders again and again, more like a massage trying to put me easy. And that's where the Power is. Knowing I'm coming into the eye of death every time I snip another wire and solder the connections tight. Each step moves closer to the Power itself, until finally the wiring's true and everything's sealed and I realize the bomb is God's own justice in the hands of humankind. Some say that's why there's war, that God invented it Himself for holy purification.

So it feels like a cave or a little church I can enter in the dark, because it's safe and warm and it's been there forever the way all caves have existed since the beginning. A couple of explorers have even found caves with drawings on the walls they figure are over a million years old. And the drawings stare into their faces with the look of wise men, as if to say, "Finally you've come to the truth. After all these years, you've found it."

And before I get too far with the bomb the Power comes through me again, but this time it sweeps up my spine and tingles along my bad ear. Whenever that happens it's like a bug racing into my head to steal all my concentration. I always know enough to stop and wait it out a minute or two, so it won't trap me into making any mistakes.

Funny thing is, while I'm waiting the sound of a radio filters through the lab door so faint I can barely hear it. It could be the ear bug playing out a trap, so I just hold my head stiff in the air, straining to hear if the music comes any louder or disappears. But a minute later it rings plain as my own voice and, even with my bad ear covered tight under a hand, the rhythms roll and slap into my brain. It's a woman singing in a deep voice with a kind of sure strength. One of Renee's blues records that she's memorized and sung a thousand times.

I open the door and walk into the livingroom where the record player's set on a bookshelf. The switches are shut off and there's no light glowing from the radio dial. And when I push my head next to the speaker, there's not a hint of vibration coming through the line. But the singing reaches up to a peak higher and higher and then snaps to a halt. It's like a whip cracking through the air sharp and fast. I twist my head around just in time to see a face flash by the door. Then it starts to call out in a light whisper:

"*Billy. B-i-l-l-y.*"

I trail it down the hall to our bedroom, touching the wall with one hand to keep steady. Somehow the whole world's gone into a dream and every step forward is rubbery and unsure.

"*Billy. Come and lie down, Billy. Just come and lie down a while, huh?*"

Is it Renee? Maybe—except her voice has gone hollow and emptied. Something strange has come into her and made her darker and tired.

"*Billy.*"

"What?" I can't quite see her yet. It's slow getting into the bedroom and my feet are sliding through each step to make sure I don't plunge straight through the floor.

"*You got to tell me something, Billy.*"

"What?"

"You got to tell me the truth."

My hand has a firm grip on the doorframe but I can't quite see her. Maybe she's under the covers already—the way she is at night sometimes when it's cold and only her nose and mouth are visible.

"Just come and lie down, okay?"

The rubber comes into my legs again and instead of walking the three steps to the bed, I have to lean over with my arms to get a firm grip on the foot board and pull myself the rest of the way. One leg catches the carpet and trips me off balance. It takes all my strength to pull myself over the blankets. Finally I flop onto my back and try to catch my breath.

"B-i-l-l-y." She's not in the bed after all. Somewhere else, just beside me, or on the floor maybe.

"You don't want it, do you?"

"Want what?" If I turn my head fast enough I can see her lips flashing past me and then out of sight. There's no body, no face, just her lips—her mouth — glowing.

"The baby."

My head lifts a few inches from the pillow to look around. The lips dart below the bed.

"I don't know," I tell her.

"Tell the truth, Billy. Just put it out straight for once."

There's something I hate about her. But I want it so bad. The way she pulls it out of me and leaves me naked with nothing but the truth on my skin.

"I don't know."

"What?"

"I don't know."

"The truth, Billy."

"Goddammit!"

Then she whispers it soft, straight into my ear: *"The truth, Billy."*

"The truth is," my voice cuts down to nothing, like it's not even my own, "the truth is that there's no baby to begin with. No baby seed inside me."

"Then you don't want it."

"There's nothing there to goddam want!"

An empty silence fills the room, and then the lips flash past two and three times, right across my face from one side to the other.

"*Then you should kill it,*" she says. "*Specially if you don't believe in it.*"

"How can I kill what's not even there?"

"*You couldn't anyhow. It's not in you.*"

"What's not in me?"

But she never explains. The lips flash down the hall and disappear with only an echo calling out again and again, "*It's not in you, it's not in you.*"

□　　　□　　　□

Maybe it's the door that startles me, or the sound of her feet slapping on the wood floor. But when I first see her in the flesh it's clear that something has changed. She's turned hard. It's as though she swallowed a pebble and it went straight to her heart and stuck there. Then it hardened the way she feels about herself and me.

"Have you started work in the lab?" Her voice is dry and brittle.

"No."

"Then we've got to hurry." Her eyes drift from my face. There's never a second when she looks straight into me.

"Why?"

"Because if we don't hit them now it'll be too late to consolidate what we've already done. The police have already broken into Steven's place."

The strength flows back into my legs and when I stand up there's no question about sinking into the floor. She walks down the hall to the kitchen and leans against the counter. A new set of ideas are running through her mind and her eyes are frozen in some deep problem.

"Why're *we* doing it?" I reach out to touch her shoulders, but she scuttles away and pours a glass of water. "Why not Steven alone?"

"I told you. Because of the nuclear power. Because of the plutonium. And because *I* work at the head office."

"All the better reason to stay clean."

"Sure, except *I* know the target." She drinks off the whole glass in one gulp and at first it looks like she might choke. Then she takes a deep breath and eyes me coldly. "I'm the logical choice. I have a pass."

"They're goddam using you, Renee, and you don't even see it."

"*Everybody's* fucking using me!" A tear runs down her face and I know that it's no rock stuck in her heart. It's something worse. "Including *you*."

"What's wrong?" I reach for her again, but she glides past me to the kitchen door.

"I'm going to have a bath," she says. Her eyes don't seem green any more. They've gone darker, almost black. "Why don't you go to the lab and start work? It's after six already."

There's nothing left to say. Steven's gone right inside and taken complete control of her. There's no room left for me to even touch her.

"Okay?" she asks.

"No."

She pulls a lip between her teeth and shakes her head. "Then why not?"

"You don't even know what size charge to use."

"Use everything. Something to blow the damn computer out of the building."

"Everything?"

"Yes." And she turns down the hallway and closes the door to the bathroom. The tub starts filling with water and she twists the faucet harder and harder until it sounds like Niagara Falls storming into the void.

I slip down the hallway to the bathroom and put my good ear to the door. There's nothing but the sound of water. Somehow I thought there'd be something else, maybe her crying, maybe some low humming or the sound of her taking out the razor blades to shave her legs. Once she tried suicide with razor blades. After Farrell raped her, she'd pulled the razor across her wrists three times and climbed into the bathtub. But instead of cutting along the line of her veins she'd done it all wrong. And the bathtub was stone dry so there was no warm water to draw the blood from her body.

When the tub's full and the noise settles down I can hear her piling clothes onto the floor.

"Are you all right?" I put my lips to the keyhole to make sure she hears me. It feels like I'm trying to kiss the door, I'm so close to the little hole.

"What are you *doing?*" She opens the door and catches me bent onto my knees. All she has on is her panties.

"You're not trying to kill yourself?"

"I'm trying to have a goddam bath. Do you mind?"

Her mouth is still glowing. I stand up and look deep into her face to be sure that her lips don't fly off again.

"Just wanted to make certain you're all right." Then something chokes into my throat and I grab her tight to my chest. There's no sense to it. I pull her in close and hold on, hoping she'll never let go. "Oh Jeezus, Renee. Don't let anything crazy happen."

And just looking at her makes me want to *stop everything*. I bend my face to her breasts and kiss them over and over. Soft, soft, so white and small and soft.

"Look. *You* have to want what I want. There's no other way." She pulls away from me and her face hardens again. "Just one more time."

She closes the door and locks it. As she slips into the tub, the water sloshes around and she calls out: "I'll see you in the lab. In about half an hour."

That settles it. At that point I decide to put all the rest of the explosives into one charge. Enough to blow the roof off the damn building.

But binding them all together isn't that easy. Specially with my hands shaking so bad. Besides, there's eleven sticks of dynamite and unless they're cinched tight enough, the ones in the centre will loosen and fall free. What you need is a watertight cannister. I dig out a can of tomatoes from the cupboard and empty them into the sink. It's a half-gallon size, so there's plenty of skinned tomatoes flopped onto the porcelain and all the seeds and red juices make it look like a disease. Then I rinse the inside of the can and put it in the oven to broil. Best thing to do is steam off any water to make sure the wiring stays completely dry. After ten minutes, I pull it out and take it down to the lab. The insides get swabbed with cotton to dry off any moisture that's condensed against the metal.

When all the explosives are loaded, I fix it so there's no free play. A few extra cotton balls tucked between the dynamite and the wall of the can tighten it up. The next step is looking after the fuses and detonators, depending on the type we want to use.

When Renee comes through the door she looks as bad as before. Cleaner, but still hard in her face and eyes.

"How's it going?" she asks.

"Why don't you put on a record. I need something to smooth

my nerves." But the music is really for her. "Put on something you like."

A half-minute later some clear blue Miles Davis music drifts into the lab. Renee sits on the little bed and locks her hands together.

"Music like that will make you even more miserable," I tell her.

"It doesn't *make* you miserable, it helps you *be* miserable."

"Same damn thing."

"Not exactly." And she starts humming with the record and it seems like old Miles Davis is going to do the trick of switching her mood. I start to check the fuses for any flaws.

"Time it for a half hour." Then she laughs with a new thought. "Or instead of that, make it thirty-three-and-a-third minutes."

"Thirty-three-and-a-third?"

"Yeah. R.P.M.s, just like a record. That way it'll be like a good luck charm."

Good luck is the last thing you want. Once you start counting on prayers and charms, you've had it.

"You really should have a remote on it. It's safer. I was planning on a remote-control detonator. Like before."

But half an hour sounds like time enough, and to make her happy I get a clock face and set it to exactly thirty-three minutes and then a touch more. When it's ready she checks the timing carefully. It's the only part she can really understand.

"The next part calls for pure nerves," I tell her. "You have to run the wiring from the clock to the battery. Then set more wires to the detonator."

All the tools are on the table in front of us. A shudder runs up her spine that shakes her by the shoulders and she grips my arm and presses her lips to my neck. "Be careful," she whispers.

There's a beauty to it I just can't explain. It makes me stand tall and suck in a deep breath of air. I push her to one side and say, "Look, if you start to shy then hide under the bunk. And most important, don't say a word."

Her head nods slow as a tiny bird's and she locks her eyes on my fingers as I start connecting the wires of the clock and soldering them into place.

After the timer's linked to the battery I rotate the hands to twelve noon and then a bit further to the contact point. When it hits, the current flies through the wire. It's perfect. I reset the clock and wire the detonator to the dynamite. The final step hooks one of the detonator lines to the battery and the other to the timer. Now that the Power has smoothed all the nerves from my hands, my fingers have become pure machines. I daub them off with the cotton balls and start the last connection.

"It's either do or die."

Renee starts to shake in the knees. "God," she says, and she backs away to the bunk.

"Get right under the bed. Face to the wall with the mattress pulled tight over your back." No one else could do this but me. Jamison and Steven are nothing when you compare it to the raw nerve it takes to set *one wire* to a charge like this. And the whole time I'm working I can see their faces, and the guys on that T.V. show, their lips rolling at the corners, ready to bite into this one last banger that I've set on the table. They can talk on and on for a century and it wouldn't touch what I do in less than ten seconds. *This* is the true Power.

When it's set, I load everything into the tomato can. The rest of the cotton is stuffed snug between the dynamite and battery and the top of the can is sealed with a layer of waterproofing and a plastic lid. Now it's just a question of connecting the clock when we get there. And that thirty-three minutes that seems like forever. No matter how long you set it for, it always takes forever.

"It's done." I flick off the spot lamp and watch her crawl out from under the bed.

"Really?"

"Yes." I feel like a god looking down on her.

"Perfect." She shoves some hair away from her eyes and looks at the bomb. "Now we just have to get a few more details ready."

And looking into her face I can see it. She's back *to me* now. All the way back.

CHAPTER 27

One of the details is the disguise. Renee figures the security at the office is bound to be tight, and to get close enough to make the strike, the bomb's got to be hidden perfect. The idea of her and a baby just won't let go and in the end she dreams it all into a flaw-less disguise. If we could wrap the bomb in a few blankets like it was a newborn child and strap it into a baby's carseat we could drive around for weeks through every police checkpoint in the country without the least suspicion. No one would wake a sleep-ing child. Even the cops have got a soft spot for kids.

She even knows where to borrow the seat and a couple of blankets. Sharon's one of the part-time workers at Renee's office. She's known her for three years. They sit five chairs apart in the same row of desks in the keypunch department. She's the only one Renee trusts, mostly because Renee helped her pay out an abor-tion when Sharon was broke and hopeless with the thought of a second kid on her hands. While the two of them are inside talking, I wait in the car until she slips free with the baby seat tucked under an arm.

Back at the apartment, everything's just the way I left it. As soon as I touch the bomb it's like being on solid ground again. It's sitting on the bench as perfect as before, calm and beautiful. Waiting.

Once it's fit into the baby seat Renee settles down to the hard facts, too. All the jokes have disappeared. She wraps it careful in a light blue blanket and puts a little tuck into the top where the head would be. When she's done, it's as natural as you please. Nobody'd take it for a bomb. Not even the chief of police.

With the baby wrapped up, there's nothing left to do but load it into the car. When the coast is clear, Renee sets the kid into the back seat and buckles the seat belt across it the way a good parent would do—fluffing the wool blanket and cooing into the tiny, wondering eyes. Everything looks so true. And all the edge of driving around with a load of T.N.T. in the car disappears because of how she's fixed it.

"See how cute it is?" she says. "See how quiet they can be?"

"Sure." But the truth is something different. It always is. And this time her ideas have turned to wild dreams, especially the idea of a baby sitting so strong in her mind.

"Think you could get used to that?" She slips into the front seat and rides her hand onto my leg and laughs like a girl holding her sex out for a few schoolboys to wonder at—and knowing none of them would dare come close to her. A woman can be like that, teasing you with the power of her sex, pulling you deep inside her with just a single look in her eye.

"Can't get used to nothing," I tell her, and gun the car along the street for half a block so she knows I'm in no mood for larking.

"Sore and silent, huh?" She's looking at the side of my face, prying away the nerve ends, trying to get to my insides. That's the way she works sometimes. Just looks at me as though she can dig into my heart and mind and see all the elements whirling and ticking away.

But I don't say a word. Feeling chatty at a time like this can burn your fingers right up to the armpits. With a big job coming up, you don't want to piss a lot of ideas out your mouth. You need *concentration*. And right now the traffic's starting to clog around a road construction zone. On the next corner there's a yellow flashing light and I have to slap through a downshift to clip past an old wino who's staggered onto the street.

I turn the radio up good and loud so we don't start talking ourselves into a corner. Renee starts tapping her fingers against her thighs to the beat of the Rolling Stones singing some phoney crap about being the Devil and then she starts thumping the dashboard with the palm of her hand. The tension's beginning to show far worse than it did on the tower job. It builds and builds until her whole body is shaking to the music. But instead of being *tuned* to the rhythm, she's off beat just enough to show she's forcing it.

"So what do you think about the baby?" In one second she cuts free of the music and turns to me with this *smile* on her face. It's as though she's using it to open me up. Smile like a knife.

"Don't think anything about it," I tell her. There's too much else to worry about. Funny how she wants to talk so much. Words are her biggest gun. In my case, all the Power's *inside* with the knowledge of making the bomb. The way Einstein had it.

"You know it's all just a guess, don't you?" She shuts off the radio and her voice turns a touch softer. Then she stubs out her cigarette and twists sideways towards me. "I mean, all that about the baby. I just missed two months. It happens to lots of women. Even the doctor doesn't have a confirmation on it yet."

"Then you shouldn't be going on about it."

"Got to you, huh?"

Let it drift. Just let it all drift by.

"Sorry. I didn't know it went all that far."

Her hand slips onto my knee again, and for a while she rides her palm back and forth on my leg and everything slips quiet and perfect along the slick sheet of asphalt. There's the humming of the wheels on the road and just a slight tingling coming into my ear. A light buzz that changes to whistling and then to humming. Once it starts humming I know someone's there. Somebody with an idea of how to make everything work out perfectly.

"Let's stop a minute, okay? I've got to pee," she says, shaking a few quarters into her hand. "Trouble is, these road stops always have pay toilets."

The Camaro pulls into the lot and Renee gets the key from the manager and walks to the washroom side of the building and out of sight. Watching her walk away is like watching the tail end of a movie. It could be that easy: she strolls away and it's the very last scene. Suddenly it clicks into my brain that she might not be coming back to the car. That maybe she'll keep going into the night, walking off somewhere, to Steven or Sharon or the safe house and leaving everything for me to do. That'd be her way of putting the challenge to me. To prove myself to her and show I could deliver the bomb with nothing but her ideas forcing me along. To prove she took me in for that one reason alone—and in the end it was the only reason that counted. That's what it would take to test that she'd stole right into my heart and locked on for good.

I turn round and look at it bundled up so perfect. It really could be a child. You wonder what it would say, being so small. I can just hear it barely through the one good ear:

"*Don't want to be like you,*" it says.

Any kid of mine would be snarky from his first word.

"*You got too lost as a baby. You got too moved around.*"

"Yeah?"

"*You had no one to pull after you and stay on your side. Couldn't even stick up for yourself when it mattered most.*"

"Don't know about that," I tell him. "You should of seen me in the Fire Eyes. I got killed once for sticking up for myself."

"*How can you get killed and come back like that?*" he says.

"Not easy. Not anybody can do it, I'll tell you. You got to be able to face up to God himself and say 'I'm going back. Ain't nobody stopping me.' "

"*You can't talk to God that way,*" he says.

"Yeah? Well, *I* did."

"*Just shows there ain't no God, if you talked like that.*"

"What?" He's a true bugger of a kid already.

"*Just shows there ain't no God!*"

Suddenly there's a tapping at the window. Renee's staring through the top of the glass, holding a can of Coke in each hand.

"What're you *doing?*"

"Just talking." She catches me off-guard, and as I twist over to the window a sharp crink stitches into my neck and shoots along my spine into the back of my bad ear. "Dammit!"

"I can *hear* you talking," she says, "but who to?"

"The kid, who else." The pain settles into a dull throbbing, and I rub the Coke can back and forth across the worst part to cool the muscle down.

"The kid?"

"Yes!" I jerk my thumb to the back seat so it's all plain as her face. Once in a while she can be stubborn by hanging onto the smallest point. "Just get into the car and let's go."

But once she's inside and I've tied us back into the freeway, she picks up a new idea to roll. She's done it before, talking just for the hell of it, the way someone would roll two dice over and over to see how many times they come up snake eyes.

"Things are pretty delicate, don't you think?" She lights up another cigarette, and the smoke pours from her nose and mouth. "I mean . . . when you think what we're doing."

She leans forward to catch my eye, but I let it all drift by. There's no way she's going to suck me into any more of it now. In half an hour we'll be playing dice with the Devil. The best thing you can do is squeeze every nerve down to nothing and hang them all somewhere outside your body like a suit of old clothes.

"Look at the two of us. I mean the two of us—it's crazy when you think about it." She takes a deep drag on the smoke.

The best plan would be to shut up, but with Renee you can't. Not now, especially when she's playing with the rope we've both been hanging onto for so long. But too many teeth are biting into my nerves. I just have to bring up the idea of her stringing me along.

"You think we should break out on our own?"

"Maybe . . . or maybe that would make things too independent for you," she says.

There's nothing to say. All the talk's gone one way. Straight to nowhere.

"That's what it is, isn't it?" She clicks the radio off and butts the cigarette into the ashtray. "The idea of being on your own, the chance that one day I won't be there for you. Or the possibility that I might take on somebody else. Even the thought that you may need me more than I need you. That terrifies you, doesn't it?"

"What in hell are you talking about?"

"Us. I'm talking about *us*."

All this yakking is really starting to shake her up. Especially talking about leaving one another and taking on someone else. So instead of cruising down the road I figure it's time to get her settled back down and I slip the Camaro off the highway onto an exit ramp. Without me holding things together, we'd be crashed into the retaining walls ten minutes ago. At the first chance, I swerve down a side street and up a few blocks until we hit a row of houses where everybody inside's asleep. Then I slip into a parking slot and cut the ignition.

Once we're stopped, she looks into my face and for a few seconds it's as though she spots something there that she's never noticed before. Her eyes keep running back and forth, washing over me again and again. They're so clear and perfect I can't say a thing, because I'm trapped so deep in them. Then they turn moist and a tear slips down her cheek and she hugs onto me with both arms wrapped around my shoulders and pushes my face next to hers.

"God, this must be—"

But she doesn't finish. Instead, she looks into my eyes again and turns her head to look outside. Then her jaw drops open and her mouth forms a little oval shape just big enough to hold a small round stone.

"Look," she says after taking a handkerchief from her pocket and wiping the tears from her eyes. "There's some things I haven't been straight with you about."

It's true. There's so much gone wrong between us that this is the first time she's really hung onto me since I got free of the army.

"I was going to just let it go on, you know, making it all work for me." She backs away and looks me in the face again. "Oh, Christ, I don't know what I'm trying to say."

She takes out two smokes and we both light up and just gaze out the windows onto the street. The street lamps show how every house has shrubs lined against the sidewalks and the driveways are loaded with two cars each. For a second I feel like I've touched down on some planet a million miles away, where I don't know a soul. I'm just a pair of eyes looking everything over, not feeling anything except the slow breathing in my chest and the sinking idea that I'm never going to make it home again.

"You know something?" she says after a few minutes.

"What?"

"You can make it on your own a lot easier than you think." She turns to look at me again. She's calmed down and there's no tears coming from her eyes any more.

"So? Who said I couldn't?"

"*You* do. You've been telling yourself that for years, probably." She sits up and twists around. "And ever since Michaels died you've been telling yourself you can't do a damn thing on your own. Did you know that? Huh?" She tucks the handkerchief in her pocket and leans forward.

I don't say a thing to her. Just stare at the street wondering where in hell I am.

"Listen to me." She pushes her face closer—just inches from mine. "*Listen to me!*" She grabs my chin in her hands and turns it around so I'm looking dead-centre into her eyes.

"All right," I tell her, yanking my head free. "Just what the hell do you want to say so damned bad?"

"That you don't need Michaels any more."

"You can't say that. You didn't even *know* him."

"That doesn't matter. The fact is you've got to walk on your own again."

"I can walk just fine," I tell her.

"Good," she says. And then in a whisper, looking straight into me as deep as she's ever done, she breathes: "And you don't need me any more either. You're free."

"But—" But nothing more comes out of my mouth. Once she's said it and laid the truth out so naked, it's as though there's no point to saying anything more at all. And the strange part, the part that runs through me like a burst of light, is the fact that it doesn't *hurt*. At least, not yet.

"And what about the baby?" I ask her after a few minutes.

She stubs out the smoke and looks off to one side. Then she turns around again. "There is no baby," she says. "There never *was* a baby—except that one." She crooks her thumb and points over her shoulder into the back seat.

I don't know what to do. I can't tell if she's gone crazy or she's turned into the sanest person I could ever hope to meet in five lifetimes. And there's no way to sort it through, no way to be *sure* of anything.

"Maybe we shouldn't go on. Maybe we should stop before it's too late."

"Stop? *No*. This is the *one* thing we should do. It's the only thing *worth* doing." She reaches over and turns the ignition. The car starts idling, just waiting. "We've got to finish it."

At first I think about training her to squeeze down all the nerves from her body the way we did in the Fire Eyes, so she'd be perfect for the office blast. But it's too late and besides, the best thing for her is the music, so I tune in the radio again and she starts nodding her head in time to the Everly Brothers and then Elvis. It's like the only thing that matters is the sound of things, the radio and her voice singing a few verses and the sound of the tires and engine and the humming that comes into the back of my ears. The night is perfect in its blackness, except for the headlights flashing like some mistaken switches in the emptiness.

Once we get to the office, the air turns raw and harsh and fills the car like cool blue gas. Renee stops singing and eyes everything carefully. I drive past the building twice and swear to myself because of Steven and the way his mind has slipped into the car like a ghost. Next door is a school yard on Mason Street with a chain-link fence wrapped around it, and we cruise by, looking for kids or any eye-witnesses hiding out. But there's nobody around, just a lot of litter and candy wrappers. Then Renee starts singing another song and I have to click the radio off to steady her down. Her voice is all nerves, and in her case the best thing I can do is turn everything serious.

Once the Camaro's parked I cut the engine and look up to the building. It's about eight floors high and set way up from the street. A huge lawn stretches in front of it and a concrete sidewalk runs straight to the road from the front gate. Bunches of prickle bushes are growing in the middle of the lawn and along the front sidewalk. All the lights in the building are switched on. It's as though they're trying to prove they can burn all the power they like just because they own the show.

Renee slips out of the front seat and stands on the curb beside me. With the few extra inches, she's taller than me. "Just set it so it works the first time," she says, "I'll do the rest."

"What else can I do?"

"Nothing. Specially without a pass." She pulls the plastic card from her pocket and pins it to her jacket. There's a black-and-white picture of her face in one corner of the card. In the picture she looks half-dead. "There's going to be no problem at all. Besides, I know half the security guards by name." And she flicks the badge with a finger and I look into the half-dead face on the card. The eyes of a ghost stare back at me.

We both get into the back seat and I go to work connecting the timer and checking to see that everything's true. The water seal is still fixed tight and all the wiring and solder connections have hardened and set. Unless she starts shaking it around, it should be okay.

"Just keep in mind what you have to do."

"I'm trying *not* to," she says.

"And don't listen to any voices when they come begging for you to run. Let your fingers do everything."

She unhitches the harness and pulls the bomb out, making sure the blankets are fit perfect for the disguise. Then she holds it tight to her chest and steps one foot onto the street and leans across the seat to me.

"I'll see you . . . when I see you." The way the street lamps catch her face it looks like her lips are glowing. Funny, nothing else stands out but her lips.

Then she backs out of the car and kicks the door closed with her heel. She's got a set of office keys in her left hand and the baby tucked under her right arm. Then she hops over the sidewalk and looks back to the car. She does a little ballet turn up a set of two stairs and whirls around to me again. And just as she turns, her handkerchief slips from her pocket and drifts to the ground.

It's crazy, all that shifting and turning, and I climb out of the back seat and whisper up to her as loud as I dare.

"Stop that assin' around, Renee. Just drop the baby off and stop that jerk-off stuff." But she's about fifty feet up the sidewalk and doesn't seem to hear me any more.

And all of a sudden a picture flashes into my head of the electrics sparking around inside the tomato can. It's as though I can see right into the guts of it. Two wires slipping free of the cotton and touching just enough to let the power arc between them.

"Set it down! Just set it next to the door!"

But before I can say another word, it's too late. She spins around and smiles like there's no care to the world and moves up the sidewalk in her dream of ballet. She points her toe to the ground once, twice—then, as she turns on one foot, the bomb explodes and breaks the night into a thousand smoking greens and yellows and reds, with a huge blast like a rocket burst echoing off the walls of the mountains. And then it's all over before you can really see it and in the end she's worse than dead because the bomb blew everything apart. There's a crater gutted into the sidewalk and suddenly all the lights in the First City Electric building black out. A minute later there's a flicker of light in the windows and then the power surges back to life. Only the front door has any sign of damage, two windows shattered from their steel frames. And along the sidewalk, halfway up from the road, her handkerchief rests where it fell. Except for that, there's nothing left at all. Not even the baby.

CHAPTER 28

It could be three hours later or three days. The way life slips into emptiness is like a dream, and when the clocks run down there's just no way of knowing about time any more.

The first thing that jogs me out of the emptiness is the telephone ringing. I just let it ring, counting the times until they bugger off. Fourteen rings on the first call, then thirty-two on the second. But the third time there's no stopping. Whoever wants to talk won't let it go, and after fifty-eight rings I lift myself from the bed and walk over to the telephone. Then for another ten or twelve blasts I just stare at the thing. Finally a touch of life comes into my hand and I pick the telephone up and place it next to the good ear.

"*Billy?*" It's a woman.

"What?" My voice has shrunk down to a whisper so small it surprises me.

"*Billy, is that you?*"

"Yeah. Who is it?"

"*Look, you've got to get out of there. It's not safe to stay there and you've got to get out fast.*"

"What're you talking about?"

"Don't take time to pack and don't take anything with you. Just leave it all behind like none of it was ever yours." She takes a deep sigh and for a second it sounds like there's traffic streaming by in the background. She's probably calling from a booth.

"Who the hell is this?" Maybe it's that woman Sharon. But the traffic starts to roar louder and I can't fix the voice to any one face.

"I can't say on the phone. Just get in the car."

After she's hung up I just stand there looking at myself in the mirror across the room. Funny how all the life gets sucked out of you so fast. The hole in my face has got dug even deeper now that Renee's left for good. First it started out as a missing piece, but now a part of my head's caved in where she used to hold everything in place. It's so bad I can't stand to see it and I reach over and grab a coffee cup and throw it straight into the mirror.

The glass shatters into hundreds of splinters, and one of them flies back at me, slicing across a finger. A trickle of blood oozes from the skin and forms a tiny red bubble on my hand. Something about the colour draws my eye down to look at it real close, and then this idea flashes into my head of how I'm still alive. It's as though I didn't *know* I was still taking in air and moving around. This one dot of blood wakes me up to the fact that nothing happened to *me*. That *I'm not dead*.

The next second I suck the red bubble onto my tongue and start racing around the apartment. First I grab my jacket and start searching for the keys to the car. Turns out they're sitting on the dresser next to a polaroid picture of Renee. Funny how it faded and how her face has gone to a blur in my own mind. Both of them gone fuzzy at once. I fold the picture in two and tuck it into my shirt pocket. After that there's nothing left to do. One last look at the apartment and I'm gone.

Outside it's the dead black of night, maybe three or four in the morning. I slip into the Camaro and turn on the ignition. In a few minutes I've got her rolling down the freeway.

Everything's slick, as though the rain just greased the road and made the whole world a nightmare of sliding down a long thin line of highway. And it greased the sidewalks and tires and the black air that sucks past the windows into the emptiness behind me. I push the shift into overdrive and fly past a few night stragglers who're all holding the speed limit.

Then I just have to figure where to do it. Taking out another car would be sure, specially if it was coming dead-on. Or the bridge posts heading out of the city, the two granite statues that look like lions on each side of the bridge entrance. Either one would be enough to do it, to kick the last breath of life away without a chance for second thoughts and a wave of fear washing through my fingers.

But when I've got the car set straight onto the statues and everything fixed automatic, a warm stream of air slips past my neck from the back seat, like someone's blowing a white cloud into the car, a cloud filled with a faint light.

"*Billy.*"

I twist my head around to see who's calling. In the back there's a shadow of someone hunched down on the floor behind me.

"*Billy, slow it down.*"

"Who the hell's there?" The statues are just a half-mile off. Everything's set dead ahead.

"*Slow it down. Ease off the peddle, Billy.*" It's that woman again. "*Just slow it down, Billy, slow it all down.*"

"Waddya want?" Something slacks my foot off the peddle and I have to tramp it hard.

"*You. I want you. I need to take you into my heart.*"

"Well, you can't!" But this time my foot pulls right off the peddle and the car begins lugging and I have to slip it into fourth and then down to third gear. "You can't!" I tell her, but she gets the cloud working into my nose and down to my lungs so her Power seeps into me. The Camaro pulls to a stop on the shoulder just a hundred yards before the lions.

Then she slips into the front seat and looks into me with the same eyes Renee used whenever she needed to pull me inside her. And when she's finished smoothing me down with her eyes she takes my hand and rubs the fingers back and forth until they warm up and all the numbness that'd built up disappears.

"*Now take us over the bridge,*" she says.

I start the car again and pull onto the bridge at a crawl so slow that a line of cars begins to pack behind me and start honking on their horns.

"*Don't worry about them. Cross the bridge and take the first road on the right.*"

It works just like she says, and after a while I build up some speed and we drift along the highway, moving deeper and deeper into the mountains past all the farms and fenced-off land, past all the lampposts, so deep into the country that there's nothing but the road and darkness and the two of us.

After a few miles the car starts pushing into the bush. When you head north like this, after an hour there's not a trace of the city. There's a few houses and farms, broken down fences, and then the wilderness. It just comes to life somehow, the green bush and the morning mist drifting timeless above the trees. Once I leave the paved road I decide to pull off onto a switchback and take a break. A valley swings below me, and in the east the sun's beginning to cut under the clouds and spread a long ray of rose-coloured light over the woods.

"You getting out, too?" I ask, climbing out of the Camaro to stretch my legs. But there's nobody there. No one sitting beside me, no one outside.

"Hey." I walk around the car, twisting my head, looking for her. "Hey!" I yell. Then again and again, until I hear it echoing back at me from the mountain walls. "Hey . . . hey . . . hey."

Nobody. I slump down against the side of the car and just stare into the rising sun. It's a helluva sight. Just what Michaels would've liked. He was always talking about breaking free somewhere up north.

A bluebird glides past the valley and into a tree. All on its own. Just the way Renee said I could make it. Funny how she figured it. No one else pulling you down, telling the world their crazy dream and trying to make you fit into it.

Then there's the sound of a branch snapping behind me. I jump up and ease past the car to a clump of bushes.

"That you behind there?" Maybe she had to have a pee.

Nothing.

I walk around the bush, slow and easy, my feet fitting perfect against the earth. In the scrub is a squirrel gnawing at some branches, his teeth biting hard and snapping the wood down into twigs. And then a funny thing happens. I just sit and watch him. He's working so damned hard, he doesn't give a thought to me. He must spend an hour running back and forth, chewing and husking the wood down, collecting seeds and storing it away somewhere behind a big rock. It's beautiful. And suddenly the whole forest opens up, and the morning light seems to break through in a way I've never seen before. It's like being in the middle of the world. Like everything was made so perfect and finally I get right into the centre of it for the first time—even though it was *always* there to see.

"Don't you see?" I yell out, almost laughing. "Don't you see it?"

And then it's a hurricane the way the truth hits in. Christ, all this time. It's impossible. "All this time," I whisper, "all this time I've been telling you this and you've even been talking back to me—*but the whole time I've just been telling myself.*"

And then the hurricane slacks and there's not a noise in the bush at all. Not a drift of wind rippling the leaves, nothing but the sound of my breathing rolling in and out, in and out. And the real beauty of it is that I can make it all last as long as I want. After a few minutes I walk back to the car, and before I head further into the bush I light up a smoke and just sit in the car and think. About the look of the world, the smell and the sound of it. The way it's all been made to work.

Then somewhere out in the woods the bark of a wild dog cuts through the trees. I twist my head around, but I can't see a thing. Then I gun the engine, pull onto the gravel road and climb up the switchback fast as I can.

Just fast enough so he can't catch me.

ACKNOWLEDGEMENTS

This book could not have been completed without the dedication and guidance of many people who believed (sometimes blindly) that *Fire Eyes* was worth the hundreds of hours of head-scratching, soul-searching, gut-wrenching and, finally, wine-toasting. I owe a debt of gratitude to my agent, Bella Pomer, for taking on a new writer at a time when new writers are extremely hard to sell. I am deeply grateful to Denise Bukowski, my editor, for the many hours she spent reading and rereading, learning the intimacies of *Fire Eyes*, and helping me shape the final manuscript. For their knowledge and expertise, I thank Dr. Guy Richmond, Dr. Harold Penner and Captain Jim Ryan (RCA), whose perspectives on psychodynamics and military affairs were indeed welcome.

Thanks is also due to "the group," who listened to chapter after chapter, night after night: Kathi, Dorothy, Romaine, Joanne, Howard and Judy. Finally, I wish to thank my wife, Audrey, for her encouragement and support during the years that *Fire Eyes* absorbed my energies.